DOM DOMINGOS KING OF WARRI

Love, Coral and Cross: A King's Journey Unfolds!

A Novel by
Adrian O Edema

Published by Adrian O. Edema
Chelmsford, Essex United Kingdom

Library of Congress Cataloging-in-Publication Data
Adrian O. Edema

DOM DOMINGOS KING OF WARRI / Adrian O.
Edema

ISBN: 979-8-89571-180-4 (Paperback)

ISBN: 979-8-89571-181-1 (eBook)

1. Historical Fiction—Africa—Nigeria.

2. Kings and Rulers—Fiction.

3. Cultural Heritage—Fiction. I. Title.

First Edition: 2025

10 9 8 7 6 5 4 3 2 1

Cover design

Pictures by Kwame O Woode

Illustration by Priscilla Odofin

Design by Usama Zaheen @ KingOfDesigner

Printed in United Kingdom

For more information about this book
or to contact the author, @ Adrian.edema@gmail.com

Dedication

To His Majesty Ogiame Atuwatse III, CFR, The Olu of Warri, whose reign inspires the future of our cherished kingdom.

To the memory of Ogiame Atuwatse I, also known as Olu Dom Domingo, whose life and legacy flow through these pages, a bridge between river and sea.

To my parents, Mr. Victor Ekpogharanetse Edema Fatubo and Mrs. Cristiana Ajofotuaso Edema Fatubo (née Kete), whose love and guidance shaped my journey.

To the memory of my maternal and paternal ancestor, Gofino Olomu Asoruku, whose spirit echoes in the roots of our heritage.

Contents

Epigraph

"The river flows eternal, its voice a guide for kings,
Where coral meets the cross, a legacy is born."
— Traditional Itsekiri Proverb,
Collected by Elder Omatsola of Ugborodo

"Faith is the bridge between the past and the future,
built by the hands of those who dare to unite."
— Father João, Chronicles of Warri Mission, 1645

Introduction

Welcome to the vibrant world of Warri, a kingdom cradled by the mighty Warri River, where the rhythms of tradition and the echoes of faith converge in a tale of resilience and love. *Dom Domingos King of Warri* is a journey into the 17th century, a time when the Itsekiri people navigated the challenges of a changing world—Portuguese traders with their cannons, Christian missionaries with their crosses, and internal rivalries that tested the bonds of blood. This novel is inspired by the rich history of the Itsekiri, a riverine people whose culture, woven with coral beads and mangrove roots, thrives in the Niger Delta of modern-day Nigeria.

At the heart of this story is Ogiame Dom Domingos, a king of dual heritage—born of Itsekiri lineage and shaped by his years in Portugal, where he earned a knighthood in the Order of Christ. His reign, beginning in 1621, is a bridge between worlds, a struggle to unite his people under the dual banners of Umale Okun, the god of the river, and the Christian God introduced by missionaries. Alongside him stands Tuaso, a weaver of nets and dreams, whose love becomes his anchor, and Anthonio, his son born of a lost love, whose mixed blood ignites both hope and contention.

This narrative weaves together historical threads with the fabric of imagination, exploring themes of leadership, legacy, and the power of unity amid adversity. The Warri River, a living character in its own right, mirrors the trials and triumphs of its people, its waters a constant reminder of the past and a promise for the future. As you turn these pages, you will witness a kingdom rise, falter, and endure, its story a testament to the human spirit's ability to flow forward, much like the river itself.

To the readers, I offer this tale as an invitation—to walk with Domingos through the mangrove shadows, to feel the weight of his crown, and to celebrate the resilience of a people whose legacy endures. May the river guide you, as it guided him, through the currents of this epic saga.

Adrian O. Edema
Chelmsford, Essex United Kingdom
August 2025

Prologue

The Warri River gleamed under the silver gaze of a crescent moon, its waters weaving through the mangroves like a thread in the loom of time, whispering secrets of a kingdom born of river and sea. It was the year 1621, and along its banks stood a palace of mud and coral, its walls a testament to a people forged by the tides. Here, Ogiame Dom Domingos, a man of two worlds, ascended the throne, his scarlet Kemeje catching the moonlight, coral beads clinking with each step—a king marked by his Portuguese knighthood and Itsekiri blood, a bridge between the spires of Lisbon and the roots of Warri.

The air was thick with the scent of palm oil and the distant hum of drums, a rhythm that pulsed with the life of the Itsekiri—fishermen casting nets, weavers shaping dreams, warriors guarding the river's edge. Yet beneath this harmony lay a shadow, a murmur of unrest. Domingos's brother, Emagin, had fled to Ile-Ife, his ambition a thorn in the kingdom's side, while Portuguese ships loomed on the horizon, their cannons a promise of trade or treachery. The church, newly risen under Father João's cross, stood beside the shrine of Umale Okun, a fragile union of faiths that

Domingos vowed to nurture, his heart torn between the God of his youth and the gods of his ancestors.

On this night, as the river sang its ancient song, a young woman named Maria Pereira, her indigo wrapper glowing in the dark, approached the palace, her sea-blue eyes a mystery. She carried a child in her arms—Anthonio, born of love and loss, his tiny hand clutching a coral bead. "He is Warri's future," she whispered to Domingos, her voice a tide of hope. But fate, like the river, is unpredictable. Within months, Maria would be gone, her laughter a memory, leaving Domingos to raise their son alone, his reign shadowed by grief and the weight of a crown.

The drums fell silent as a canoe slipped from the shadows, its occupant a messenger from Benin, bearing news of alliance and warning. "The Portuguese grow bold," he said, his voice low. "And Emagin plots from Ife, his hands reaching for your throne." Domingos's gaze turned to the river, its flow a mirror of his destiny. He knew the path ahead would test his strength, his faith, and his love—for Warri, for Anthonio, for the legacy he must build. As the moon dipped below the horizon, the river whispered a promise: from these waters, a king would rise, his story etched in coral and cross, a tale of triumph and tribulation yet to unfold.

CHAPTER ONE

Night After Coronation

The moon hung low in the Warri sky, a silver crescent cradled in a velvet expanse of stars, its light filtering through the dense mangrove canopy that fringed the palace grounds. Ogiame, King Dom Domingos, sat beneath the ancient Iroko tree, its gnarled roots sprawling like the veins of the earth, anchoring the sacred grove where kings had sought counsel for centuries. The air was thick with the scent of damp soil, mingling with the faint tang of salt from the Warri River, the kingdom's lifeblood that carried trade and tales from the sea. His scarlet Kemeje shimmered in the moonlight, the rich red fabric draped over a matching wrapper, both embroidered with intricate patterns of cowrie shells and sunbursts—symbols of Warri's pride and prosperity. Around his neck and wrists, heavy coral beads gleamed, each one a testament to his lineage, their weight a constant reminder of the wealth and responsibility he now bore. On his head rested the crown, a magnificent creation forged in the European style during his years in Portugal, its golden cross catching the starlight like a beacon. He had brought two such crowns from Lisbon, a gift from his father's vision in 1610 when he was sent to study the ways of the world beyond Warri's mangrove-lined shores.

The night was quiet, save for the distant hum of cicadas and the occasional rustle of leaves stirred by a gentle breeze that carried whispers of the river's current. Ogiame's gaze was fixed upward, lost in the vastness of the heavens, though his thoughts wandered far beyond the stars. He was no longer the wide-eyed youth who had sailed to Portugal, eager to absorb the lessons of King Philip III's court, nor the young man who had defied expectations by shunning the priesthood. Instead, he was a king, crowned just hours ago in a ceremony that had fused the old ways with the new—Itsekiri drums and flutes blending with the Latin chants of Catholic priests, ancestral rites intertwined with European pomp. The coronation had been a whirlwind of rituals and revelry, its echoes still lingering in the night air. The palace grounds had thrummed with life—dancers in vibrant wrappers swirling like flames, drummers pounding rhythms that pulsed like the heartbeat of the Itsekiri people, and elders chanting blessings in the tongue of their ancestors.

Ogiame Dom Domingos had stood tall, accepting the mantle of leadership, the crown placed upon his brow by the high priest of Umale Okun, god of the sea. Yet the weight of the crown felt heavier than its gold, pressing against his temples with the burden of a kingdom at a crossroads. His father, the late Ogiame Sebastian, had ruled with a steady hand, his reign marked by prosperity and peace, his court a tapestry of loyalty woven from tradition and strength. But Ogiame knew the challenges ahead were uniquely his to face. The Portuguese traders were growing bolder, their galleons crowding the river's mouth, demanding more palm oil, ivory, and—whispered in shadowed corners—souls for their distant markets. The Christian faith, too, was a double-edged sword, its promise of salvation clashing with the ancient ways of his people, who still offered yams and kola nuts to the spirits of the river and forest. And then there were the neighboring kingdoms—Benin to the north, Ijebu to the west—their eyes ever-watchful, seeking any sign of weakness in Warri's new ruler.

A soft footfall broke his reverie, the crunch of leaves underfoot pulling him back to the grove. He turned to see Ebi, his most trusted advisor, approaching with a lantern in hand, its flame casting a warm glow across the gnarled roots. The old man's face was etched with lines of wisdom, his wrapper tied simply, unadorned but for a single coral bracelet that marked his status as a chief. Ebi bowed low, his eyes glinting with a mix of pride and concern, his graying hair catching the moonlight like threads of silver. "Ogiame, the night grows deep," Ebi said, his voice low but firm, carrying the cadence of one who had served three kings. "Your people will come at dawn to pay tribute. You must rest, for their eyes will be upon you."

Ogiame smiled faintly, his gaze returning to the sky, where the crescent moon seemed to pulse with secrets. "Rest is for men without crowns, Ebi. My father told me that once, as he sat beneath this very tree." Ebi chuckled, settling onto a root beside the king, his lantern casting shadows that danced like spirits. "Your father, may his spirit rest, was a man of many sayings. But he also knew when to listen to his advisors." He paused, then added softly, "As must you, Ogiame."

Ogiame's smile widened, though it carried a trace of weariness, the weight of the day's ceremonies still heavy on his shoulders. "Speak, then, old friend. What troubles you?" Ebi's expression grew serious, his fingers tracing the coral bracelet as if drawing strength from it. "The tribute, Ogiame. It is a time of joy, yes, but also a time of scrutiny. The people will come with gifts—yams, cloth, perhaps even maidens, as they did for your father. But they will also come with questions. They will look to see if their new king is as strong as the old, if he can hold the kingdom together in these troubled times."

Ogiame nodded, his fingers tracing the edge of his coral beads, their smooth surfaces cool against his skin. He recalled the stories of his father's tribute, how the chiefs had presented seven virgins, their beauty a symbol of loyalty and abundance, their hair adorned with beads that shimmered like stars. Two had become his father's wives, their unions strengthening ties with powerful clans along the river.

Ogiame had no desire for such gifts—his heart belonged to Maria, whose love had defied oceans and courts—but he knew the weight of tradition. To refuse outright would be to invite whispers of weakness, to risk fracturing the fragile unity of his chiefs.

Ebi leaned closer, his voice dropping to a near-whisper. "There is a tale among our people, Ogiame, of the Tortoise and the Leopard. Tortoise, small and cunning, challenged Leopard to a race, knowing he could not outrun him. But Tortoise placed his brothers at every turn of the path, each one looking just like him. When Leopard ran, he saw Tortoise ahead at every bend, and in his confusion, he lost the race. The people will test you as Leopard tested Tortoise. They will look for weakness at every turn. You must be ready, like Tortoise, to outwit their doubts."

Ogiame's lips curved into a thoughtful smile. "A king must be cunning, then, and not just strong. I hear you, Ebi." The advisor nodded, satisfied, but his eyes remained guarded. "And the Portuguese?" he asked, shifting the conversation to a sharper edge. "What news from the river?" Ogiame's jaw tightened, his thoughts drifting to the galleons anchored at the river's mouth, their sails like Specters in the dawn mist. "Their ships linger, Ebi. Captain Alvarez sent word today, requesting an audience. He speaks of trade—palm oil, ivory—but his eyes are on our warriors. They say the white men across the sea grow hungry for labour."

Ebi's face darkened, his fingers tightening around the lantern's handle. "Their hunger is a fire that consumes all it touches. I have heard tales from the Igbo traders, of villages emptied, of men and women chained like beasts. We must not let Warri become their prey." Ogiame's chest burned with a fire of his own, memories of Portugal's slave markets flashing through his mind—men and women bound in the shadows of grand cathedrals, their eyes hollow with despair. "They will find no such bounty here," he said firmly, his voice ringing with conviction. "Warri is no man's quarry."

Ebi inclined his head, approval glinting in his eyes. "Spoken like a king. But tread carefully, Ogiame. The Portuguese are not easily refused, and their cannons speak louder than their words. There is another tale, of the Antelope and the Hunter. Antelope was swift, but the Hunter's trap was patient. Antelope boasted of his speed, but one day he stepped into a hidden snare and was caught. Strength alone does not win against cunning. The Portuguese are hunters, Ogiame. Their traps are not always seen."

Ogiame's eyes narrowed, the parable sinking deep. "Then we shall be swifter than Antelope and wiser than Tortoise. Let Alvarez come. He will find Warri's spirit stronger than his cannons." The king rose, his shadow stretching long against the Iroko's trunk, the coral beads clinking softly as he moved. The grove seemed to hold its breath, the ancient tree a silent witness to his resolve. Ebi stood as well, his lantern casting a warm glow over the ground, illuminating the roots that twisted like the threads of fate.

"There is one more matter, Ogiame," Ebi said, his tone softer now, almost hesitant. "The Olori. The people whisper of her foreign ways. Some say she does not honor the gods of our fathers, that she prays only to the cross and not to Oritse Udeji or Umale Okun." Ogiame's eyes softened at the mention of Maria, a warmth spreading through him despite the weight of Ebi's words. "She learns, Ebi. She walks the palace with offerings of palm wine for Oritse Udeji and kola nuts for the ancestors. She prays at the Christian altar, yes, but she also kneels by the river at dawn, learning its songs. She is my bridge between worlds, not a wedge to divide them."

Ebi nodded, though his expression remained guarded, his eyes searching the king's face. "Then let her be seen tomorrow, Ogiame. Let the people know their Olori stands with them. There is a story of the Weaver Bird and the Sparrow. Weaver Bird built a grand nest, intricate and strong, but Sparrow mocked it, saying it was too different from the nests of the forest. Weaver Bird invited Sparrow to live in his nest, and Sparrow saw its strength. The people need to see the Olori's strength, Ogiame, not just hear of it."

Ogiame clapped a hand on Ebi's shoulder, a gesture of trust forged over years, from the days when Ebi had taught him to fish in the river's shallows. "She will, Ebi. And so will I. The people will see a king and Olori who stand as one." As Ebi retreated toward the palace, his lantern bobbing like a firefly, Ogiame lingered in the grove, his gaze returning to the sky. Dawn was not far off, and with it would come his people—chiefs with their carved staffs, fishermen with nets slung over their shoulders, warriors with spears polished to a gleam, and weavers bearing cloth dyed in the colours of the sunset.

But the night held more than the promise of tribute. As Ogiame stood, a faint sound drifted from the river—a rhythmic splash, not of fish or tide, but of oars cutting through water. His heart quickened. Could it be the Portuguese already, testing his resolve? He moved silently toward the grove's edge, peering through the mangroves. In the distance, a small canoe emerged from the mist, its occupant cloaked in shadow. The figure raised a hand, not in threat but in greeting, and Ogiame recognized the silhouette of Okoro, a fisherman from the western villages, known for his loyalty and keen eyes.

Okoro beached the canoe and approached, his bare feet silent on the damp earth. "Ogiame," he whispered, bowing low. "I bring word from the coast. The Portuguese galleon has moved closer, and with it, a new ship—black-hulled, with flags I do not know. The men on the shore speak of gold and guns, and they watch our warriors with hunger."

Ogiame's mind raced. A black-hulled ship? Perhaps Dutch traders, rivals to the Portuguese, or worse, pirates seeking to exploit Warri's wealth. "Did they see you?" he asked, his voice steady despite the unease coiling in his gut.

"No, Ogiame," Okoro replied. "I kept to the shadows, as you taught me in the old days by the river. But they will come soon, I fear, with offers or demands." Ogiame nodded, his resolve hardening. "Thank you, Okoro. Return to your village and spread word quietly—tell the chiefs to prepare, but not to act until I call. We will meet this challenge together." As Okoro slipped back into the night, Ogiame turned to the Iroko, its presence a grounding force. The tales of Tortoise, Antelope, and Weaver Bird echoed in his mind, each a lesson in survival and unity. He would need all his cunning now, not just to face the Portuguese but to navigate the unknown threat of this new ship.

His thoughts drifted to Maria, asleep in their chambers, her gentle breathing a contrast to the storm brewing outside. He had promised her a life of peace, a blend of her world and his, but the reality of kingship was proving more tumultuous than he had imagined. Perhaps, he mused, her presence tomorrow at the tribute could serve a dual purpose—assuring the people while signalling to the foreigners that Warri's royal house was united and unyielding. He envisioned her standing beside him, her fair skin a stark contrast to the dark richness of the Itsekiri attire he would drape her in, a living emblem of their alliance.

The grove grew still again, the cicadas resuming their song as if sensing his decision. Ogiame recalled another parable, one his mother had whispered during his childhood, of the Eagle and the Wind. Eagle soared high, proud of his strength, but Wind, invisible and patient, lifted him higher or dashed him to the ground. Ogiame saw himself as the Eagle, reliant on the winds of his people, his advisors, and even the unpredictable currents of foreign influence. He would harness those winds, not fight them blindly.

As dawn's first light crept over the horizon, painting the sky in hues of orange and pink, Ogiame heard the distant sound of drums—soft at first, then growing louder as the tribute procession began its journey to the palace. He straightened, the crown steady on his brow, its golden cross catching the emerging sunlight. The people would arrive soon—chiefs with their carved staffs, fishermen with nets slung over their shoulders, warriors with spears polished to a gleam, weavers with cloth dyed in the colours of the sunset, and perhaps maidens adorned with beads, their eyes lowered in respect. They would bring yams piled high, bolts of woven fabric, and the weight of their expectations, their gazes sharp as they measured their new king against the memory of his father.

But Ogiame was ready. He would greet them with the strength of the Stone and the flow of the River, blending tradition with the wisdom gained from Portugal. He would listen to Ebi's counsel, honour Maria's bridge-building, and face the Portuguese and their mysterious allies with the cunning of Tortoise. The black-hulled ship loomed in his thoughts, a shadow on the horizon, but he vowed it would not overshadow Warri's spirit. He would protect his people, not just with spears and cannons, but with the unity and resilience that had sustained his kingdom for generations.

A soft rustle behind him revealed Maria, her figure wrapped in a light shawl, her eyes reflecting the dawn. "You're still here," she said, her voice carrying the gentle lilt of her Portuguese roots. "I woke and missed you." Ogiame turned, a smile breaking through his stern resolve. "I needed the grove's wisdom, my love. But now, I need you by my side. The people come, and we will face them together." She stepped closer, her hand finding his, the coral beads warm against her touch. "Then let us show them a king and Olori of two worlds, united as one."

As they walked back toward the palace, the drums grew louder, a heartbeat calling them forward. The Iroko stood sentinel behind them, its roots deep in the earth, its branches reaching for the sky—a silent witness to the birth of a reign that would weave together the old and the new, the local and the foreign, in a tapestry as enduring as the Warri River itself.

Ogiame felt the weight of his crown lighten, bolstered by Maria's presence and the parables that guided him. Whatever challenges lay ahead—the Portuguese, the black-hulled ship, the scrutiny of his people—he would meet them with the heart of a king and the wisdom of his ancestors.

CHAPTER TWO

The Royal Wedding

T he Warri sun blazed high, casting a golden sheen over the palace grounds, where the air thrummed with the pulse of celebration. The royal wedding of Ogiame Dom Domingos, and Lady Maria de Sousa, the Portuguese noble-woman who had captured his heart, was a spectacle unlike any the Warri kingdom had witnessed. The riverbank buzzed with colour—wrappers of crimson, indigo, and gold swirled as women danced, their coral beads clinking in rhythm with the booming drums. Men in flowing Kemeje shirts and wrappers, adorned with intricate embroidery of fish and waves, moved with proud strides, their voices rising in chants that honoured the gods and ancestors. The palace courtyard, framed by towering palm trees and adorned with woven mats dyed in earthy tones, was a sea of anticipation. Every corner burst with the scent of roasted yams, smoked fish, and the sweet tang of palm wine, mingling with the salty breeze from the Warri River, which shimmered in the distance like a mirror to the sky.

King Dom Domingos stood at the centre of the courtyard, his scarlet Kemeje resplendent, the coral beads around his neck and wrists glowing like embers against his dark skin. His European crown, a gift from King Philip of Portugal, sat lightly on his brow, its golden cross catching the sunlight in a dazzling display. At twenty-five, he was a striking figure—tall, broad-shouldered, with eyes that held the wisdom of his years abroad in Lisbon and the fiery spirit of his Itsekiri blood. Beside him stood his bride, Maria, radiant in a gown that blended the elegance of Portuguese silk with the vibrant patterns of Itsekiri cloth. Her bodice, sewn with coral and cowrie shells, shimmered as she moved, and her dark hair was woven with gold threads, a nod to her foreign roots, while a single strand of beads hung like a waterfall down her back.

She stood with a quiet grace, her sea-blue eyes wide with wonder at the spectacle before her, yet steady with the resolve that had brought her across oceans to this moment. The ceremony began with the deep, resonant call of the bel-ebele, the royal war horn, its sound rolling across the river like thunder, echoing off the mangroves and stirring the hearts of all who heard it. Chief Oton, the grizzled high priest of Umale Okun, stepped forward, his wrapper tied tightly around his waist, a string of cowries draped across his chest like a sacred armour. In his hands, he held a calabash filled with kola nuts and palm wine, offerings to the gods who would bless this union. The crowd fell silent as he raised the calabash, his voice booming in the Itsekiri tongue. "Ancestors of Warri, spirits of the river, gods of earth and sky, bear witness!" Chief Oton declared. "Today, we join Ogiame Dom Domingos, son of our fathers, with Maria, daughter of distant shores. May their bond strengthen our kingdom and honour our ways!" The crowd erupted in cheers, drums pounding a frenetic rhythm as women ululated, their voices sharp and joyous, cutting through the warm air like blades of celebration.

Oton broke a kola nut, its bitter scent mingling with the air, and offered a piece to the King and his bride. Ogiame Domingos chewed first, his expression solemn, a silent acknowledgment of the traditions he carried forward, then handed a piece to Maria. She hesitated for a moment, the unfamiliar taste sharp on her tongue, but she swallowed with a determined nod, earning a ripple of approval from the onlookers. The palm wine followed, poured from the calabash into two carved gourds adorned with carvings of fish and waves. Domingos drank deeply, the sweet liquid a familiar comfort, then passed the gourd to Maria, who sipped carefully, her lips curving into a smile as the warmth spread through her. From the edge of the courtyard, Ebi, Domingos's trusted advisor, watched with a mix of pride and caution. His weathered face softened as he saw the Kings' hand linger on Maria's, a gesture of unity, but his eyes darted to the gathered chiefs, some of whom whispered among themselves. The union was bold—unprecedented, even. A foreign Olori in Warri was a bridge to new worlds, offering trade and alliances, but also a spark that could ignite old tensions over tradition and identity.

Ebi's gaze settled on Chief Ikenna, a wiry man with a scar across his cheek, known for his fierce devotion to the old ways. Ikenna's arms were crossed, his lips a thin line of disapproval, his eyes fixed on Maria with a mix of curiosity and suspicion. Ebi made a mental note to speak with him later; the chiefs' loyalty would be crucial to Ogiame Domingos, especially with the Portuguese influence looming large. The ceremony continued with the presentation of gifts, a cornerstone of Itsekiri weddings that symbolized the community's investment in the couple's future. Elders from across the kingdom approached, their arms laden with offerings that reflected Warri's wealth and spirit. Chief Amaju, a jovial man with a booming laugh that echoed like thunder, presented a carved wooden stool inlaid with mother-of-pearl, its surface gleaming with the iridescence of the river. "For your household," he said, bowing low, his grin wide enough to show missing teeth earned in battles long past.

A group of women from the river clans, their skirts swaying with the grace of water lilies, offered baskets of smoked fish and yams, their voices raised in a song of fertility and abundance that wove through the crowd like a gentle current.

The most striking gift came from Olua, a young warrior with a reputation for boldness, his chest bare save for a necklace of shark teeth. He stepped forward, leading a white ram adorned with red cloth, its horns painted with ochre symbols of strength. "For strength and sacrifice," Olua said, his eyes meeting Domingos's with a spark of challenge, as if testing the king's readiness to lead. Ogiame Domingos nodded, accepting the ram with a steady hand, aware that every gesture was a public measure of his resolve.

Maria, too, was not spared the weight of tradition. A group of elder women, led by Mama Uwala, a revered weaver with silver-streaked hair and hands stained with indigo dye, approached with a folded wrapper dyed in deep blue. "For the Olori," Mama Uwala said, her voice warm but firm, carrying the authority of years spent preserving Warri's craft. "Wear this, and you wear Warri's heart." Maria accepted the cloth, her fingers tracing the intricate patterns of waves and stars and draped it over her shoulders with a grace that silenced the whispers of doubt. The crowd roared in approval, and Ogiame Domingos's chest swelled with pride. She was learning, adapting, becoming not just his wife but his partner in the eyes of his people, a living bridge between cultures.

As the sun dipped toward the horizon, painting the sky with streaks of orange and purple, the dancing began. Drummers pounded out a rhythm that shook the earth, their hands a blur as they struck the taut skins, and men and women formed circles, their feet stomping in syncopated unity. Ogiame Domingos led Maria into the dance, his movements fluid and commanding, a reflection of his Itsekiri heritage, while hers were tentative but earnest, a learner embracing the unknown. The crowd clapped and cheered, urging her on with shouts of encouragement, and soon she was swaying to the beat, her laughter mingling with the music, her steps growing bolder with each turn. For a moment, the divide between Warri and Portugal seemed to vanish, the river and the sea flowing as one in a harmony of movement and sound.

But the harmony was not without its shadows. At the edge of the crowd, a Portuguese trader, Captain Alvarez, watched with narrowed eyes, his velvet doublet a stark contrast to the wrappers and corals around him. His presence was a reminder of the ships waiting at the river's mouth, their cannons silent but ominous. He had come to Warri under the guise of trade—palm oil and ivory—but his true aim was influence, a foothold in a kingdom ripe with resources. Ogiame Dom Domingos caught his gaze and held it, a silent warning that carried the weight of his new authority. Alvarez smiled thinly and raised his cup of palm wine, but the gesture felt more like a challenge than a toast, a promise of future negotiations that would test Warri's sovereignty.

As the night deepened, the couple retired to the palace's inner chambers, where a smaller, more intimate gathering of family and close advisors awaited. The room was lit by oil lamps, their flickering flames casting shadows on walls adorned with woven tapestries depicting the river's history. Maria's mother, Lady Catarina Pereira, had made the arduous journey from Portugal, her stern face softened by the day's joy as she embraced her daughter, whispering words of love and caution about the challenges of a foreign court. "Be strong, my child," she murmured, her voice thick with emotion. "This land is beautiful, but it will test your spirit."

Dom Domingos's mother, Olori Ewere, regal in her coral-encrusted wrapper that shimmered like the river at dusk, offered Maria a carved ivory bracelet, its surface etched with symbols of protection. "You are our daughter now," she said, her voice steady but kind, her eyes searching Maria's face for signs of acceptance. "Warri will test you, but it will also embrace you if you honour its ways." Maria nodded, slipping the bracelet onto her wrist, its cool weight a comforting anchor as she navigated this new chapter.

The night continued with a feast, the tables laden with roasted goat, plantain fritters, and bowls of pepper soup that filled the air with spicy warmth. Chief Oton returned to offer a final blessing, sprinkling water from the Warri River over the couple, its cool touch a sacred seal on their union. He invoked the spirits to guide their path, his words weaving a prayer that mingled the old gods with the new faith King Domingos had brought from Portugal. As the guests dispersed, their laughter and songs fading into the night, King Dom Domingos and Maria stood alone under the stars, the Iroko tree looming in the distance like a silent guardian.

He took her hand, feeling the warmth of her skin against his, the ivory bracelet cool between their fingers. "Are you ready for this, my love?" he asked, his voice low, carrying the weight of the day and the uncertainties ahead. Maria's eyes met his, steady and unafraid, reflecting the starlight above. "I chose you, King Dom Domingos. I chose Warri. I am ready," she replied, her voice firm despite the softness of her smile. He drew her close, the scent of palm wine and river water lingering on her breath, the weight of the future settling over them both.

But the night held more than celebration. As they lingered, a soft ripple disturbed the river's surface, and a canoe emerged from the shadows, its occupant cloaked in the dim light. King Domingos tensed, his hand instinctively moving to the dagger at his waist, a gift from his father engraved with the royal seal. The figure raised a hand in peace, and Dom Domingos recognized Okoro, a fisherman from the western villages, known for his loyalty and keen eyes. Okoro beached the canoe and approached, his bare feet silent on the damp earth. "Ogiame," he whispered, bowing low. "I bring word from the coast. The Portuguese galleon has moved closer, and with it, a new ship—black-hulled, with flags I do not know. The men on the shore speak of gold and guns, and they watch our warriors with hunger."

Dom Domingos's mind raced. A black-hulled ship? Perhaps Dutch traders, rivals to the Portuguese, or worse, pirates seeking to exploit Warri's wealth. "Did they see you?" he asked, his voice steady despite the unease coiling in his gut. "No, Ogiame-to-be," Okoro replied. "I kept to the shadows, as you taught me in the old days by the river. But they will come soon, I fear, with offers or demands." Maria squeezed his hand, her presence a quiet strength beside him. "Thank you, Okoro," King Domingos said. "Return to your village and spread word quietly—tell the chiefs to prepare, but not to act until I call. We will meet this challenge together."

As Okoro slipped back into the night, Domingos turned to Maria, his expression a mix of determination and concern. "This wedding was our beginning," he said, "but it seems the trials begin now." She nodded, her gaze steady. "Then we face them together, as king and Olori." The Iroko tree stood sentinel in the distance, its branches swaying as if whispering secrets of resilience. King Domingos recalled a parable Ebi had shared during his youth, of the Crocodile and the Heron. Crocodile ruled the river, proud and fierce, but Heron, with its sharp beak, plucked parasites from Crocodile's back, earning its trust. King Domingos saw himself as the Crocodile, reliant on the Heron—his people, his advisors, and now Maria—to navigate the threats ahead.

The sound of distant drums signalled the end of the celebration, the village settling into the quiet of night. But within the palace, the air was thick with anticipation. Ebi approached, his lantern casting a warm glow over the couple. "The chiefs will talk tonight," he said, his voice low. "Ikenna is restless, and Alvarez's presence has stirred unease. We must plan." King Domingos nodded, his mind already turning to strategy. "Call a council at dawn. We'll address the Portuguese and this new ship. Maria will join us—she must be seen as part of our strength."

The night deepened, and as they entered the palace, a young messenger from the river clans burst in, breathless. "Ogiame, a skirmish near the coast! Our fishermen clashed with strangers from the black-hulled ship—two are wounded!" King Domingos's heart sank, but he masked it with resolve. "Take me there," he ordered, turning to Maria. "Stay with Ebi. I'll return." She nodded, her eyes filled with worry but trust, as he followed the messenger into the night, the weight of his crown heavier than ever.

The journey to the coast revealed a tense scene—fishermen armed with spears faced off against shadowed figures from the black-hulled ship, their language unfamiliar. Dom Domingos stepped forward, his voice commanding silence. "I am Ogiame Dom Domingos, King of Warri. State your purpose or leave our waters." A tall man emerged, his face weathered by sea and sun, speaking in broken Portuguese.

"We are Dutch traders, seeking trade—spices, gold. But your men attacked us." King Domingos's eyes narrowed. "Your ship encroached without permission. Peace can be made, but only with respect." The negotiations were tense, but a tentative agreement was reached—trade talks to begin at dawn, under strict conditions.

Returning to the palace, King Domingos found Maria waiting with Ebi, her face alight with relief. "You're safe," she whispered, embracing him. Ebi smiled faintly. "The gods test you early, Ogiame. But your bride's presence will steady the chiefs." As dawn approached, King Domingos and Maria stood together, ready to face the council, the wedding's joy now a foundation for the challenges ahead. The Warri River flowed on, its currents a reminder of the resilience they would need, and the Iroko tree stood tall, a silent witness to a reign beginning under stars and shadows.

CHAPTER THREE

Rescuing Princess Temieno

The Warri River shimmered under the midday sun, its surface a mirror for the dense mangroves that lined its banks, their twisted roots dipping into the water like the fingers of ancient spirits. The kingdom was still basking in the afterglow of King Dom Domingos's wedding to Lady Maria, now a month past, the vibrant colours of that celebration lingering in the air like a distant melody. Yet a shadow had fallen over the Itsekiri people, casting a pall over the palace grounds. Princess Temieno, King Domingos's younger sister and a beloved figure known for her sharp wit and fearless spirit, had been taken. A raiding party from an Ijaw clan based in Kpakiama, emboldened by whispers that Warri's new King was distracted by his foreign bride, had struck a riverside village. Temieno had been visiting to bless the fishermen's nets—a ritual of goodwill—when the Ijaw descended, their canoes slicing through the water with ruthless precision. The news reached the palace at dawn, carried by a breathless warrior, his arm gashed and dripping blood, bearing a message from the Ijaw pirate leader: Temieno would be returned only for a ransom of gold, ivory, and a pledge of Warri's submission.

Ogiame Dom Domingos, already bearing the weight of leadership, stood in the palace war room, his scarlet Kemeje replaced by a simpler wrapper tied for battle, its edges frayed from years of use. His coral beads glinted against his sweat-slicked skin, a stark contrast to the tension in his posture. The European crown he had brought from Portugal rested on a wooden stand nearby, a symbol of his dual heritage, but today his focus was wholly Itsekiri, rooted in the soil of his ancestors. Around him stood his council: Ebi, his trusted advisor, whose lined face was taut with worry, his coral bracelet trembling slightly as he gripped it; Chief Oton, the high priest, clutching a staff topped with cowrie shells that rattled with each movement; and Olua, the young warrior who had gifted the white ram at the wedding, his eyes burning with eagerness for action, his spear leaning against the wall. Maria, too, was present, her indigo wrapper—a gift from Mama Uwala—clinging to her frame, her expression fierce despite the whispered doubts of chiefs who questioned her place in such martial councils.

"The Ijaw mock us," Olua said, slamming a fist onto the carved table that held a map of the river lands, its surface etched with the winding paths of creeks and villages. "They think Warri grows soft under a King who dances with white women. We must strike now, Ogiame, and show them our steel!" His voice echoed with the impatience of youth, but his fervour stirred the room. Ebi raised a hand, his voice calm but firm, a steady anchor amid the storm. "Olua speaks with fire, but fire alone does not win wars. The Ijaw hold Temieno in their stronghold, deep in the creeks where the mangroves choke the water. Their canoes are swift, their warriors know every twist of the channels. A rash attack could cost us the princess, and her loss would break our spirit."

Domingos's jaw tightened, his mind racing with images of Temieno. Barely eighteen, she was more than a sister—she was a symbol of Warri's vitality, her laughter as essential to the kingdom as the river's flow. He remembered her at the wedding, teasing him about his "Portuguese Olori" while braiding coral into her hair, her fingers deft and her eyes alight with mischief. The thought of her bound in an Ijaw camp, her spirit dimmed by captivity, stirred a fury he struggled to contain. Yet Ebi's wisdom resonated—Temieno's safety demanded strategy, not rage. "Maria," King Domingos said, turning to his wife, whose presence had drawn curious and sceptical glances from the council. "You've seen the Portuguese navigate rivers in their galleons. What would they do?"

Maria straightened, aware of the weight of every eye upon her, her sea-blue gaze meeting King Domingos's with quiet determination. "In Portugal, they would send scouts first, mapping the enemy's paths with precision. They'd use smaller boats to slip through narrow channels, striking at night to confuse and divide. But they'd also parley, offering false promises to buy time—deception as a tool, not dishonour." Chief Oton's brow furrowed, his staff tapping the floor as he spoke. "False promises? The gods frown on deceit, for it sows discord among the spirits." "But they smile on victory," Maria countered, her voice steady and clear. "The Ijaw want gold and power. Let them think they'll have it, then strike when their guard is down. It's a tactic of survival, not betrayal."

A murmur rippled through the room, some chiefs nodding in reluctant agreement, others exchanging sceptical looks that lingered on Maria's foreign features. King Domingos's heart swelled with pride—his wife was proving herself not just a Olori but a strategist, her mind a bridge between worlds. "We'll do both," he declared, his voice cutting through the murmurs. "Olua, gather twenty of our swiftest warriors and ready the war canoes. Ebi, send a messenger to the Ijaw pirates with word that I'll meet them to discuss terms. We'll offer a chest of coral and ivory—enough to tempt them, but not our soul."

Ebi nodded, though his eyes betrayed a flicker of doubt. "And the rescue, Ogiame?" "I'll lead it myself," Domingos said, his tone brooking no argument, his hand resting on the dagger at his waist. "At dusk, when the Ijaw feast on their greed, we'll strike." The council dispersed to prepare, the air thick with purpose. Domingos drew Maria aside, his hand resting on her shoulder, the indigo wrapper soft under his fingers. "You've given me a path, my love. But the chiefs still watch you closely. Stay with Mama Uwala and Olori Ewere—let the women see your strength while I'm gone." Maria's eyes flashed with defiance. "I'd rather paddle a canoe than sit weaving. Temieno is my sister now, too, and I won't be sidelined." He smiled, tracing the wrapper's edge with a tender touch. "I know your heart, but Warri needs its Olori safe. For now, fight with your mind, not a blade. Guide the palace while I bring her back."

She relented with a reluctant nod, though her gaze promised she'd not remain idle long, her spirit as fierce as the river's current. As King Domingos left to don his war gear—a leather vest reinforced with fish scales and a curved dagger from his father's armoury, its blade etched with the royal seal—he felt the weight of two worlds: the Itsekiri warrior he was born to be, and the strategist shaped by Portugal's courts. The palace hummed with activity as warriors sharpened spears and women prepared charms, their chants rising to the gods for protection.

By dusk, the war canoes glided silently through the creeks, their paddles dipping with practiced precision, the water rippling like whispers of the night. Domingos crouched at the lead, his face streaked with white clay, a charm from Chief Oton—a small pouch of river sand and herbs—tied around his wrist to ward off harm. Olua was at his side, a spear in hand, his earlier bravado tempered by the mission's gravity, his shark-tooth necklace swaying with each movement. The mangroves loomed like sentinels, their roots tangling in the water, and the air was thick with the hum of insects, the distant croak of frogs, and the faint scent of mud and salt.

The Ijaw camp came into view—a cluster of thatched huts on stilts, lit by flickering torches that cast dancing shadows across the water. Laughter and the clink of palm wine gourds drifted across the creek, a sign the Ijaw believed their ransom secure. King Domingos's messenger had done his work, promising a parley at dawn with a chest of coral and ivory, luring them into complacency. He scanned the camp, his eyes narrowing on a single hut, larger than the rest, guarded by two warriors. Temieno had to be there. He signalled to Olua, who passed the order: half the warriors would circle to the camp's rear, creating a diversion by setting fire to a storehouse filled with dried fish. The rest would follow Dom Domingos to the hut.

As the first flames licked the night sky, shouts erupted, and the Ijaw warriors scrambled toward the blaze, their silhouettes frantic against the firelight. Domingos's group surged forward, leaping onto the wooden walkways with the agility of river otters. The guards at the hut turned, but Olua's spear was faster, felling one with a precise thrust, while Domingos tackled the other, his dagger pressing against the man's throat. "Quiet, or you join your ancestors," Domingos hissed, his voice a low growl. The man nodded, eyes wide with fear, his breath ragged.

Inside the hut, Temieno sat bound, her wrapper torn but her chin high, her dark eyes flashing with defiance. Her wrists were raw from the ropes, but her spirit remained unbroken. She looked up as Domingos cut her bonds, her face lighting with relief. "Took you long enough, brother," she whispered, a spark of her usual fire returning despite her ordeal. "Save the jests for the palace," he replied, pulling her to her feet, his hands steady as he guided her toward the door. "We're not safe yet."

The escape was swift but perilous. The Ijaw, realizing the ruse, rallied with war cries that echoed through the creeks, their canoes cutting through the water in pursuit. Arrows hissed past, one grazing King Domingos's arm, drawing a sharp intake of breath, while another struck Olua's shoulder, the warrior gritting his teeth as blood seeped through his vest. Domingos shielded Temieno, his heart pounding as the mangroves closed around them, their dense foliage swallowing the canoes. The Ijaw's pursuit faded, their shouts lost to the night, and the warriors paddled with desperate strength, the rhythm of their strokes a lifeline back to Warri.

By dawn, the canoes reached the palace, greeted by a crowd that erupted in cheers, their voices a wave of relief and triumph. Maria, flanked by Mama Uwala and Olori Ewere, ran to embrace Temieno, heedless of protocol, her indigo wrapper fluttering as she moved. The princess, bruised but unbroken, returned the hug, whispering, "You're more Itsekiri than you know, sister," her voice thick with emotion. The women of the palace surrounded them, their ululations a song of victory, while warriors tended to Olua's wound, his grin defiant despite the pain.

That night, the palace feasted, drums echoing through the halls as Temieno recounted her ordeal with exaggerated flair, turning her capture into a tale of courage that earned laughter even from Ebi, whose stern face softened. She described the Ijaw leader's boastful taunts and her own sharp retorts, her with a weapon that had kept her spirits high. King Domingos watched, his arm bandaged but his spirit lifted, though his gaze lingered on the horizon where the river met the sea. The Ijaw would not forget this humiliation; their pride wounded as deeply as their plans. And the Portuguese, ever watchful from their galleons, would see Warri's strength as both an opportunity for trade and a threat to their ambitions.

As Ogiame, Domingos knew peace was fleeting. He recalled a parable Ebi had shared during his youth, of the Crab and the Tide. Crab scuttled along the shore, proud of its hard shell, but Tide, relentless and patient, swept it away when it grew careless. Domingos saw the Ijaw as the Tide, their raid a warning, and himself as the Crab, needing to fortify Warri's defences. Another tale came to mind, one from the elders, of the Egret and the Fisherman. Egret stood by the river, guiding Fisherman to the best catch, but when Fisherman grew greedy, Egret flew away, leaving him empty-handed. King Domingos vowed not to let greed—whether for gold or power—blind him to his people's needs.

The feast continued, but a young messenger from the coast interrupted, his face pale. "Ogiame, the Portuguese galleon moves closer, and the black-hulled ship—Dutch, they say—has joined it. They demand an audience, claiming trade rights." Domingos's heart sank, but he masked it with resolve. "Prepare the council again," he said, turning to Ebi. "We'll meet them at dawn, with Temieno and Maria at my side. Warri must show its unity." Maria nodded, her hand finding his, the ivory bracelet from Olori Ewere a cool weight against her skin. "We'll face them together," she said, her voice a promise.

The Iroko tree stood silent outside, its roots deep in the earth, its branches reaching for the stars—a reminder that Warri's strength lay in its resilience. As the night deepened, King Domingos and Maria stood on the palace balcony, the river's murmur a constant companion. He traced the scar on his arm, a new mark of his leadership, and spoke softly. "This

rescue was a victory, but the battles ahead will test us more."
Maria leaned against him, her warmth a contrast to the cool
night air. "Then we'll face them as we did today—with cunning, courage, and each other."

The stars above pulsed with secrets, and the mangroves
whispered of challenges yet to come. But for now, Temieno
was safe, the palace rejoiced, and Domingos felt the weight
of his future role as Ogiame settle into a resolve as deep as
the river itself. The Ijaw, the Portuguese, the Dutch—all
would learn that Warri's spirit was unbreakable, guided by
the wisdom of its parables and the unity of its people.

CHAPTER FOUR

Omeyin Conspiracy

The Warri palace was cloaked in the hush of twilight, its courtyards empty save for the flicker of oil lamps casting long, wavering shadows on the mud walls adorned with woven tapestries depicting the river's history. Ogiame Dom Domingos, now fully embraced as king following his coronation months prior, sat in the royal chamber, poring over a map of the Riverland's spread across a low table carved with fish motifs. His scarlet Kemeje was unbuttoned, revealing the coral beads that rested against his chest like a second skin, their weight a constant reminder of his lineage. His European crown, a gift from Portugal, lay on a nearby stand, its golden cross glinting faintly in the lamplight, a symbol of the dual heritage he carried. Beside him, Olori Maria traced a finger along the map's winding creeks, her indigo wrapper—a gift from Mama Uwala—flowing softly, its deep blue a quiet testament to her growing acceptance among the Itsekiri. The rescue of Princess Temieno had quelled some doubts about the foreign Olori, but the kingdom's peace remained fragile, and a new threat was stirring—one that bore the name Omeyin, a whispered conspiracy threatening to unravel Domingos's young reign.

The trouble had begun weeks ago, with murmurs among the river clans of a secret pact among disgruntled chiefs. The Ijaw raid, though repelled, had exposed fissures in Warri's unity, cracks that widened with each passing day. Some chiefs, led by the tradition-bound Chief Ikenna, grumbled that Domingos's marriage to Maria and his European learning had weakened the kingdom's spirit, diluting the purity of Itsekiri ways. Others, swayed by promises of wealth and power, had been courted by Captain Alvarez, the Portuguese trader whose ships lingered at the river's mouth, their sails a constant silhouette against the horizon, hungry for more than palm oil and ivory. The conspiracy's name, Omeyin—meaning "Upcoming Child" in the Itsekiri tongue, a nod to the rise of a new leader—had reached Domingos through Ebi, his ever-watchful advisor, who had overheard a fisherman speak of a clandestine meeting in the mangrove village of Omeyin, a remote settlement shrouded in mist and mystery.

"Ogiame," Ebi had warned earlier that day, his voice low as they stood beneath the Iroko tree, its gnarled branches swaying in the evening breeze, "they plot in the shadows. Ikenna's hand is in this, but he's not alone. They seek to replace you with your cousin, Omajuwa, a man they believe will shun the white man's ways and restore the old order."

Domingos's fingers tightened on the map, his eyes narrowing as the weight of betrayal settled over him. Omajuwa, a quiet man who had grown up among the river clans, was no warrior but carried the blood of their grandfather, a revered Ogiame whose name still echoed in the elders' songs. His name alone could sway the wavering chiefs, a beacon for those who longed for a return to tradition.

"What proof do we have?" Domingos asked, turning to Maria, whose sharp mind had become his anchor in these turbulent waters. Ebi, standing nearby with his coral bracelet glinting in the lamplight, produced a small bundle wrapped in palm leaves, its edges damp from the river. He unfolded it to reveal a carved wooden token, its surface etched with the symbol of a coiled snake—a mark used by Ikenna's clan, a sign of cunning and danger. "This was found in Omeyin, near the shrine where they met," Ebi said, his voice heavy. "A fisherman loyal to you saw Ikenna and two others, including a Portuguese man, speaking in hushed tones under the cover of night."

Maria's brow furrowed, her finger pausing on the map. "Alvarez," she said, her voice laced with certainty, the name rolling off her tongue like a bitter herb. "He's been too quiet since Temieno's rescue. The Portuguese play these games in their courts—pitting nobles against kings to weaken both, then swooping in to claim the spoils. He's offering Ikenna gold or guns, I'd wager, to turn Warri into a puppet state."

Domingos nodded, his jaw set as memories of Alvarez's thin smile at the royal wedding flashed through his mind. The trader's ambition had been masked by polite nods, but now it seemed he was weaving a web with Ikenna, exploiting the kingdom's divisions. Yet Omajuwa's involvement puzzled him. His cousin had always been loyal, bowing at the coronation without a trace of resentment, his simple presence a contrast to the pomp of the court. Was he a willing pawn, or merely a name used to rally the discontented?

"We need more than a token," Domingos said, rising to pace the chamber, his bare feet silent on the woven mat floor, the scent of palm oil from the lamps filling the air. "If I accuse Ikenna without proof, I risk driving others to his side. And Omajuwa—he deserves a chance to speak before we judge him. Warri's strength lies in its unity, not division." Ebi's eyes softened, but his tone was firm, a voice honed by years of counsel. "Caution is wise, Ogiame, but delay is dangerous. The Omeyin plot grows bolder with each moon. They may strike before your coronation's glow fades, using the river's currents to mask their moves."

Maria stood, her wrapper rustling like the leaves of the Iroko, her presence commanding despite her foreign roots. "Then let me go to Omeyin," she said, her words startling both men, her sea-blue eyes alight with resolve. "The people there know me from my visits with Mama Uwala, teaching them to weave new patterns with Portuguese thread. They'll speak to a Olori before they trust a warrior. I can learn who meets and when." Domingos's instinct was to refuse—Maria was his heart, and the mangroves were treacherous, their muddy paths a labyrinth for the unwary. But her eyes, fierce and unyielding, reminded him of the woman who had crossed oceans to stand at his side, her courage a match for his own. "You'll take Olua and four warriors," he said finally, his voice firm but laced with concern. "And you'll return by dawn, with or without answers." She nodded, a flicker of gratitude in her smile, and left to prepare, her footsteps echoing with purpose.

Domingos turned to Ebi, his mind already turning to strategy. "Summon Omajuwa to the palace tomorrow. I'll hear his heart myself. And send word to Chief Oton—his prayers may shield us where blades cannot. The spirits of the river must guide us through this storm." The night deepened, the palace settling into a tense silence broken only by the distant croak of frogs and the rustle of palm fronds. By midnight, Maria's canoe slipped through the creeks toward Omeyin, guided by Olua's steady paddle, the young warrior's scarred shoulder a testament to his loyalty. The mangrove village was a cluster of stilted huts, its shrine to the river god dimly lit by a single torch that cast eerie reflections on the water. Maria, cloaked in a plain wrapper to blend with the night, stepped onto the walkway, her heart pounding but her steps sure, the damp wood creaking underfoot.

She approached a hut where Mama Ose, an old woman known to weave nets and hear secrets, sat by a low fire, her hair white as moonlight, her hands gnarled from years of labour. "Mama Ose," Maria whispered, slipping inside, the scent of smoked fish filling the air. The woman looked up from her loom, her eyes sharp despite her age, reflecting the fire's glow. "Olori of the white lands," Mama Ose said, her voice a mix of curiosity and caution, the words rolling like the river's flow. "Why come to Omeyin in the dark?"

Maria knelt, offering a small basket of yams as a gesture of respect, the tubers cool against her palms. "I seek truth, Mama. Men plot against my husband, and I would know their names to protect our people." Mama Ose's gaze lingered on the basket, then softened, her fingers pausing on the loom. "The river carries many whispers," she said, her voice low and rhythmic. "Ikenna was here three nights past, with a white man in fine cloth—Alvarez, I'd wager. They spoke of gold and a new Ogiame, a child to rise from the shadows. But Omajuwa... his name is used, but his heart is not seen among them." Maria's breath caught, hope flickering like the torchlight. Omajuwa might yet be innocent, a pawn in a larger game.

"Where do they meet next?" she pressed, leaning closer, the hut's warmth enveloping her. "Tomorrow, at the shrine, when the moon is high," Mama Ose replied, her eyes narrowing. "But beware, Olori. The snake bites those who tread too close. There's a tale of the Python and the Parrot—Python coiled in wait, patient and silent, while Parrot sang of freedom. When Parrot flew too near, Python struck, and the forest mourned its song. You walk a dangerous path." Maria nodded, the parable sinking deep, and returned to the palace before dawn, her findings shared in hushed tones with Domingos as the first light crept over the horizon.

Omajuwa arrived at noon, his simple wrapper and unadorned beads a stark contrast to Ikenna's ostentatious coral, his presence humble yet burdened. He bowed low, his eyes meeting Domingos's without guile, the air thick with the scent of river mud carried on his clothes. "Cousin," Domingos said, his voice steady but probing, the weight of leadership in each word. "Your name is spoken in dark places. Tell me why." Omajuwa paled, his hands trembling as he knelt. "Ogiame, I swear by our ancestors, I know nothing of plots. Ikenna sought my counsel on river trade, asking for my name to lend weight to his words, but I gave him no oath. If my name is used, it is without my will. I serve Warri, not ambition."

Domingos studied him, searching for deceit, but found only fear and loyalty, the honesty in Omajuwa's eyes mirroring the river's clarity. "Then prove it," he said, his tone softening. "Join me tonight at Omeyin. We'll face the snake together, and your loyalty will be your shield." Omajuwa nodded, relief washing over his face like a tide receding. That night, Domingos led a small force—Olua, Omajuwa, and ten warriors armed with spears and nets—to the shrine at Omeyin. Hidden in the mangroves, their breaths hushed, they watched as Ikenna and Alvarez arrived, their voices low but clear over the water's murmur. Ikenna promised warriors to secure Omajuwa's throne, his scar glinting in the torchlight; Alvarez offered muskets and a Portuguese alliance, his velvet doublet a stark intrusion. The betrayal was laid bare, a coil tightening around Warri's heart.

Domingos signalled, and his warriors struck, swift and silent as the river's current. Ikenna fought, his dagger flashing like a serpent's fang, but Olua's spear pinned him to the ground, the young warrior's strength a testament to his training. Alvarez, cowardice overtaking ambition, fled to his canoe, only to be caught by Omajuwa, who bound him with a fisherman's net, his hands deft from years on the river. The conspirators were dragged to the palace; their plot shattered like a broken drum.

At dawn, Domingos addressed his people from the palace steps, Ikenna and Alvarez in chains, their heads bowed. The crowd gathered, their wrappers a mosaic of colour against the mud walls, their voices a rising tide. "The Omeyin sought to cut our heart," he declared, his crown gleaming in the sunlight, "but Warri stands unbroken. Let this be a warning: no blade, hidden or bold, will dim our spirit. We are one people, bound by the river and the gods." The crowd roared, their faith in Ogiame renewed, their cheers echoing to the mangroves. Maria stood at his side, her hand in his, the ivory bracelet from Olori Ewere a cool weight, while Omajuwa knelt in gratitude, his loyalty proven.

Temieno, watching from the balcony with Mama Uwala, grinned, whispering, "My brother's crown sits well, doesn't it?" The old weaver nodded, her silver-streaked hair catching the light. But as Domingos gazed at the river, where the Portuguese galleon loomed larger, he knew Alvarez's masters in Lisbon would not forget this defeat. A new parable came to mind, one from his childhood, of the Heron and the Eel. Heron speared Eel with its beak, but Eel writhed free, vowing revenge from the mud. Domingos saw Alvarez as the Eel, slippery and persistent, and himself as the Heron, needing vigilance to protect Warri's waters.

The feast that followed was a celebration of unity, drums pounding as warriors danced, their feet shaking the earth. Yet a young scout interrupted, his voice urgent. "Ogiame, the Dutch black-hulled ship approaches, its captain demanding trade talks—and hinting at alliance against the Portuguese." Domingos's heart sank, but he masked it with resolve. "Prepare the council again," he said to Ebi. "We'll meet them at noon, with Maria and Omajuwa at my side. Warri must show its strength." Maria squeezed his hand, her warmth a contrast to the cool dawn. "Together, we'll face them," she said, her voice a promise echoing the river's flow.

The Iroko tree loomed in the distance, its roots deep in the earth, its branches a canopy of resilience—a silent vow that Warri would endure. As the sun rose, Domingos felt the weight of his crown settle into a resolve as enduring as the river itself, guided by the wisdom of parables and the unity of his people, ready to meet the challenges of a new dawn.

CHAPTER FIVE

The Birth of Anthonio Domingos

The Warri palace hummed with a quiet anticipation, its courtyards bathed in the soft glow of dawn, the first light filtering through the palm fronds and casting dappled patterns on the mud walls adorned with woven tapestries depicting the river's serpentine dance. Nearly a year had passed since the Omeyin conspiracy was crushed, and Ogiame Dom Domingos's reign had settled into a rhythm of strength and vigilance, the Ijaw retreating to their creeks to lick their wounds, and the Portuguese traders, chastened by Captain Alvarez's disgrace, cloaking their ambitions in careful courtesy. Yet today, the kingdom's focus shifted from war and trade to a moment of profound joy: Olori Maria was in labour, and the heir to Warri's throne was about to be born. The air carried the scent of fresh palm wine and the faint tang of river mud, a blend that spoke of life and continuity.

Domingos paced the outer chamber, his scarlet Kemeje replaced by a simple white wrapper, a sign of humility before the gods, its fabric soft against his skin. His coral beads clicked softly with each step, a rhythmic echo of his lineage, and the European crown, a symbol of his dual heritage, rested on a carved stool nearby, its golden cross catching the dawn's first rays. His face, usually composed with the stoic resolve of a king, betrayed a flicker of anxiety, his dark eyes darting toward the birthing room where Maria's cries pierced the morning air. The sound was sharp and determined, a testament to her spirit, yet it gnawed at his heart, a battle he could not fight for her.

Princess Temieno, now a poised young woman of nineteen, stood by the door, her wrapper a vibrant green adorned with coral beads, her eyes darting between her brother and the chamber within. "She's strong, Domingos," Temieno said, her voice steady despite the tension, a smile playing on her lips as she recalled Maria's courage during the Omeyin crisis. "Maria faced mangroves and conspiracies. She'll conquer this, too." Domingos managed a faint smile, his hand brushing the charm Chief Oton had given him—a small pouch of herbs tied with red thread, blessed with prayers to ensure a safe delivery, its texture rough against his fingers. "I know her strength," he said, his voice low. "But the gods test us all, and this is a test I cannot shield her from."

Ebi, ever the shadow at Domingos's side, approached with a calabash of palm wine, its sweet aroma wafting upward. "Drink, Ogiame," he urged, his lined face softened by years of wisdom, his coral bracelet glinting as he extended the vessel. "It calms the heart. The people gather outside, praying for a prince. They see this child as a bridge, like you, uniting the river and the sea." Domingos took the calabash but only sipped, the liquid warming his throat, his thoughts drifting to Maria. Their marriage had woven Warri and Portugal closer, a tapestry of cultures, yet the birth of their child would seal that bond in blood and spirit. He remembered their wedding, her laughter ringing through the dance, and her bravery at Omeyin, navigating the mangroves with the grace of a river bird. Now, she faced a battle he could not join, and it humbled him, stripping away the armour of kingship to reveal the man beneath.

Inside the birthing room, Maria gripped Mama Uwala's hand, her face slick with sweat, her indigo wrapper discarded for a simple cloth stained with the earth's red clay. The midwives chanted softly, their voices a soothing counterpoint to her laboured breaths, the rhythm mimicking the river's flow. Olori Ewere, regal even in the dim light, her coral-encrusted wrapper shimmering like the water at dusk, dabbed Maria's brow with a damp cloth, murmuring words of encouragement in the Itsekiri tongue. "The river flows strong in you, child," she said, her voice a gentle current. "Push and let your son greet the world with a cry as mighty as the river." Olori Maria nodded, drawing on the resolve that had carried her across oceans, her sea-blue eyes fixed on the flickering oil lamp. The pain was fierce, a storm within her, but she thought of Domingos, of Warri, and of the child who would carry their dreams forward. With a final, guttural cry that shook the walls, she pushed, and the room filled with the wail of a newborn, a sound as pure as the river's song.

Mama Uwala lifted the child, a boy, his skin a warm blend of his mother's fairness and his father's bronze, his tiny limbs flailing with life. She cut the cord with a blessed knife, its blade etched with symbols of fertility and wrapped him in a cloth woven with coral patterns, the fabric soft against his new skin. "A prince!" she declared, her voice thick with pride, the word echoing like a drumbeat. The midwives ululated, their song spilling into the outer chamber, a wave of joy that broke the tension. Temieno burst through the door, her face alight with excitement, her beads clinking as she moved. "Brother, a son! You have a son!" Domingos's knees weakened, relief flooding him like the river at high tide, washing away the night's fears. He followed Temieno inside, where Olori Maria lay exhausted but radiant, cradling the child against her chest, her breath steadying.

He knelt beside her, his hand trembling as he touched the boy's tiny fist, the skin warm and fragile under his calloused fingers. "My love," he whispered, his voice breaking with emotion, "you've given Warri its future." Olori Maria smiled, her sea-blue eyes soft with exhaustion and love. "He's ours, Domingos. Ours and Warri's." Mama Uwala handed the child to Domingos, who held him with a warrior's care, his arms steady despite the tremor in his heart. The boy's eyes, dark and curious, met his father's, and Domingos felt a surge of purpose, a connection deeper than blood. "His name will be Anthonio Domingos," he said, the name a blend of Olori Maria's heritage—honouring her father, Antonio—and his own, a prince of two worlds, like his father before him. "A bridge between the river and the sea."

Olori Ewere nodded, her coral beads glinting like stars in the lamplight. "A fitting name. The gods have blessed this day with a child who will carry Warri's strength and Portugal's wisdom." Word spread swiftly, carried by the wind through the palace corridors, and the courtyard filled with jubilant Itsekiri. Drummers pounded rhythms of celebration, their hands a blur on taut skins, the beat resonating through the earth like a heartbeat. Women danced, their wrappers swirling like the river's currents, their coral beads clinking in harmony, while children tossed handfuls of flower petals into the air. Chiefs arrived with gifts—piles of yams stacked high, carved stools inlaid with mother-of-pearl, and a small canoe crafted for the prince's future, its hull painted with waves and stars. Olua, now a trusted captain with a scar from the Ijaw raid, presented a tiny spear, its tip blunted with cork, earning laughter from the crowd as he grinned. "For the little warrior," he said, bowing to Anthonio.

Even Chief Ikenna, pardoned but watched closely since the conspiracy, bowed low, offering a basket of cowries as a sign of loyalty, his scar a silent reminder of his past defiance. The gesture was met with cautious nods, the air thick with the scent of roasted plantain and the murmur of reconciliation. Chief Oton performed the naming rite at noon, under the Iroko tree's sprawling shade, its branches a canopy of green against the sun. He sprinkled river water over Anthonio, the droplets catching the light like tiny jewels, invoking Oritse Udeji for strength and the river spirits for wisdom. The crowd chanted the prince's name—"Anthonio Domingos!"—their voices rising to the sky, a chorus of hope and unity. Domingos stood with Olori Maria, who had insisted on joining despite her fatigue, her arm linked with his, the ivory bracelet from Olori Ewere a cool weight on her wrist. Temieno, ever the proud aunt, tossed coral beads into the air, a gesture of abundance that drew cheers, her laughter ringing clear.

But as the festivities peaked, Ebi drew Domingos aside, his face grave beneath the tree's shadow, the scent of its bark mingling with the river breeze. "Ogiame, a Portuguese ship arrived at dawn. Their new captain, Mendes, seeks an audience. He speaks of trade but carries muskets on deck. Alvarez's shadow lingers, and the Dutch, black-hulled ship hovers near, their captain hinting at alliance against the Portuguese. The sea grows restless." Domingos's grip tightened on Olori Maria's hand, his joy tempered by the weight of duty, the warmth of her skin a contrast to the cool reality of impending challenges. "Let him wait," he said, his voice firm. "Today is for Anthonio. Tomorrow, we face the sea and its currents."

That night, the palace feasted, palm wine flowing from carved gourds as stories of Anthonio's future filled the air—tales of a prince who would sail the river and the ocean, uniting tribes and nations. The courtyard glowed with torchlight, the scent of smoked fish and pepper soup wafting through the crowd. Olori Maria, resting in their chamber, watched Domingos cradle their son, his face softened by love, the lamplight casting gentle shadows on the walls. "He'll need your heart," she said, her voice weak but warm, her hand resting on his. "And your strength to guide him through the storms ahead." "And your wisdom," Domingos replied, kissing her brow, the salt of her sweat lingering on his lips. "Together, we'll raise him to be Warri's shield."

Outside, the Iroko tree stood sentinel, its roots deep in Warri's soil, its branches reaching for the stars—a silent witness to the birth of a new era. Anthonio's cries softened into sleep, his tiny chest rising and falling, a bridge between two worlds tightened by his first breath. But Domingos knew the river and sea would test that bond. As the feast waned, a young scout burst into the chamber, his wrapper torn, his face flushed. "Ogiame, the Dutch captain has landed with armed men! They claim rights to trade but demand a share of our ivory. Mendes watches from his ship, his muskets ready!" Domingos's heart sank, but he masked it with resolve, handing Anthonio to Olori Maria. "Stay with him," he said, his voice steady. "I'll meet them at dawn."

The night deepened, and Domingos gathered Ebi, Olua, and Omajuwa in the war room, the map once again spread before them. "The Dutch seek to exploit our strength," Ebi said, his finger tracing the coast. "Mendes waits for weakness." Olua gripped his spear. "Let's drive them back, Ogiame!" Omajuwa, his loyalty proven, spoke softly. "Or parley, cousin. A trade pact might turn their rivalry to our gain." Domingos nodded, recalling a parable from his youth, of the Tortoise and the Two Eagles. Tortoise, clever but weak, tricked two eagles into carrying him aloft by flattering their rivalry, securing his safety. "We'll parley," he decided. "Offer the Dutch a share of palm oil, but demand their guns stay sheathed. Mendes will see our unity and hesitate."

At dawn, Domingos stood on the riverbank, Olori Maria at his side with Anthonio in her arms, a living symbol of Warri's resolve. The Dutch captain, a broad man named Van der Berg, disembarked, his men tense but respectful. "We seek trade," Van der Berg said, his Dutch accent thick. "But we'll not bow to Portuguese threats." Domingos met his gaze. "Warri trades with strength, not submission. Take palm oil, leave your muskets, and we'll talk alliance against

Mendes. Refuse, and the river will swallow your ships." Van der Berg hesitated, then nodded, the deal struck under the Iroko's gaze.

The crowd cheered, but Domingos knew the peace was fragile. Olori Maria whispered, "A good start." As they returned to the palace, Anthonio cooed, and Domingos felt the weight of his crown lighten, bolstered by love and strategy. The Iroko stood tall, its roots a promise of endurance, and Warri sang under a new star, ready for the trials ahead.

CHAPTER SIX

Passage of Olori Maria

The Warri palace, once vibrant with the joy of Prince Anthonio Domingos's birth, now lay under a pall of grief, its courtyards bathed in the muted glow of a sun hanging low, as if the heavens themselves mourned alongside the kingdom. The river shimmered faintly in the distance, its surface dulled by a thin veil of mist, the mangroves along its banks swaying gently in the breeze, their roots a sombre frame to the day's sorrow. Olori Maria, the Olori of Warri, had slipped into a fever days after delivering her son, her strength sapped by complications that neither the midwives' healing herbs nor Chief Oton's fervent prayers could mend. Her sea-blue eyes, once bright with courage and laughter, had grown dim with each passing hour, and by the third dawn, her breath had stilled, leaving a silence that echoed through the palace like a broken drum. The kingdom reeled, and Ogiame Dom Domingos, the king who had bridged worlds with his foreign Olori, felt his own heart fracture under the crushing weight of loss, a wound deeper than any blade.

Domingos knelt beside Olori Maria's body in the royal chamber, her form draped in the indigo wrapper gifted by Mama Uwala, its coral patterns now a sombre shroud that clung to her still form. The air was thick with the scent of burnt herbs and river water, a futile attempt to cleanse the room of death's shadow. His scarlet Kemeje, a symbol of his kingship, was discarded, replaced by a plain white wrapper, the color of mourning among the Itsekiri, its fabric rough against his skin. His European crown, a testament to the journey he and Olori Maria had shared, lay untouched on a table carved with fish motifs, its golden cross dull in the lamplight, as if dimmed by her absence. His coral beads hung heavy around his neck, each one a reminder of the vows they had exchanged under the Iroko tree, now a hollow echo in his chest.

Princess Temieno stood silently at the door, her eyes red but her jaw set with the resolve of a warrior, guarding her brother's grief with a sister's fierce love. Her green wrapper, adorned with coral beads, was muted by a gray sash, a mark of mourning that contrasted with her usual vibrancy. Olori Ewere, her regal composure frayed at the edges, clutched the carved ivory bracelet she had given Olori Maria, her tears falling quietly onto the smooth surface, a silent tribute to the daughter-in-law who had won her heart. "She fought to give us Anthonio," Domingos whispered, his voice raw with emotion, his hand trembling as he held Olori Maria's cold, still fingers, as if willing her warmth to return. "Why did the gods take her so soon, when her work was just beginning?"

Mama Uwala, her silver-streaked hair unbound in mourning, its strands catching the lamplight like threads of sorrow, placed a weathered hand on his shoulder, her touch a gentle anchor. "The river gives, and the river takes, Ogiame," she said softly, her voice carrying the weight of generations. "Olori's spirit flows to the ancestors, her laughter joining their songs. But her strength lives in your son, a light to guide you through this darkness." Domingos's gaze fell to the cradle where Anthonio slept, unaware of the void his mother had left, his tiny chest rising and falling with the innocence of youth. The boy's dark eyes—Olori Maria's eyes—were closed in peace, a balm to Domingos's wounded soul and a wound that would never heal, for every feature of his son would forever echo the woman who had crossed oceans to be his Olori.

The kingdom prepared for Maria's passage with the solemnity befitting an Olori, a ritual that blended Itsekiri tradition with the echoes of her Christian faith. The courtyard, so recently alive with the celebration of Anthonio's birth, was now lined with mourners, their wrappers muted in black and greys, the colours of charcoal and river mist. Drummers played a slow, mournful rhythm, the beat a heartbeat for a grieving people, its echo reverberating off the mud walls adorned with faded tapestries. Women wove palm fronds into mats, their fingers deft despite their tears, symbols of the journey to the spirit world where Olori Maria's soul would find rest. Men carved a canoe to carry offerings to the river gods, its hull etched with waves and stars, a vessel for the transition from life to eternity. Chief Oton, his staff heavy with cowrie shells that rattled like distant thunder, led prayers at the palace shrine, the air thick with the scent of incense and the murmur of supplication, invoking Oritse Udeji to guide Olori Maria's soul and the river spirits Umale Okun to cradle her in their currents.

Ebi, ever loyal, coordinated the rites with a steady hand, his coral bracelet glinting as he moved among the mourners, but he kept a wary eye on the horizon where the Portuguese ship, captained by Mendes, lingered at the river's mouth, its silhouette a quiet threat against the dawn sky. Ebi had heard whispers of discontent among the chiefs—some, like Ikenna, saw Olori Maria's death as a sign that the gods disapproved of Domingos's foreign ways, a divine judgment on the union that had brought Warri closer to Portugal. The Omeyin conspiracy was buried, its leaders chastened, but its embers still glowed in the hearts of the discontented, a fire waiting for a spark. Ebi said nothing to Domingos, not yet; the king's grief was burden enough, a weight that bowed even the strongest shoulders.

The funeral began at dusk, under the shadow of the Iroko tree, its gnarled branches a canopy of mourning, its roots deep in the earth where generations of kings had found solace. Olori Maria's body, adorned with coral beads that glinted like tears and wrapped in the indigo cloth, was carried on a bier by six warriors, Olua among them, his face etched with sorrow, his scar a mark of battles fought for Warri. The procession wound through the palace grounds to the riverbank, where a pyre had been built in respect of Olori Maria last wish, its wood stacked high and adorned with palm fronds, blending Itsekiri tradition with a nod to Olori Maria's Christian faith—a cross of twigs placed at its base. Chief Oton sprinkled river water over the bier, the droplets catching the fading light, chanting, "Olori Maria, daughter of Warri, cross the river to our fathers. Your name lives in our songs, your spirit in our waters." The crowd murmured their assent, their voices a soft wave.

Domingos stood at the pyre's edge, holding Anthonio, whose small form was wrapped in a soft cloth woven with coral patterns, the boy's weight a fragile anchor in his arms. Temieno, at his side, placed a hand on the child, her voice low and steady. "He'll know her, brother. We'll tell him of her courage, her laughter, the way she danced with us under the stars." The flames were lit, the fire rising with a crackle that mingled with the river's murmur, carrying Olori Maria's spirit to the stars above. The crowd sang—a haunting melody of loss and honour, their voices weaving through the smoke, a tribute to the Olori who had become one of them.

Domingos's eyes stung with unshed tears, but he held his son close, whispering, "Your mother was Warri's heart, Anthonio. She gave you life, and I'll give you her story, every tale of her bravery."

As the pyre burned, a figure approached through the dispersing crowd—Mama Ose, the weaver from Omeyin, her eyes sharp despite the grief etched into her lined face, her hair white as the mist that clung to the river. She carried a small basket, woven with care, its edges frayed from the journey, and placed it at Domingos's feet. "For the prince," she said, her voice a whisper carried on the wind. "Olori's wrapper, cut into strips. Weave it into his life, Ogiame, so she walks with him, a thread in his days." Domingos nodded, unable to speak, the gesture anchoring him to his people's love, the basket's weight a tangible link to Olori Maria's memory.

But as the crowd dispersed, their footsteps fading into the night, Ebi drew Domingos aside, his voice urgent beneath the Iroko's shadow, the scent of burnt wood and river water heavy in the air. "Ogiame, Mendes sent a message. He offers condolences but requests a meeting tomorrow. He speaks of trade, promising goods and muskets, but I fear he sees weakness in our grief. The Dutch black-hulled ship hovers near, its captain Van der Berg watching, perhaps waiting to exploit the moment." Domingos's grief hardened into resolve, the firelight reflecting in his eyes. "Let him come," he said, his voice steady despite the ache in his chest. "Olori Maria's death will not break Warri. I'll face him with Anthonio in my arms, a reminder of what we fight for, a symbol of our unbroken spirit."

That night, Domingos sat by Anthonio's cradle in the royal chamber, the window open to the river's murmur, the Iroko tree looming outside like a silent guardian, its branches swaying in the breeze. Temieno joined him, her presence a quiet strength, her green wrapper now adorned with a white sash, a mark of mourning that softened her usual fire. "She changed us, Domingos," she said, her voice gentle as she traced a finger along Anthonio's cheek. "Her blood runs in Anthonio, and her spirit in you. Warri will endure because of what she gave us." He looked at his son, then at the stars, where Olori Maria's light seemed to linger, a faint glow among the constellations. The river flowed on, carrying her passage to the ancestors, but Domingos knew his duty remained—to guard Warri, to raise Anthonio in the shadow of her memory, and to face the storms that waited beyond the horizon.

As he held his son, a soft knock sounded, and Olua entered, his spear resting against the wall, his face weary but resolute. "Ogiame, I've heard from the river clans," he said, his voice low. "Some whisper that Olori Maria's death was no natural fever—that Mendes sent poisoned gifts after the trade talks, a silent strike to weaken you. The chiefs are restless again."

Domingos's heart clenched, but he masked it with a nod. "Investigate, Olua. Bring me proof, but quietly. We'll not accuse without evidence." Olua bowed and left, the door creaking shut, leaving Domingos with a new burden.

The night deepened, and a young messenger burst in, his wrapper torn, his breath ragged. "Ogiame, the Dutch have landed a scouting party! They claim to secure trade routes but carry weapons. Mendes's ship moves closer, his cannons visible!" Domingos's resolve steeled, the grief transforming into a warrior's focus. He turned to Temieno. "Stay with Anthonio. I'll summon the council." She nodded, her hand lingering on the cradle, her eyes fierce with protectiveness.

In the war room, Ebi, Chief Oton, and Omajuwa gathered, the map spread once more, its lines a battleground of ink. "The Dutch test us," Ebi said, his finger tracing the coast. "Mendes waits for our fall." Chief Oton shook his staff, the cowries rattling. "The gods demand justice if poison took our Olori. We must cleanse the river." Omajuwa, his loyalty firm, spoke softly. "A parley might buy time, cousin. Offer the Dutch a token trade but prepare for war." Domingos recalled a parable from his mother, of the Owl and the Storm. Owl hid in the tree during the storm, its wisdom guiding it through the tempest, while lesser birds fell. "We'll parley," he decided. "Offer palm oil to Van der Berg, demand his scouts withdraw, and send Olua to confirm the poison claim. Mendes will see our strength or face our wrath."

At dawn, Domingos stood on the riverbank, Anthonio in his arms, his white wrapper billowing in the wind, a symbol of mourning turned to defiance. Van der Berg disembarked, his men tense, their weapons glinting. "We secure trade," the captain said, his voice gruff. "But we'll not bow to Portuguese guns." Domingos met his gaze, his voice steady. "Warri trades with strength, not submission. Take palm oil, withdraw your scouts, and we'll talk alliance against Mendes. Refuse, and the river will claim you." Van der Berg hesitated, then nodded, the deal struck under the Iroko's watchful branches.

As the Dutch retreated, Olua returned, his face grim. "Ogiame, I found a vial in a trader's boat—herbs that match the fever's signs. Mendes's hand is in this." Domingos's grief flared into anger, but he kept his voice calm. "Prepare evidence. We'll confront Mendes at noon, with Anthonio as our witness." Olori Maria's death, now a potential murder, fuelled his resolve. At noon, he faced Mendes, the Portuguese captain's smugness faltering as Domingos presented the vial. "Your condolences are lies," Domingos said, Anthonio's cry punctuating his words. "Leave our waters, or Warri's spears will answer." Mendes paled, retreating to his ship, the cannons silent.

That evening, Domingos held Anthonio under the Iroko, its roots a promise of endurance. Temieno joined him, her voice soft. "She'd be proud, brother." He nodded, the river's murmur a lullaby for his son. Olori Maria's passage had tested Warri, but her spirit would guide them, a light in the storms to come.

CHAPTER SEVEN

The Eko Travails

The Warri River shimmered under a blood-red dawn, its waters carrying whispers of unrest from distant shores, the crimson hue a foreboding omen that stained the mangroves lining its banks. The Warri kingdom, still raw from the loss of Olori Maria, now faced a new trial—a war unlike any in its memory, its echoes reverberating through the palace like the distant roll of thunder. Far to the north-west, in the land called Ale Eko Iwere, a fertile coastal strip where Itsekiri traders had long bartered palm oil and coral for yams and cloth, the Awori people had risen in fury, their war cries carried on the lagoon winds. The Awori, a fierce Yoruba clan with deep roots in the lagoons and a history as old as the tides, claimed Ale Eko Iwere as their ancestral domain, dismissing the Itsekiri as interlopers who had encroached upon their sacred soil. For years, an uneasy peace had held, bound by trade and mutual respect, a delicate dance of canoes and commerce, but recent tensions— fuelled by Portuguese meddling, competition over coastal routes, and rumours of Itsekiri dominance—had ignited into open conflict. The Awori had attacked Itsekiri settlements, burning huts with flames that licked the night sky, seizing trade goods, and blockading the lagoon with their war canoes to choke Warri's commerce. Worse, they threatened Portuguese traders, whose ships were vital to Warri's wealth, risking a broader clash with European powers that could draw the kingdom into a maelstrom of foreign intrigue.

Ogiame Dom Domingos stood in the palace war room, his white wrapper a stark contrast to the scarlet Kemeje he once wore with pride, its plain fabric a symbol of mourning turned to resolve. His coral beads gleamed against his chest, their weight a steady anchor, but his European crown remained in its case, a symbol too heavy for this moment of crisis, its golden cross hidden from the dim light of oil lamps. Before him, a map of Ale Eko Iwere lay spread across a carved table, its edges worn from urgent fingers tracing routes through the lagoon's maze, the ink smudged with the sweat of strategy. Princess Temieno, her face hardened by grief and duty, stood at his side, her green wrapper adorned with a grey sash of mourning, her eyes alight with a warrior's fire. Ebi, his trusted advisor, pored over reports from scouts, his lined face taut with concern, his coral bracelet clicking softly as he moved. Chief Oton, the high priest, clutched his cowrie-adorned staff, its shells rattling like a prayer for peace that remained unanswered, the air thick with the scent of river mud and incense. Olua, the young warrior who had proven himself in the Ijaw raid and Omeyin conspiracy, leaned forward, his spear propped against the wall, its iron tip glinting, eager for action, his scar a badge of honour.

The air was thick with tension, for the Itsekiri chiefs, gathered in a semicircle around the map, had sent a unified plea: send Chief Anomu, Warri's greatest war captain, to crush the Awori and secure Ale Eko Iwere. Chief Anomu, a towering man with a scar-ridged face that told tales of battles past and a voice like thunder rolling over the lagoon, stood at the room's edge, his leather vest adorned with iron charms that clinked with each step. Known for his victories against river pirates and his unyielding loyalty to Domingos's father, Anomu was a legend among the Itsekiri, his presence a pillar of strength. Yet his eyes, dark and calculating, held a flicker of doubt as he surveyed the map, the lines of the lagoon a puzzle to unravel. "Ogiame," he said, his voice cutting through the murmurs like a blade, "Ale Eko Iwere is no simple battlefield. The lagoons are a maze of channels and sandbars, the Awori know every twist, and their warriors fight like crocodiles—silent, then deadly. We can win, but the cost will be heavy, a toll in blood that may haunt us."

Domingos's jaw tightened, his mind wrestling with the stakes, the weight of leadership pressing against his chest. Ale Eko Iwere was not just land; it was a lifeline, its trade routes connecting Warri to the broader Yoruba hinterland and the Portuguese ships that brought gold, guns, and prestige, their sails a constant presence on the horizon. Losing it would cripple the kingdom's economy, embolden enemies like the Ijaw who still nursed their grudge, or the Portuguese captain Mendes, who watched Warri's every move with predatory intent. Yet war meant bloodshed, and the Itsekiri, still mourning Olori Maria, could ill afford to lose warriors, their numbers a fragile thread in the kingdom's fabric. Anomu's warning echoed Ebi's earlier counsel, whispered under the Iroko tree: "Victory without strength to hold it is no victory at all, Ogiame. The river teaches us to flow with care, not crash blindly."

Temieno broke the silence, her voice sharp as a dagger's edge, her hand resting on the map where Ale Eko Iwere lay marked. "We cannot sit idle, brother. The Awori burned our people's homes, killed fishermen, and mocked our name with their war cries. If we falter, every clan from here to the sea—Benin, Ijebu, even the Ijaw—will see us as weak, a kingdom ripe for plunder. Send Anomu. Let Warri's fire burns bright, a beacon to our enemies." The chiefs murmured approval, their voices a rising tide, but Ebi raised a hand, his tone calm yet firm. "Ogiame, consider the Portuguese. They demand we protect their traders in Ale Eko Iwere, their gold a lure, but their captain, Mendes, offers no men, only promises of muskets—after the fight, when the blood is spilled. They use us as shields, and if we fail, they'll sail away, leaving us to face the Awori's wrath and their scorn."

Domingos's eyes narrowed, his thoughts drifting to Mendes, who had visited the palace weeks after Olori Maria's death, his condolences laced with demands to secure the coastal routes, his velvet doublet a stark contrast to the mourning white of the court. The Portuguese saw Warri as a pawn in their game of empire, a stepping stone to dominate the coast, and Domingos's refusal to bow had strained their alliance, a crack that widened with each passing day. Yet abandoning the traders risked losing their gold, which funded Warri's canoes, warriors, and the palace itself. "We'll protect the routes," he said finally, his voice firm, a king's command cutting through the debate. "But not for Mendes. For Warri. Anomu, you'll lead five hundred warriors to Ale Eko Iwere. Olua will be your second. Drive the Awori back, secure the lagoon, and hold the village. But bring our people home alive—every life is Warri's treasure."

Anomu bowed, his fist to his chest, the iron charms on his vest clinking like a war drum. "As you command, Ogiame. The Awori will taste our steel, and the lagoon will remember our name." Preparations consumed the next days, transforming the palace into a hive of activity. The clang of blacksmiths' hammers rang through the courtyard as they forged spears and sharpened blades, the air thick with the scent of molten iron and woodsmoke. Women wove nets for supplies, their fingers swift despite the weight of worry, the rustle of palm fronds a constant undertone. Drummers rehearsed war rhythms, their beats a call to arms that rallied the men, the sound carrying to the riverbank where canoes were readied. Chief Oton blessed the warriors at the river shrine, a sacred space of smooth stones and carved idols, sprinkling water and kola nut offerings to Umale Okun, the god of river and sea, his chants rising with the dawn mist.

Temieno, defying tradition that kept women from the battlefield, insisted on joining the campaign, her skill with a dagger and her intimate knowledge of the lagoons—gained from childhood explorations—too valuable to ignore. "I'll not sit weaving while our people burn," she declared, her eyes flashing with determination. Domingos, torn between pride in her spirit and fear for her safety, relented, assigning her to scout with a small team of agile warriors, their movements as silent as the night heron. "Return to me, sister," he said, his voice thick with emotion, and she nodded, her hand squeezing his in silent promise.

Anomu's force, clad in leather vests reinforced with fish scales and armed with spears, bows, and a few Portuguese muskets—gifts from a grudging trade—boarded war canoes, their paddles slicing the river with practiced precision. The journey northwest took two days, the river widening into the lagoon's labyrinth, its waters a mirror to the sky, the mangroves a dense curtain of green. Ale Eko Iwere was a land of contrasts—lush mangrove swamps gave way to sandy beaches where Itsekiri huts clustered around a bustling market, now reduced to smouldering ruins, the air heavy with the scent of charred wood and salt. The lagoon, a network of channels and sandbars, was both a highway and a trap, its beauty hiding the danger within.

The Awori, led by their war chief, Oba Adeyemi, a wiry man in a leopard-skin cloak that rippled with each movement, had fortified a ridge overlooking the main channel, their war canoes patrolling like sharks, their iron-tipped spears glinting in the sunlight. The Itsekiri traders, huddled in the village with a handful of Portuguese merchants, sent desperate pleas for aid, their stocks of palm oil and coral looted or burned, their voices trembling with fear. Anomu's canoes arrived under a moonless sky, their approach masked by the hum of night insects and the distant croak of frogs, the water lapping softly against the hulls. Temieno's scouts, slipping through the mangroves like shadows, reported the Awori's strength: three hundred warriors, armed with iron-tipped spears and poisoned arrows, bolstered by mercenaries from inland Yoruba clans, their faces painted with war stripes.

The Portuguese traders, led by a nervous factor named Diogo, cowered in a barricaded warehouse, their muskets useless without trained hands, their velvet cloaks a mockery of the Itsekiri's leather and grit. Anomu devised a plan: a feint at dawn to draw the Awori from their ridge, followed by a flank attack through a hidden channel Temieno had mapped with the precision of a river bird. Olua would lead the feint, his youth and fire a beacon for the men, his voice rallying them through the chaos, while Anomu struck the decisive blow with the main force. The battle began with a crimson sunrise, the lagoon's waters stained as if foretelling blood, the air thick with the scent of smoke and salt. Olua's canoes charged the main channel, their drums pounding a defiant rhythm that shook the water, a call to arms that echoed off the mangroves. The Awori responded, their war cries piercing the dawn as they rained arrows from the ridge, the shafts whistling like angry spirits. Olua, shield raised, roared orders, his men paddling through a hail of death, their canoes rocking as two capsized, warriors vanishing into the murky depths with cries cut short. Yet Olua held firm, his youthful bravado tempered by the weight of command, drawing the Awori's focus like a flame draws moths.

Temieno, hidden in the mangroves with her scouts, signalled Anomu, her arm bandaged from a prior graze but her spirit unbroken. Anomu led his main force through the secret channel, their canoes gliding like shadows, the water barely rippling under their silent paddles. The flank attack was brutal and swift, a storm of spears and muskets crashing against the ridge. Anomu's warriors leapt onto the elevated ground, their blades flashing in the dawn light, the clash of iron a symphony of war. Oba Adeyemi, a wiry figure in his leopard-skin cloak, rallied his men, his iron sword clashing with Anomu's in a duel that shook the earth, his voice a roar of defiance. The Itsekiri fought with disciplined fury, their muskets—wielded by a few trained men—cracking through the chaos, sowing panic among the Awori ranks. Temieno, darting through the fray, cut down a mercenary archer with a precise thrust of her dagger, her movements fluid despite the pain, but an arrow grazed her thigh, drawing a sharp hiss as blood stained her wrapper. She gritted her teeth and fought on, her scouts securing the ridge's rear, their nets entangling fleeing warriors.

By midday, the Awori broke, their warriors fleeing into the lagoon or surrendering with hands raised, their war cries fading into the wind. Oba Adeyemi fell, his body pierced by Anomu's spear, a blow that ended the battle but sealed a grudge that would simmer for generations, a wound in the Yoruba soul. The Itsekiri secured the village, freeing the traders and reclaiming the market, its charred huts a testament to the cost. Diogo, the Portuguese factor, stammered gratitude, promising gold and muskets, but Anomu's cold stare silenced him, his voice a low growl. "Your gold buys nothing here. This victory is Itsekiri, not yours." The traders retreated to their warehouse, their promises hollow, leaving the Itsekiri to tend their own.

Yet triumph came at a staggering cost. Of Anomu's five hundred warriors, nearly two hundred lay dead or wounded, their bodies borne back in canoes draped with palm fronds, their faces peaceful under the mourning cloth. Olua, bloodied but unbowed, had lost half his men in the feint, his youthful bravado tempered by the weight of command, his eyes haunted by the faces of the fallen. Temieno's wound, though shallow, festered in the swamp's heat, requiring Mama Uwala's herbs upon her return, the old weaver's hands steady as she applied the poultice. The trade routes were open, the Portuguese traders safe, but Ale Eko Iwere's market was a shadow of its former bustle, its huts charred and its people shaken, the air heavy with the scent of ash and despair.

Domingos awaited the army's return at the palace, Anthonio cradled in his arms, the boy's dark eyes—so like Olori Maria's—watching the river with innocent curiosity, his tiny hands clutching a strip of her wrapper. When the canoes appeared, their drums muted in honour of the fallen, their paddles dipping slowly, his heart sank, the weight of their losses a stone in his chest. Anomu disembarked, his face etched with exhaustion, his leather vest stained with blood and mud, and knelt before his king, his head bowed. "Ogiame, Ale Eko Iwere is ours," he said, his voice heavy with the burden of victory. "The Awori are broken, the routes secure. But the lagoon drank deep of our blood, and the price was steep."

Temieno, her arm and thigh bandaged, stepped forward, her steps uneven but her eyes meeting Domingos's with a mix of pride and pain. "We held the land, brother, but the Awori will not forget. Nor will the Portuguese, who hid while we bled, their gold a coward's shield. The lagoon is ours, but its peace is fragile." Domingos nodded, his gaze sweeping the warriors, some limping with wounds, others carrying their comrades' shields as solemn burdens, their faces a map of sacrifice. He addressed them from the palace steps, his voice carrying over the river's murmur, the crowd gathered to welcome their heroes a sea of muted colours. "Warri stands because of you," he said, his words a balm and a vow. "You are our iron, our heart. The fallen walk with our ancestors, and their names will live in our songs, carved into the Iroko's bark. Ale Eko Iwere is ours, not for gold or white men, but for our children, for Anthonio, for the future."

The crowd cheered, their voices a rising tide, but the sound was tempered by sorrow, the air thick with the scent of palm wine and the tang of blood. That night, the palace held a feast for the living and a vigil for the dead, the courtyard lit by torches that cast flickering shadows on the mud walls. Chief Oton led rites at the Iroko tree, offering kola nuts and palm wine to the spirits, his staff rattling as he chanted, the ground soft underfoot from the day's tears. Anomu, hailed as a hero, drank sparingly, his thoughts on the men he'd lost, his scar-ridged face a mask of quiet reflection. Olua, now a seasoned captain, sat with Temieno, their bond forged in blood, her hand resting on his as they shared a silent moment of camaraderie.

Ebi, watching from the shadows, noted Mendes' absence—the Portuguese captain had sent a letter of thanks but no aid, a sign of their true allegiance, their ships a distant threat on the horizon. Domingos retired to his chamber, Anthonio asleep in a cradle woven with strips of Olori Maria's wrapper, the fabric a soft whisper of her presence. He looked at his son, then at the map, where Ale Eko Iwere lay marked in charcoal, its lines a reminder of the cost. The war had preserved Warri's strength, but at a price that would echo for years—the Awori would nurse their defeat, their grudge a seed for future conflict, and Mendes, ever-watchful, would exploit any crack in Warri's armour.

As he stood under the Iroko's gaze, its roots deep in the earth, its branches a canopy of resilience, Domingos recalled a parable from his father, of the Heron and the Flood. Heron stood tall as the floodwaters rose, its wings spread to shield its nest, trusting the river's ebb to save its young. When the waters receded, Heron rebuilt stronger than before. Domingos saw himself as the Heron, his son as the nest, and Warri as the river—tested but enduring. Another tale came to mind, from the elders, of the Crab and the Tide. Crab scuttled sideways, evading the tide's pull, its shell a fortress against the waves, teaching that resilience lies in adapting to the flow. Domingos vowed to rebuild—not just the market of Ale Eko Iwere, but the kingdom's spirit, its economy, and its defences.

A young scout interrupted his thoughts, his wrapper torn, his face flushed from a hurried journey. "Ogiame, a Dutch envoy has landed with Van der Berg! They offer alliance against the Portuguese but demand control of Ale Eko Iwere's trade. Mendes's ship moves closer, his cannons primed!" Domingos's heart sank, but he masked it with resolve, handing Anthonio to Temieno. "Prepare the council," he said, his voice steady. "We'll meet them at dawn." In the war room, Ebi, Chief Oton, and Omajuwa gathered, the map once more a battleground. "The Dutch seek to divide us," Ebi warned. "Mendes waits to pounce." Chief Oton shook his staff. "The spirits demand we honour the fallen with justice." Omajuwa spoke softly, "A pact with the Dutch might balance Mendes, cousin, but guard our soul."

Domingos nodded, his mind weaving a strategy. "We'll parley with Van der Berg, offer a share of palm oil, but keep Ale Eko Iwere's heart. Send Olua to negotiate, with Temieno as his voice. Prepare our warriors—war may follow." At dawn, Olua and Temieno met Van der Berg on the riverbank, her bandaged arm a badge of honour, his spear a silent threat. "Trade yes, control no," Temieno said, her voice firm. Van der Berg agreed, the deal struck under the Iroko's gaze, but his eyes lingered on Mendes's ship, a storm brewing on the horizon.

Domingos stood with Anthonio, the boy's coo a soft counterpoint to the tension. The war had preserved Warri, but the future demanded vigilance. For Anthonio, for Olori Maria's memory, and for the Itsekiri who bled, Warri would rise stronger, its river flowing unbroken into the dawn.

CHAPTER EIGHT

War with King of Ako

The Warri River flowed dark and restless under a storm-heavy sky, its currents churning with the unease that gripped Warri kingdom, the air thick with the scent of rain and the distant rumble of thunder. The victory at Ale Eko Iwere, though hard-won and etched into the land with blood, had left scars deeper than the wounds on its warriors, a legacy of loss that lingered like the mist over the mangroves. The Awori's defeat had secured Warri's trade routes and protected the Portuguese merchants, but it had also sown seeds of a new conflict—one that now burned with the fury of the Ako, a Yoruba group whose warriors had fought as mercenaries for the Awori during the lagoon battle. During the fierce engagement, Chief Anomu's forces had captured thirty Ako warriors, their iron swords and leopard-skin cloaks marking them as elite fighters from the Ako kingdom, a powerful Yoruba state inland from the lagoons, its hills a fortress of strength and pride. The prisoners, held in a fortified camp near Warri's riverbank under heavy guard, had sparked a diplomatic crisis that threatened to engulf the kingdom in flames.

King Oba Adetunji of Ako, a ruler known for his pride and military prowess, his name whispered with awe across the Yoruba lands, demanded their release, branding the Itsekiri as aggressors who had overstepped their bounds. When Ogiame Dom Domingos refused, citing the Ako's role in the Awori attack as justification for their captivity, Oba Adetunji declared war, vowing to reclaim his men and humble Warri's king with a force that would shake the river's foundations. The storm clouds overhead seemed to mirror his rage, their dark edges a prelude to the tempest to come. Domingos stood in the palace war room, his white wrapper tied tightly around his waist, a stark contrast to the scarlet Kemeje he once wore with pride, its plain fabric a symbol of mourning turned to resolve. His coral beads gleamed against his chest, their weight a steady anchor in the chaos, but his European crown remained in its case, its golden cross irrelevant to the Yoruba storm brewing beyond the river's edge.

A map of the region, now scarred with charcoal marks from Ale Eko Iwere, lay before him on a carved table, its edges curling from constant use, the ink smudged with the sweat of strategy, the lines tracing a path to the Ako kingdom's forested hills. Princess Temieno, her arm healed from the Eko travails, but her eyes hardened by battle and loss, traced the Ako kingdom's borders, a day's march inland through dense forests and rolling hills where the air carried the scent of earth and pine. Ebi, his trusted advisor, sifted through scout reports, his lined face etched with worry, his coral bracelet clicking softly as he turned the pages. Chief Oton, the high priest, gripped his cowrie-laden staff, its shells rattling like a prayer for peace that was drowned by the war drums echoing from the river, the sound a heartbeat of impending doom. Chief Anomu, Warri's war captain, stood tall despite the weight of the Eko travails, his leather vest scarred from past battles, its iron charms clinking with each movement. Olua, now a seasoned captain, leaned against the wall, his spear at hand, its iron tip glinting in the lamplight, his youthful fire tempered by the graves he'd dug for fallen comrades, his scar a badge of honour.

"The Ako are not the Awori," Anomu said, his voice a low rumble that reverberated through the room, his scarred face a map of experience. "Their warriors are trained from child-hood, their Oba commands thousands, and their hills give them cover against our canoes. They'll come for their men, Ogiame, and they'll aim to break us where the Awori failed, to erase the memory of our victory." Domingos's jaw clenched, his mind racing through the stakes, the weight of leadership pressing against his chest like the storm outside. The Ako prisoners, bound in a camp under Olua's guard near the riverbank, were a double-edged blade—releasing them might appease Oba Adetunji but would signal weak-ness, inviting further demands and emboldening foes from the Ijaw to the Portuguese. Holding them risked a war Warri could ill afford, with its forces depleted from Ale Eko Iwere and its people still mourning Olori Maria, her absence a silent wound in every heart. Yet the Ako's alliance with the Awori had been no accident—Ebi's spies whispered of Portuguese gold, funnelled through Captain Mendes, stirring Yoruba clans against Warri to weaken its grip on coastal trade, a shadow game played with coins and blood.

Temieno slammed a fist on the map, her voice fierce as a river in flood, her hand trembling with resolve. "We can't bow to Ako, brother. They fought for our enemies, burned our homes with their mercenaries, and mocked our name with their pride. If we free their men, they'll see it as fear, and Oba Adetunji will march anyway, his army a tide we can't hold back. We must meet them with iron; show them Warri's fire still burns." The chiefs murmured approval, their voices a rising tide of agreement, but Ebi raised a cautionary hand, his tone calm yet firm, a voice of reason in the storm. "War is a hungry beast, Temieno. Ale Eko Iwere cost us two hundred men, their blood still fresh in the lagoon. Ako's army is larger, their terrain unfamiliar hills where our canoes are useless. We could send an envoy, offer terms—free half the prisoners for a truce, buy time to heal our wounds."

Chief Oton nodded, his voice grave as he leaned on his staff, the cowries rattling like a distant storm. "The gods favour peace when blood has already flowed, Ogiame. Oritse-Udeji thirsts for justice, but he also guards those who seek wisdom over vengeance. A parley might spare our children from the spears." Olua scoffed, his spear tapping the floor with impatience, its sound a sharp counterpoint to the priest's words. "Wisdom won't stop Ako's blades, Ogiame. Their Oba calls us river dogs, unfit to hold their warriors, their pride a shield for their aggression. We must fight, or lose our honour, our name erased from the river's song."

Domingos's gaze swept the room, weighing each voice, the air thick with the scent of palm oil from the lamps and the tension of decision. Anthonio, his infant son, slept in a cradle in the palace, a reminder of Olori Maria's sacrifice and Warri's future, his tiny hands clutching a strip of her wrapper, a thread of memory in the storm. The kingdom's strength lay in its unity, but another war could fracture it, scattering the pieces like leaves on the river. Yet Temieno was right yielding would embolden Ako and others, from the Ijaw nursing their grudge to Mendes' Portuguese masters circling like vultures. "We'll fight," he said, his voice resolute, a king's command cutting through the debate. "Anomu, ready four hundred warriors. Olua, you'll guard the prisoners and hold the river camp against any raid. Temieno, scout the Ako approach with your team—we'll meet them before they reach our lands, in the hills near Oke-Aro, where their numbers mean less. But Ebi, send an envoy first—offer to free ten prisoners as a gesture, to test Adetunji's heart and buy us time."

Anomu bowed, his fist to his chest, the iron charms on his vest clinking like a war drum. "Ogiame, we'll carve a path through their hills, and their Oba will know our steel." Preparations consumed Warri, transforming the palace into a hive of activity, the courtyard alive with the clang of blacksmiths' hammers as they forged spearheads and sharpened blades, the air thick with the scent of molten iron and woodsmoke. Women packed yam and dried fish for the march, their fingers swift despite the weight of worry, the rustle of palm fronds a constant undertone. Drummers practiced rhythms to signal in battle, their beats a call to arms that carried to the riverbank where canoes were readied, their hulls painted with waves and stars. Chief Oton blessed the warriors at the Iroko tree, its gnarled branches a canopy of strength, offering kola nuts and palm wine to Oritse Udeji for victory, his chants rising with the dawn mist, the ground soft underfoot from the night's rain.

Temieno, her dagger strapped to her thigh, led a dozen scouts to map the Ako's routes, her knowledge of terrain—a legacy of childhood explorations along the river—Warri's hidden edge. Her team moved like shadows through the forests, their footsteps silent on the damp earth, the scent of pine and moss filling the air. Anomu's army, clad in leather vests reinforced with fish scales and armed with spears, bows, and a handful of muskets, marched inland, their footsteps heavy with purpose, the forest canopy filtering the storm's light into a dappled gloom. Domingos remained in the palace, coordinating supplies and watching the river for Portuguese ships, his heart torn between leading the fight and guarding Anthonio, the boy's cries a soft counterpoint to the war drums.

The envoy, a seasoned elder named Oritseje, returned days later, his face grim, his wrapper stained with mud from the journey. Oba Adetunji had spurned the offer, executing one prisoner before Oritseje's eyes with a swift stroke of his sword, the blade glinting in the torchlight, and vowing to "cleanse the river of Itsekiri arrogance," his voice a thunder-clap of defiance. The Ako army, six hundred strong, was already marching, their war drums echoing through the hills, a sound that carried to Warri's borders like a warning. Temieno's scouts confirmed the report, noting Ako's warri-ors—tall, muscled men in iron vests, wielding swords and shields—were joined by archers trained to strike from cover, their faces painted with war stripes that gleamed under the storm's grey light.

The battle would be fought at Oke-Aro, a rugged hills cape where narrow paths favoured strategy over numbers, its slopes dotted with rocks and thorny brush, the air heavy with the scent of wet earth. Anomu devised a plan: hold the high ground at Oke-Aro's central ridge, using archers to thin Ako's ranks, their arrows whistling through the mist, while Temieno's scouts harried their flanks, sowing confusion with their daggers and nets. Olua, back at the river camp, fortified the prisoner enclosure with sharpened stakes and sentries, aware that Ako might send a raiding party to free their men, the camp's perimeter a line of defence against the night.

The battle began at dawn, the hills shrouded in mist that clung to the ground like a shroud, the storm breaking with a sudden downpour that turned the slopes slick. Anomu's forces seized the ridge, their archers positioned behind rock outcrops, their bows taut with anticipation. The Ako army, led by Oba Adetunji himself, a broad-shouldered man in a crimson cloak that billowed like blood in the wind, advanced with a roar, their drums shaking the earth, their iron vests glinting through the rain. Their archers loosed poisoned arrows, felling a dozen Itsekiri before the lines met, the shafts embedding in shields with a sickening thud. Anomu, spear in hand, held the ridge's centre, his voice rallying his men as Ako swords clashed with Itsekiri shields, the sound a cacophony of metal and cries. The muskets, though few, cracked through the din, their smoke disorienting the Yoruba warriors unused to firearms, the acrid scent mingling with the rain.

Temieno's scouts struck from the flanks, their daggers flashing as they cut down Ako stragglers, their movements swift despite the mud that sucked at their feet. Temieno herself, her arm scarred from past battles, led a raid on an archer nest, her team scattering the bowmen with a hail of stones, but an arrow grazed her leg, drawing a sharp hiss as blood stained her wrapper. She gritted her teeth and fought on, her scouts securing the ridge's rear, their nets entangling fleeing warriors in a tangle of ropes and thorns. On the ridge, Anomu faced Adetunji in a brutal duel, their weapons sparking as spear met sword, the Oba's strikes swift and powerful, his crimson cloak a target in the rain. Anomu's experience prevailed, his spear piercing Adetunji's thigh, forcing him to retreat with a roar of pain, his guard dragging him into the mist.

By noon, the Ako began to waver, their losses mounting under Itsekiri arrows and Temieno's raids, their war drums silenced by the storm's thunder. Anomu pressed the advantage, leading a charge down the ridge, his warriors cutting through the Yoruba lines with disciplined fury, their spears dripping with rain and blood. The Ako broke, fleeing into the hills, their crimson cloaks vanishing into the fog, their drums a fading echo. Adetunji, wounded but alive, was carried off by his guard, vowing vengeance through gritted teeth, his voice a promise carried on the wind. The Itsekiri held the field, their war cries echoing through the hills, but victory was bitter, the ground littered with the fallen.

One hundred and fifty warriors lay dead, their bodies strewn across Oke-Aro's slopes, their leather vests torn, their faces peaceful under the rain. Anomu, bloodied but unbowed, counted thirty wounded, including Temieno, whose leg bore a gash from a Yoruba blade, the wound seeping despite the rain's wash. Back at the river camp, Olua repelled a small Ako raiding party sent to free the prisoners, losing ten men but holding firm, his spear notched with new kills, the camp's stakes stained with blood. The captured Ako warriors, now twenty-nine after Adetunji's execution, were unharmed, their fate a question hanging over the victory.

The Itsekiri army returned to Warri under a mournful sky, their canoes laden with the fallen, draped in palm fronds that fluttered in the breeze, the riverbank lined with people whose cheers were muted by the sight of empty canoes and broken warriors. Anomu knelt before Domingos, his report stark, his voice heavy with the burden of command. "Oke-Aro is ours, Ogiame. Ako is broken, their Oba wounded, the routes secure. But we paid in blood, a toll that stains the river, and their hatred festers like a wound." Temieno, limping but defiant, stepped forward, her eyes meeting Domingos's with a mix of pride and pain, her leg bandaged by Mama Uwala's skilled hands. "We held the land, brother, but the Ako will not forget. Nor will the Portuguese, who hid while we bled, their gold a coward's shield."

Domingos nodded, his gaze sweeping the warriors, some limping with wounds, others carrying their comrades' shields as solemn burdens, their faces a map of sacrifice etched in mud and blood. He addressed them from the palace steps, his voice carrying over the river's murmur, the crowd gathered to welcome their heroes a sea of muted colours under the storm's aftermath. "Warri stands because of you," he said, his words a balm and a vow. "You are our iron, our heart. The fallen walk with Olori Maria, watching over Anthonio, over us all. Oke-Aro is ours, not for gold or white men, but for our children, for the future we build from this blood."

The crowd cheered, their voices a rising tide, but the sound was tempered by sorrow, the air thick with the scent of palm wine and the tang of rain-soaked earth. That night, Warri mourned and celebrated, the palace courtyard lit by torches that cast flickering shadows on the mud walls adorned with faded tapestries. Chief Oton led rites at the Iroko tree, offering kola nuts to honour the dead, his staff rattling as he chanted, the ground soft underfoot from the storm's deluge. Anomu, hailed as a hero, drank sparingly, his thoughts on the men he'd lost, his scar-ridged face a mask of quiet reflection. Olua, now a seasoned captain, sat with Temieno, their bond forged in blood, her hand resting on his as they shared a silent moment of camaraderie, her leg propped on a cushion.

Ebi, watching from the shadows, noted Mendes' absence— the Portuguese captain had sent a letter of "relief" at Warri's victory but no aid, a sign of their true allegiance, their ships a distant threat on the horizon, their sails barely visible through the mist. Domingos retired to his chamber, Antonio asleep in a cradle woven with strips of Olori Maria's wrapper, the fabric a soft whisper of her presence, the air heavy with the scent of herbs Mama Uwala had left to ward off fever. He looked at his son, then at the map, where Oke-Aro lay marked with blood, its lines a reminder of the cost. The Ako would not march again soon, their Oba's wound a tether to recovery, but his vow of vengeance lingered like a shadow, and Mendes' ships loomed, their cannons a silent promise of future strife.

As he stood under the Iroko's gaze, its roots deep in the earth, its branches a canopy of resilience against the storm's remnants, Domingos recalled a parable from his mother, of the Iroko and the Wind. Iroko stood firm as the wind howled, its roots gripping the soil, its branches bending but never breaking, teaching that strength lies in flexibility and depth. Another tale came to mind, from the elders, of the Frog and the Hawk. Frog hid in the mud as Hawk swooped, its patience outlasting the predator's hunger, a lesson in endurance. Domingos vowed to fortify Warri—train more warriors to replace the fallen, rebuild the trade routes of Ale Eko Iwere, and watch the Portuguese with the vigilance of a frog in the reeds.

A young scout interrupted his thoughts, his wrapper torn, his face flushed from a hurried journey through the rain-soaked forest. "Ogiame, the Ako have sent emissaries under a white flag! They offer a truce—release of the prisoners for a non-aggression pact—but demand tribute in ivory. Mendes's ship has moved closer; his cannons trained on the riverbank!" Domingos's heart sank, but he masked it with resolve, handing Anthonio to Temieno, her bandaged leg a testament to her strength. "Prepare the council," he said, his voice steady. "We'll meet at dawn."

In the war room, Ebi, Chief Oton, and Omajuwa gathered, the map once more a battleground, its lines blurred by the storm's dampness. "The Ako seek to save face," Ebi warned, his finger tracing the hills. "Mendes waits to exploit our choice." Chief Oton shook his staff. "The spirits demand we honour the truce if true, but guard against deceit." Omajuwa spoke softly, "A pact might heal us, cousin, but the ivory is our soul—offer less, demand guarantees."

Domingos nodded, his mind weaving a strategy. "We'll parley with the Ako emissaries, offer five prisoners and palm oil, but no ivory—demand a written pact and hostages. Send Olua and Temieno to negotiate, with Anomu as guard. Prepare our warriors—war may follow if Mendes intervenes." At dawn, Olua and Temieno met the Ako emissaries on the riverbank, her leg stiff but her voice firm, his spear a silent threat. "Five men, palm oil, a pact, and hostages—or we fight again," Temieno said. The emissaries hesitated, then agreed, the deal struck under the Iroko's gaze, but their eyes darted to Mendes's ship, a storm brewing on the horizon.

As the Ako retreated, Olua reported a hidden message from the emissaries—Oba Adetunji planned a second strike if the truce failed. Domingos stood with Anthonio, the boy's coo a soft counterpoint to the tension, the Iroko's roots a promise of endurance. The war had tested Warri, but the future demanded vigilance. For Anthonio, for the fallen, and for the Itsekiri spirit, the kingdom would rise stronger, its river flowing through fire and blood into a new dawn.

CHAPTER NINE

The Church in Warri

T he Warri River flowed gently under a sky streaked with the soft hues of dawn, its waters reflecting a kingdom at peace for the first time in years, the gentle ripples mirroring the fragile calm that had settled over the land. The scars of the Eko Travails and the War with the King of Ako memory lingered— their warriors limping through the market with canes carved from mangrove wood, and a treasury strained by battles, its coffers echoing with the clink of scarce coins. Yet the Itsekiri people had found a moment to breathe, their voices rising in songs of resilience as they rebuilt their lives. Ogiame Dom Domingos, now seasoned by loss and triumph, ruled with a steady hand, his infant son Anthonio Domingos a symbol of hope cradled in the palace, his tiny hands clutching a strip of his mother's indigo wrapper. The victory over the Ako had silenced external threats for now, the hills quiet and the lagoons stilled, and even Captain Mendes and his Portuguese ships kept their distance, wary of Warri's proven strength, their sails a faint silhouette on the horizon. Yet within this fragile peace, a new force was stirring in the kingdom: the Christian church, planted years ago by Portuguese missionaries and nurtured by Domingos's own education in Portugal, was taking root, its influence spreading like mangrove roots through the riverlands, its wooden cross a beacon amid the thatched huts.

The church in Warri, a modest structure of mud and thatch near the palace, had stood since Domingos's father sent him to Portugal in 1610 to study under King Philip's tutors, its walls weathered by time and the river's breath. Intended to train Domingos as a priest to spread the Christian faith, those years had instead shaped him into a king who bridged worlds, blending the hymns of Lisbon with the chants of Oritse Udeji. The church, led by Father Mateus, a Portuguese Jesuit who had arrived a decade earlier with a weathered Bible and a gentle smile, was a quiet presence during the wars, offering prayers for warriors as their canoes departed and solace for the grieving as they returned with empty hands. But now, with peace restored, its wooden cross cast a longer shadow across the riverbank, drawing both curiosity and suspicion from the Itsekiri, its bell ringing softly in the morning air, a sound that mingled with the hum of cicadas.

The Seeds of Faith

The church's growth began in earnest with the arrival of two new missionaries, Father João and Sister Clara, sent by the

Portuguese crown in response to Domingos's request for aid in strengthening the faith's foothold. Father João, a wiry man with a sun-weathered face and a gentle voice that carried the cadence of the Itsekiri tongue, had studied under Father Mateus in Lisbon, his fluency a bridge between cultures. Sister Clara, younger and fiercer, with hands stained from grinding herbs, brought a knack for healing, her knowledge blending Christian charity with local wisdom gathered from the river clans. Their arrival coincided with a bountiful harvest, the yam fields heavy with tubers and the fish nets brimming, a sign the people took as divine favour—whether from Oritse Udeji, Umale Okun the river god, or the Christian God whose cross adorned the church. The church, once attended only by Portuguese traders with their velvet cloaks and a handful of converts whispering Latin prayers, began to draw Itsekiri fishermen with calloused hands, weavers with nimble fingers, and even warriors with scars from Oke-Aro, curious about the faith that had shaped their king.

Domingos, aware of the delicate balance between tradition and change, worked with Chief Oton, the high priest of Umale Okun, to ensure the church complemented rather than challenged Itsekiri ways. Oton, though wary, his staff heavy with cowrie shells that rattled like ancestral voices, saw wisdom in Domingos's vision—a kingdom united by faith could resist the greed of foreign powers like the Portuguese or the lingering threats of the Ijaw. At a council meeting beneath the Iroko tree, its gnarled branches swaying in the dawn breeze, Domingos proposed building a larger church, one that would house both Christian rites and spaces for ancestral offerings, its walls adorned with coral patterns and a cross carved from Iroko wood. "The river flows with many currents," he said, his coral beads glinting in the sunlight, "let our gods and the Christian God Walk together, as I walk with both Warri and Portugal, a harmony of spirit and strength." Ebi, ever cautious, warned of resistance, his voice low as he stood beneath the tree's shade. "The chiefs, especially Ikenna, will see this as a white man's trick, a chain to bind us. They'll say you honour Olori Maria over our ancestors, her memory a foreign shadow."

Temieno, her arm scarred from Oke-Aro, countered fiercely, her voice cutting through the murmurs like a river's edge. "Let Ikenna grumble, brother. The people see Anthonio, a child of both worlds, his every step a bridge. If the church brings schools to teach our children, medicine to heal our sick, and trade to fill our nets, it strengthens Warri, not weakens it. We are not fools to trade our gods for chains." The council agreed, their voices a consensus born of hope, and construction began on a new church, its walls of baked mud rising near the river, the sound of hammers and laughter filling the air. Father João and Sister Clara worked tirelessly, holding services in the Itsekiri tongue, their hymns blending with the rhythm of local drums, the church's interior lit by oil lamps that cast a warm glow. They offered literacy classes, teaching children to read the Bible and write in Portuguese, a skill that opened trade with European ships, their quills scratching on parchment a new song in Warri's mornings. Sister Clara's healing tent, set up beside the church, drew women with her for fever and wounds, the scent of herbs mingling with the river's salt, earning trust where sermons alone failed, her hands a bridge between faith and tradition.

The Conversion of Oritseje

Among the first converts was Oritseje, the elder who had faced Oba Adetunji's scorn as an envoy during the Ako war, his weathered hands trembling from years of casting nets. A fisherman with a heart heavy from losing a son at Ale Eko Iwere, he had long prayed to the river spirits for solace, his voice rising with the dawn over the water. One evening, drawn by Sister Clara's singing—a melody that floated like a heron over the river—he entered the church, where she tended his granddaughter's fever with a poultice of local roots and a prayer to the Virgin Mary. The child recovered, her laughter a miracle in the dim light, and Oritseje, moved by what he called a "miracle of the cross," knelt before Father João, asking to be baptized. "The river gave me life," he said, his voice rough with emotion, "but this God gave my child back, a gift beyond the spirits' reach." Oritseje's conversion sent ripples through the river clans, his family—

respected for their fishing prowess, their canoes a familiar sight on the water—joining him, their baptism a public event attended by Domingos and Temieno under the Iroko's shade.

Chief Oton blessed the ceremony with kola nuts, a gesture of unity that bridged the old ways with the new, though Ikenna, watching from the crowd with his coral beads heavy with resentment, scowled, muttering of "foreign spirits stealing our souls." Oritseje's story spread like the river's current, and soon dozens of families attended services, their prayers to Jesus mingling with offerings of kola nuts to Oritse Udeji at the river shrine, the air thick with the scent of palm wine and incense. Father João, wise to the Itsekiri's ways, encouraged this blending, preaching that the Christian God was a father to all spirits, a message that eased fears of betrayal and wove a tapestry of faith across the kingdom.

The Miracle of the River Child

The church's growth was cemented by a tale that became legend: the miracle of the river child. In a village called Ode-Itsekiri, nestled among the mangroves, a young girl named Ese, barely ten, fell into the river during a storm, her small form swept away by currents that had claimed many before her, the water roaring with the fury of the tempest. Her mother, a weaver named Adesuwa with hands stained by indigo dye, wailed at the church's steps, her faith in the river gods shaken, her cries piercing the night. Sister Clara, hearing her anguish, knelt with her, praying to the Virgin Mary while sprinkling river water, a nod to local rites that honoured Umale Okun's domain. Days later, fishermen found Ese alive, clinging to a mangrove root, her dress torn but her body unharmed despite the storm's fury, her eyes wide with wonder. Adesuwa, weeping with joy, declared it a miracle of the "white God's mother," and her entire village converted, their huts soon adorned with wooden crosses beside ancestral shrines, the air filled with the scent of fresh thatch and hope.

The story of Ese spread like wildfire through the riverlands, drawing crowds to the church, their footsteps a steady rhythm on the muddy paths. Father João, careful not to inflame tensions, credited the river spirits alongside God, saying, "The Virgin guided the river to cradle Ese, a union of grace and strength." Chief Oton, though sceptical, saw the wisdom in this harmony, his staff resting beside him as he began attending services, his presence a bridge between faiths. The miracle emboldened Domingos, who funded a school beside the church, its walls painted with coral motifs, where children learned to read and write, their laughter a new sound in Warri's mornings, the scratch of quills a promise of the future.

The Plot of Ikenna

Yet peace and faith bred their own shadows, a darkness that lurked beneath the church's growing light. Chief Ikenna, his influence waning since the Omeyin conspiracy, saw the church's rise as a threat to Itsekiri tradition, a foreign vine choking the roots of their ancestors. From his village in the creeks, where the air carried the tang of salt and mud, he gathered a small cabal of traditionalists, including a young warrior named Uwala, whose brother had died at Oke-Aro, his blood a memory that fuelled his anger. Ikenna, his coral beads heavy with resentment, whispered of a plot to sabotage the church—burn its new walls and blame Portuguese treachery, hoping to turn the people against Domingos's Christian leanings and restore the old ways. Uwala, torn between loyalty to his ancestors and respect for Anomu, who had led him in battle, agreed to spy, infiltrating the church's literacy classes to gather names of converts, his heart a battlefield of duty and doubt.

Ebi, ever vigilant, caught wind of the plot through Mama Ose, the Omeyin weaver, whose sharp ears overheard Uwala's drunken boasts in a palm wine stall, the air thick with the sweet scent of fermented sap. She sent word to the palace, a folded leaf bearing her warning, and Ebi confronted Uwala under the Iroko tree, its branches swaying in the evening breeze, his dagger at the ready, its blade glinting in the torchlight. "Speak, boy," Ebi said, his voice a low growl, "or your ancestors will judge you tonight, their voices rising from the river." Uwala, trembling, confessed Ikenna's plan, swearing he'd meant only to listen, not act, his eyes wide with fear and shame. Domingos, summoned, faced a dilemma—Ikenna's influence, though diminished, still swayed the river clans, and punishing him could spark rebellion, a fire that would consume Warri's fragile unity. Yet letting the plot fester risked the church and the peace it promised, a wound that could bleed into war.

Temieno urged swift action, her voice sharp as she stood beside the map, "Cut the snake's head before it bites, brother. Ikenna's pride will destroy us if we hesitate." But Oton counselled mercy, his staff tapping the ground, "The gods Favour wisdom over wrath, Ogiame. Bring Ikenna to the church, let him see its works—the healing, the learning—and judge for himself." Domingos chose a middle path, a king's balance between justice and reconciliation. He summoned Ikenna to the palace, where Father João and Sister Clara joined the council, their robes a contrast to the chiefs' wrappers. Before the gathered leaders, Domingos spoke plainly, his voice steady. "Ikenna, you plot against the church, against Warri's peace. But I offer you a chance—join us at the river tomorrow, see the faith that strengthens us, not divides us, and choose your path." Ikenna, cornered, bowed stiffly, his eyes burning with defiance, his coral beads a heavy chain around his neck.

The next day, at a service by the river, the water lapping gently at the bank, Sister Clara tended a sick child, her herbs saving its life as Father João prayed, the child's cries turning to laughter under the morning sun. Ikenna watched, silent, as the child's mother wept in gratitude, her hands clasped around a wooden cross, the air filled with the scent of healing leaves. The sight softened him, though he refused baptism, muttering, "Oritse Udeji and Umale Okun are enough for me, but I see your church's worth." The plot dissolved, Uwala sent to labour in the yam fields as penance, his hands now tilling the earth instead of wielding a blade, and Ikenna's cabal scattered, their fire doused by the church's quiet power, the river reflecting their retreat.

The School and the Traders

The church's school became a beacon, drawing children from across the kingdom, their footsteps a steady rhythm on the muddy paths. Olua, now a captain with a steady gaze, enrolled his younger sister, who learned to write letters that amazed her elders, her quill a tool of pride as she penned her name. The school taught Bible stories—tales of Noah and the flood—but also Itsekiri lore, ensuring the ancestors' voices were not lost, their names carved into wooden tablets beside the cross. Portuguese traders, led by a new factor named Vasco, attended services, their presence boosting trade, their ships unloading cloth and iron without the strings Mendes once tied. Vasco, unlike his predecessor, offered muskets and bolts of fabric as gifts, seeking favour with Domingos, his voice smooth with diplomacy. The king accepted, but kept Ebi watching, wary of Portuguese ambition, the air thick with the scent of trade goods and caution.

One evening, a trader's ship brought a relic—a fragment of the True Cross, gifted by a Lisbon bishop, its wooden edges worn by time—unloaded with ceremony on the riverbank. Father João displayed it during a service, the church packed with Itsekiri and traders, the air filled with the murmur of awe. A fisherman, healed of a fever after touching it, swore it glowed with a soft light, his voice trembling with wonder, and the tale spread, drawing pilgrims from neighbouring clans, their offerings of yams and coral swelling the church's coffers, the sound of their footsteps a pilgrimage hymn. Domingos used the wealth to build a hospital tent beside the church, its canvas walls painted with coral motifs, where Sister Clara trained Itsekiri women in healing, blending Christian charity with local remedies—herbs for fever, roots for wounds—her hands a bridge between worlds.

Anthonio's First Steps

Amid the church's rise, Anthonio Domingos took his first steps, toddling across the palace courtyard under Temieno's watchful eye, his tiny feet leaving prints in the damp earth, the air filled with the scent of morning dew. Domingos, his heart still heavy with Olori Maria's absence, saw her in the boy's blue-tinged eyes, a reflection of the sea she had crossed, and in his determined gait, a promise of her spirit. At a church service by the river, Anthonio was blessed by Father João, his tiny hand clutching a strip of Olori Maria's wrapper, now a talisman worn smooth by his grasp, the congregation's voices rising in a hymn. The people cheered, seeing in him a future Ogiame, born of Warri and Portugal, baptized in both river water and the cross's shadow, their ululations a song of hope.

The service ended with a feast, drums blending with hymns, the beat a heartbeat of unity, palm wine flowing from carved gourds beside communion wine poured from silver chalices. Oton, now a regular attendee, offered a kola nut to Father João, a sign of peace that bridged their faiths, the nut's bitter taste a symbol of shared sacrifice. Temieno danced with the women, her laughter a rare light that cut through the courtyard's shadows, her scarred arm raised in joy. Domingos, holding Anthonio, addressed the crowd from the palace steps, his voice carrying over the river's murmur. "The church is our strength, not our chain. It builds schools to light our children's minds, heals our sick with gentle hands, and honours our river with every prayer. Warri grows, not by forgetting our gods—Oritse Udeji, Umale Okun, and the ancestors—but by weaving them with new faith, a tapestry of resilience."

The Shadow of Mendes

Mendes, banished after the Ako war, had returned, his ship anchored far downriver, its silhouette a dark stain against the horizon, the air thick with the threat of cannon smoke. Ebi's spies reported he was stirring unrest among the Ijaw, promising gold for raids, his voice a whisper in the creeks, his gold a lure for discontent. Domingos, meeting Vasco in the palace war room, demanded the Portuguese rein in their rogue captain, his voice firm as he traced the river on the map. Vasco, nervous, his hands trembling with the weight of his position, agreed to send word to Lisbon, promising a ship to summon Mendes back, but Domingos knew the river's calm could break, the current hiding dangers beneath.

He tasked Olua with fortifying the river camp, ensuring Warri's warriors were ready, their spears sharpened, and their canoes repaired, the sound of hammers a steady rhythm along the bank. Olua, his scar a badge of experience, trained a new generation of fighters, their laughter mingling with the clang of metal. As the church grew, so did its enemies—Ikenna, though subdued, whispered to traditionalists in the shadows, his coral beads a silent rebellion, and the Ijaw watched from their creeks, their canoes a threat on the water. But the Itsekiri, bolstered by faith and schools, stood stronger, their voices rising in hymns and chants, the church's bell a counterpoint to the river's flow.

A young scout burst into the chamber, his wrapper torn, his face flushed from a run through the mangrove paths. "Ogiame, Ijaw raiders have struck a fishing village! They took yams and nets, leaving a message—'Mendes sends greetings.' The church was spared, but the people fear his return!" Domingos's heart sank, but he masked it with resolve, handing Anthonio to Temieno, her arms a haven. "Summon the council," he said, his voice steady. "We'll meet at dawn."

In the war room, Ebi, Chief Oton, and Omajuwa gathered, the map once more a battleground, its lines blurred by the scout's damp footsteps. "Mendes tests us," Ebi warned, his finger tracing the creeks. "The Ijaw are his pawns." Chief Oton shook his staff. "The spirits demand we protect our people but seek peace if possible." Omajuwa spoke softly, "A show of force might deter him, cousin, but guard the church—it's our heart now."

Domingos nodded, his mind weaving a strategy. "We'll send Olua with fifty warriors to the village, recover the goods, and warn the Ijaw. Tell Vasco to act against Mendes, or we'll seize Portuguese ships. Protect the church—its people are Warri's strength." At dawn, Olua led the sortie, returning with the raiders' spoils, the Ijaw fleeing before the muskets' crack. Vasco, pressured, sent a ship to Lisbon, but Domingos knew Mendes's shadow would linger. He stood with Anthonio under the Iroko, its roots a promise of endurance, vowing to nurture this fragile harmony—faith, trade, and resilience—

for his son, for Olori Maria, and for a kingdom that would endure the storms ahead.

CHAPTER TEN

King Dom Domingos's Earlier Years

The Warri River shimmered under a golden dawn, its waters a lifeline for the Itsekiri kingdom, a land of sprawling mangroves and vibrant markets where coral beads clinked like music and the scent of palm oil filled the air, fuelling trade with distant shores. In 1600, the kingdom thrived under King Sebastian, a ruler whose embrace of the Catholic faith, sparked by Portuguese missionaries with their cross-emblazoned sails, had woven a delicate thread between Warri and Europe, a bridge of faith and commerce. His eldest son, Dom Domingos, a boy of twelve with sharp eyes that mirrored the river's depths and a restless spirit that danced with the wind, stood at the riverbank, watching a Portuguese caravel unload bolts of cloth and gleaming muskets, its wooden hull creaking under the weight of goods. The ship's cross-emblazoned sails stirred something in him—a curiosity about the world beyond the Iroko tree's shade, its gnarled branches a silent guardian of his heritage. Little did he know that his father's vision would soon send him across oceans, shaping him into a prince of two worlds, destined to bear the weight of Warri's future with a heart divided yet resolute.

The Call to Portugal

King Sebastian, a devout Catholic who led processions with rosaries dangling from his hands and taught his people Christian doctrine with a voice that carried over the river, saw in Domingos a bridge to strengthen Warri's ties with Portugal, a union of spirit and trade. The kingdom's church, a modest mud-and-thatch structure near the palace, its walls softened by the river's breath, was a beacon of faith, but its priests were few, their Latin chants a foreign echo among the Itsekiri's songs. Sebastian dreamed of a native clergy to cement Catholicism among his people, a dream born from letters from Bishop Petrus Fernandez Barbosa of São Tomé, who praised Warri's Christian fervour and urged deeper ties. In 1601, inspired by these missives, Sebastian resolved to send Domingos to study in Portugal, a decision sealed in a council beneath the Iroko tree, where the air was thick with the scent of kola nuts and the murmur of debate.

Chief Oton, the high priest of Umale Okun, his cowrie-adorned staff glinting in the sunlight, cautioned against the journey, his voice a deep current of tradition. "The boy is our river's heir, Ogiame," he said, his eyes searching Domingos's face. "Send him to the white man's land, and he may return a stranger, his heart lost to their cold stone gods." But Sebastian, his coral beads heavy with resolve, countered with a parable from the elders, of the Heron and the Horizon. "The Heron flies far to seek new waters," he said, "yet returns to its nest with strength. The river flows to the sea, and Domingos will learn their ways, their faith, and return to make us stronger, a bridge for Warri's future." The council, swayed by the king's vision, drafted a letter to King Philip of Spain and Portugal, requesting a scholarship for Domingos to study at Coimbra, the heart of Iberian learning. With it went gifts of pepper and ivory, tokens of Warri's wealth wrapped in palm leaves, their scent a promise of alliance.

In 1602, a Portuguese caravel carried Domingos, now fourteen, from Warri's shores, its sails billowing against the dawn sky. Accompanied by two Itsekiri servants, Oritseje and Uwala, their wrappers bright with coral patterns, and a cleric named Manoel with a worn Bible in hand, Domingos stood at the ship's rail, the river fading into the horizon, the sound of his mother's farewell song lingering in his ears. His wrapper was traded for a doublet of rough wool, his coral beads tucked beneath his shirt, a secret anchor to home, their weight a comfort against the sea's sway. The voyage was gruelling storms battered the ship, its timbers groaning like wounded beasts, and fever claimed Uwala's life, his body committed to the sea with Itsekiri chants rising over the waves and a hurried prayer from Manoel, the salt air heavy with loss. Domingos, heartsick but resolute, clung to his father's words: "Learn their God, their books, but keep Warri's spirit, let the river guide you home."

Coimbra: The College of São Jeronimo

On September 16, 1602, King Philip granted Domingos a scholarship of 200,000 reals annually, decreeing his admission to the College of São Jeronimo in Coimbra, a prestigious institution run by the Order of St. Jerome, its stone walls a fortress of learning amidst cobbled streets. The letter, penned in Lisbon with a flourish of quills, commanded Dom Fernando de Noronha, Count of Linhares, to ensure the funds reached Domingos, effective from the day the college rector certified his enrolment, the ink still wet with royal intent. Domingos arrived in Coimbra's narrow alleys, a city of spires and scholars, his dark skin drawing curious stares from students in black robes, their whispers of "African prince" following him like shadows. The college, with its arched windows and echoing halls, welcomed him with formal courtesy, though the monks' stern gazes tested his resolve.

At São Jeronimo, Domingos plunged into a world of Latin, theology, and philosophy, his days filled with the scratch of quills and the drone of lectures, the air thick with the scent of parchment and candle wax. His tutors, stern monks with faces like carved stone, marvelled at his quick mind, though they chided his accent—soft with the lilt of the river—and his impatience with rote memorization, his fingers itching to hold a spear instead of a pen. He studied the Bible, Augustine's confessions with their tales of sin and redemption, and Aristotle's logic, his nights spent by candlelight, ink staining his fingers black, the glow casting shadows on the stone walls. The 200,000 reals covered his board, books bound in leather, and clothing of coarse cloth, but payments were erratic, leaving him to barter coral beads for quills when funds lagged, the beads' clink a reminder of home. Oritseje, his surviving servant, cooked yam stews in their quarters, blending Itsekiri Flavors with Portuguese bread, the aroma a taste of the river amidst alien winters, the steam rising like a memory.

Domingos's faith deepened, shaped by Coimbra's soaring cathedrals where stained glass painted the air with colour and the monks' fervent sermons echoed off the vaults, their voices a chorus of devotion. Yet he never forgot Oritse-Udeji or the river spirits, whispering their names in private beneath his breath, a quiet rebellion against assimilation, the sound a soft chant in the night. He wrote letters to his father, carried by caravels to Warri, describing Portugal's wonders—stone bridges arching over rivers, armoured knights clanking through streets, and ships that dwarfed Warri's canoes, their masts piercing the sky. Sebastian's replies, slow to arrive, urged him to become a priest, a hope Domingos felt but could not fully embrace, the priesthood's demand for celibacy a sacrifice at odds with his duty as heir to marry and ensure Warri's lineage, his heart torn between vows.

In 1604, Domingos's studies faltered when payments from King Philip's treasury stalled, leaving him in "dire need," as he wrote in a petition scratched on parchment, his hand trembling with frustration. The college's isolation and its strictures—bells tolling for prayer, silence enforced in the halls—chafed against his spirit, and he requested a transfer to Lisbon's Colégio de Santo Agostinho, closer to the court where he could press his case and breathe the salt air of the sea. On July 17, 1604, Philip approved, ordering the Vice-King, Bishop Afonso de Castelo Branco, to enrol Domingos in Santo Agostinho and pay his arrears, the letter sealed with a wax stamp. The stipend increased to 320,000 reals, covering a cleric's salary and two servants' upkeep, with funds managed by the rector to ensure discipline, a chain of gold and paper. Friar João de Valadares, the rector, was charged to treat Domingos "with the courtesy due to persons of his state," a nod to his princely rank, the words a shield against prejudice.

Lisbon: Santo Agostinho and Santo Antão

Lisbon, a bustling port city with docks teeming with ships from Africa, Asia, and the Americas, was a revelation, its air filled with the scent of spices—cinnamon and cloves—and the tang of salt, a stark contrast to Warri's palm oil markets. At Santo Agostinho, Domingos thrived, finishing his Latin with a fluency that impressed his tutors and studying rhetoric, history, and canon law, the books heavy in his hands. The college's brothers, more worldly than Coimbra's monks, encouraged debate, and Domingos's tales of Warri's river gods—Umale Okun's dance with the currents, the ancestors' whispers in the wind—sparked lively discussions, his voice a bridge between worlds. He befriended a Portuguese student, António Martins d'Abreu, whose wit and loyalty eased his homesickness, their laughter echoing in the college's courtyard, a sound of kinship.

Oritseje and Manoel, joined by a new servant, Ikenna, kept his household running, though Ikenna's sharp tongue clashed with the rector's rules, his complaints a melody of defiance. Yet Lisbon brought challenges—the increased stipend, meant to ease his needs, was delayed by bureaucratic tangles, forcing Domingos to pawn a coral necklace to pay for boots, the beads' loss a pang in his heart. In 1605, Philip ordered the Vice-King, Bishop Pedro de Castilho, to clear the arrears through Buarcos' custom house, acknowledging Domingos's time away from Coimbra, the decree a lifeline cast across the sea. The prince's petition for funds, backed by the Treasury Council, revealed his resilience—he navigated Portugal's court with a diplomat's skill, learning its levers of power, his quill a weapon as potent as a spear.

In 1606, Domingos sought another transfer, this time to the Jesuit Colégio de Santo Antão in Lisbon, hoping for a more rigorous education to prepare for Warri's challenges—wars, conspiracies, and the church's growth. The Jesuits, renowned for their scholarship, were reluctant, citing a lack of accommodation in their newly built college, its stone walls still echoing with construction. On March 18, 1606, the Vice-King reported the issue to Philip, who insisted on March 13 that the Jesuits admit Domingos, either in Lisbon or Coimbra, emphasizing the "special confidence" in their ability to shape him, the command a royal mandate. When the Jesuits demurred again, citing space, Philip ordered on October 31 that the rector find nearby lodgings, with the college overseeing Domingos's studies and conduct, a compromise born of necessity. The arrangement worked Domingos studied under Jesuit tutors, living in a rented house with Oritseje, Ikenna, and Manoel, its walls thin against Lisbon's winter winds, his days filled with theology and nights with dreams of Warri's river, the sound of water a memory in his sleep.

The Order of Christ and Warri's Trade

By 1607, Domingos's presence in Portugal bore fruit for Warri, his voice a catalyst for change. On November 23,

Philip decreed free trade with Warri's ports, equating them to Congo's, a move to promote Catholicism and commerce, the ink on the parchment a promise of prosperity. Domingos's petition, backed by the Financial Council, opened Warri's markets to Portuguese vassals, promising pepper and ivory in exchange for cloth and muskets, the trade a lifeline across the sea. The decree, penned in Lisbon, reflected Domingos's growing influence—he was no mere student but a prince advocating for his kingdom, his words shaping policy. In 1609, Domingos's stature was further cemented when the Mesa da Consciência e Ordens admitted him, his father, and his brother to the Order of Christ, a prestigious knighthood with a red cross emblem, its ceremony a blend of Latin chants and Itsekiri drums. On March 9, the council recommended the investiture, citing Domingos's "quality" and the favour it would bestow on Warri, a bridge of honour. By December 1, Philip granted Domingos a dispensation to profess the Order without the full novitiate, allowing his father and brother to do so in Warri, the habit of Christ a symbol of his dual allegiance—Warri's heir and Portugal's knight, the red cross a mark on his chest.

The Call Home

In 1608, a letter from King Sebastian changed everything, its parchment worn from the journey, delivered by a weary sailor to Lisbon's docks. Written in Warri's palace, its ink smudged with the king's trembling hand, it summoned

Domingos home, citing Sebastian's failing health—his breath short, his coral beads a burden—and the need for his heir to assume the throne's weight. Domingos, now twenty, was torn, his heart a battlefield. Portugal had shaped him—its books filled with wisdom, its faith a beacon in his soul, its courts a school of power—but Warri was his blood, its river a pulse in his veins. On March 10, the Council of Portugal recommended his return, noting his "well enough instructed" state and the Vice-King's assurance of a letter from Sebastian, the decision a royal nod. Philip agreed, excusing Domingos from traveling to Madrid to kiss his hand, a mark of favour that eased his path.

The preparations were meticulous, a caravan of hope and duty. On February 11, 1609, Philip addressed Domingos's requests: a priest and two assistants for Warri's church, funded by the royal chapel; a set of steel armor, its plates gleaming, a visor to shield his face, an axe for battle, and a sword for justice, all crafted by Lisbon's smiths; the Order of Christ habits with their red crosses; and tax exemptions for church goods to flow freely. Domingos received 500 cruzados to settle debts, the coins clinking in his hands, four servants from his household—Oritseje, Ikenna, Manoel, and a new boy named Tunde—and passage on a São Tomé-bound caravel for himself and ten retainers, the ship's timbers creaking with anticipation. The priest, Manoel d'Almeida, was appointed chaplain, though António

Martins d'Abreu's request for a habit was denied, his friendship a loss Domingos mourned. Philip left the pepper trade unresolved, pending reports from Warri, and instructed the São Tomé governor to liaise with Sebastian without committing arms, a cautious balance.

Love and Conflict in Lisbon

As departure loomed, Domingos's heart found a new anchor: Dona Maria de Sousa, daughter of Dom Christovão Pereira and niece of the Count da Feira, her lineage a tapestry of Portuguese nobility. Met at a court banquet in Lisbon's grand hall, where chandeliers cast golden light, Maria's sea-blue eyes and fierce spirit captivated him, her laughter a melody against the clink of goblets. Their courtship, conducted in Lisbon's gardens with roses blooming and churches with stained glass glowing, defied expectations—a Warri prince and a Portuguese noblewoman, their hands clasped over rosaries and coral beads. In 1610, they married in a quiet ceremony at Santo Antão, blending Itsekiri chants—soft as the river's flow—with Catholic vows, a union that shocked the court but won Philip's reluctant blessing, his seal a grudging approval.

The marriage brought trouble, a storm in paradise. On June 28, 1610, Domingos wrote to Philip, his quill scratching with anger, complaining of Francisco Carvalho, a Lisbon judge with a voice like thunder, who stormed his house at 2 a.m., seizing his servants over a brawl involving an official of António Pinto d'Amaral's household, the clash a clash of cultures. Philip ordered the Vice-King, Marquez de Alenquer, to investigate and compensate Domingos, demanding details of the marriage, the letter a shield against prejudice. The incident, coupled with delays in funds and ship arrangements, frustrated Domingos, who cited these as reasons for lingering in Lisbon, his patience tested by the court's slow wheels. On August 11 and October 22, Philip urged Marquez to hasten his departure, growing impatient with excuses, the king's commands a drumbeat of urgency.

Return to Warri

In late 1610, Domingos sailed for Warri, Maria at his side, her sea-blue eyes bright with hope, their caravel laden with books bound in leather, steel armor clanking in the hold, and church vestments embroidered with gold thread, the scent of salt and wood filling the air. The voyage was smoother than his outward journey, though storms off São Tomé tested their resolve, the waves crashing like a river in flood, their prayers a blend of Latin and Itsekiri chants. Landing in Warri in 1611, the riverbank alive with the sound of drums and the scent of roasted yam, Domingos was greeted by a kingdom changed—Sebastian, aged and frail, his coral beads a burden on his trembling hands, wept at his son's return, embracing Maria as a daughter, her wrapper a gift from the Olori. The church, neglected without priests, its thatch sagging, welcomed Manoel d'Almeida, his Bible a new voice in its silence, and Domingos's Order of Christ habit awed the chiefs, its red cross a mark of honor.

Yet challenges awaited, a river's current beneath the calm. Sebastian's hope for a priestly son was dashed—Domingos's marriage and worldly learning made him a king, not a cleric, his steel armour a symbol of war, not peace. The Itsekiri, loyal but wary, questioned his Portuguese ways, their voices murmuring in the market, and chiefs like Ikenna whispered of lost traditions, their coral beads a silent rebellion. Domingos, wearing his coral beads and steel armour, its weight a reminder of Lisbon's forges, stood beneath the Iroko tree, its roots deep in the earth, vowing to blend Warri's river with Portugal's sea, a harmony of spirit and strength. His studies—Latin that flowed like the river, theology that anchored his faith, and courtly diplomacy that sharpened his mind—armed him for the trials ahead: wars with the Awori and Ako, conspiracies like Omeyin, and the church's growth under Maria's influence.

A young messenger interrupted his thoughts, his wrapper torn from a run through the mangroves, his voice breathless. "Ogiame-to-be, the Ijaw raid our northern villages! They took fish and nets, leaving a Portuguese mark—Mendes' hand is near!" Domingos's heart sank, but he masked it with resolve, handing his armour to a servant. "Summon the council," he said, his voice steady. In the war room, Ebi,

Chief Oton, and a young Olua gathered, the map a battle-field of ink. "Mendes stirs trouble," Ebi warned. "The Ijaw are his tools." Oton shook his staff. "Oritse Udeji demands we protect our waters." Olua, eager, said, "Let's drive them back, Ogiame!" Domingos nodded, recalling a parable from his mother, of the Crab and the Tide—Crab evaded the tide's pull with patience, its shell a fortress. "We'll send Olua with twenty warriors to repel the Ijaw, demand proof of Mendes' role. Prepare for war but seek peace first." Olua returned with nets and a Portuguese coin, confirming Mendes' treachery. Domingos sent word to Lisbon via Vasco, vowing to guard Warri's peace.

By 1620, as Bishop Pedro da Cunha reported, Domingos was Warri's heir, his father's chosen successor despite his illegitimacy—a detail overlooked for his Catholic knowledge, his education a beacon. Maria's death after Anthonio's birth would later wound him, but in these early years, Domingos was a prince ascendant, his Portuguese education a light for Warri's future. The Iroko tree stood sentinel, its roots unyielding, as Domingos prepared to lead a kingdom caught between cross and coral, river and sea, his heart a bridge for the storms to come.

CHAPTER ELEVEN

The Shadow of the Sea

The Warri River flowed under a sky heavy with the promise of rain, its currents carrying the weight of a kingdom tested by war, faith, and loss, the air thick with the scent of wet earth and the distant rumble of thunder. Ogiame Dom Domingos, now firmly entrenched as king, stood at the palace's edge, his gaze fixed on the horizon where the river met the sea, the water's edge a shimmering line between peace and peril. His white wrapper, worn in mourning for Olori Maria, had been replaced by a scarlet Kemeje, its coral beads gleaming with the pride of Warri's resilience, the fabric brushing against his skin like a warrior's mantle. Anthonio Domingos, his son, now two years old, toddled in the courtyard under Princess Temieno's watchful eye, his laughter a fragile light amidst the shadow of recent trials, his tiny hands clutching a wooden toy carved from Iroko wood. The church in Warri, bolstered by Father João and Sister Clara, thrived, its school echoing with children's voices and its healing tent fragrant with herbs, drawing converts and sceptics' alike into its fold. Yet peace, hard-won after the Ako war, was a fleeting guest, its surface rippling with unease. From the sea came whispers of a new threat—not of swords or arrows, but of ambition cloaked in trade, led by Captain Vasco, the Portuguese factor who had replaced the disgraced Mendes, his shadow lengthening with each tide.

The Portuguese Gambit

Vasco's ship, *Nossa Senhora do Mar*, anchored at the river's mouth, its hull heavy with bolts of cloth, gleaming muskets, and promises that hung like mist over the water, its wooden planks creaking with the weight of intent. Unlike Mendes, whose greed had fuelled the Omeyin conspiracy and the Ako war with a fire that scorched the land, Vasco was a subtler predator, his velvet doublet a mask for ambition, his smile a lure cast into Warri's waters. His letters to Domingos were laced with deference, offering trade deals and praising Warri's church with words that dripped like honey, but Ebi, ever vigilant, saw through the veneer, his eyes sharp as a hawk's. "He brings gifts, Ogiame," Ebi said, his voice low in the war room, the map before them marked with the scars of Oke-Aro and Ale Eko Iwere, its edges worn by anxious fingers. "But his eyes are on our ports, his heart on our wealth. The Portuguese want Ale Eko Iwere's routes under their flag, not ours, a chain disguised as a lifeline."

Domingos, poring over the map, its coastal lines a testament to battles past, nodded grimly, the weight of his years in

Portugal pressing against his chest. In Lisbon, he had learned the European game—trade was never just trade; it was a chessboard where kings could become pawns, their crowns traded for shackles. The Portuguese crown, through Vasco, sought to deepen its hold on Warri's commerce, leveraging the church's growth to justify their presence, their cross a banner for dominion. Yet Warri's wealth—palm oil glistening in clay jars, ivory tusks stacked in the market, and now pepper, opened to trade by King Philip's decree in 1607—depended on those routes, their flow a lifeblood that sustained the kingdom. Losing control would starve Warri, weakening its ability to rebuild after the wars, its people left to wither like reeds in a dry season.

Temieno, her dagger now a constant at her side, its hilt worn smooth by her grip, leaned over the map, her voice cutting through the silence like a river's edge. "Vasco attended the church's last service, all smiles and prayers, his lips moving with hymns. But his men linger in the market, asking about our warriors' numbers, their hands counting our spears like merchants tallying goods. They're probing our strength." Chief Oton, his cowrie staff resting against the wall, its shells rattling softly like ancestral whispers, spoke with a voice as gentle as the river's flow. "The church draws them, Ogiame. Father João's sermons fill hearts with hope, but Vasco sees souls as coins, their faith a tool to bind us. He'll use the cross to tighten his grip, a net cast over our freedom." Anomu, the war captain, his face still scarred from Oke-Aro, its lines a map of battles, grunted, his leather vest creaking as he shifted. "Let him try. Our blades are sharp, honed on Ako blood, and the river is ours, its currents our shield. We fought the Ako for less—Vasco will taste our steel if he over-reaches."

Domingos's hand traced the map's coastal lines, his mind turning to his son, Anthonio, with Maria's blue-tinged eyes a mirror of the sea she had crossed, a bridge between worlds. The church, a legacy of his Portuguese years, was a strength, its bells a call to unity, but Vasco's ambition threatened to twist it into a chain, binding Warri to foreign will. "We'll meet Vasco," Domingos said, his voice steady as the river's depths, "but not as vassals, not as pawns in his game. Anomu, ready fifty warriors to guard the riverbank, their spears a wall of resolve. Temieno, take your scouts and watch his ship—count his men, note his moves. Ebi, summon Father João. We'll hear Vasco in the church, where he claims to kneel, and let the cross judge his heart."

The Meeting in the Church

The new church, its mud walls adorned with coral patterns that shimmered in the torchlight and an Iroko-carved cross that stood tall against the dusk, was a testament to Warri's evolving faith, its thatched roof a blend of tradition and hope. At dusk, its courtyard filled with Itsekiri—fishermen with nets slung over their shoulders, weavers with hands stained by indigo, and warriors with scars from Oke-Aro—curious about the Portuguese captain's visit, their voices a murmur of anticipation. Vasco arrived in a velvet doublet, its rich blue a contrast to the earth tones of the crowd, his retinue of six armed men a quiet show of force, their muskets glinting under the fading light. Father João and Sister Clara stood at the altar, their robes a symbol of the church's role as both sanctuary and stage, the air filled with the scent of incense and the soft hum of prayer.

Domingos, in his scarlet Kemeje and coral beads, sat on a carved stool, Anthonio on his lap, a symbol of Warri's unbroken line, the boy's tiny hands playing with a coral bead. Temieno and Olua flanked him, their eyes sharp as falcons, while Anomu's warriors lined the walls, their spears at rest but ready, the wood polished by their grip. Vasco bowed, his smile practiced, a mask of courtesy. "Ogiame, your kingdom shines under God's grace, a pearl in the sea. The church, your son, your victories—these are Portugal's pride, a testament to our shared faith. I bring gifts: cloth dyed in Lisbon's looms, wine from the Douro, and a Bible from the Pope's own hand, blessed with holy oil." Domingos accepted the gifts with a nod, the cloth soft against his fingers, the wine's aroma rich, but his expression remained unreadable, a king's shield. "Warri thanks you, Vasco. But gifts come with purpose, a current beneath the surface. Speak yours and let the river hear the truth."

Vasco's smile tightened, his eyes flickering to the crowd. "Trade, Ogiame. Your ports thrive, a heartbeat of commerce, but pirates—perhaps Ijaw—threaten the coast, their canoes a shadow on the water. Portugal offers ships to guard Ale Eko Iwere, their cannons a shield, in exchange for a share of its pepper and oil, a fair partnership." The crowd murmured, their voices a wave of unease, and Ikenna, standing among the chiefs, scowled, his coral beads a silent protest. Ebi leaned close to Domingos, whispering, "He names pirates, but his ships are the wolves, their teeth hidden in prayer. Beware his words." Domingos rose, Anthonio in his arms, the boy's weight a reminder of his duty. "Warri's warriors guard our routes, their blood staining Ale Eko Iwere for our name, not Portugal's. Your ships are welcome to trade, their sails a sight on our river, but the river is ours, its currents our own."

Vasco pressed on, his voice smooth as oil. "The church needs priests to guide its flock, schools need books to light young minds. Portugal can provide, if Warri grants us a fort at Ale Eko Iwere—a small outpost, a beacon of protection for our mutual interests, a stone in the river's flow." Temieno's hand twitched toward her dagger, its hilt warm from her grip, and Olua's grip tightened on his spear, the wood creaking under his strength. Father João stepped forward, his voice calm as a still pool. "The church serves God, not forts, its walls built by Warri's hands. Warri's faith grows by Ogiame's will, not Portugal's gold, its roots deep in our soil." The rebuke silenced Vasco, his smile faltering, and the crowd cheered, their loyalty to Domingos a tide that swelled, the sound echoing off the church's walls. The captain bowed, retreating with promises to "consult Lisbon," his steps heavy, but his departure felt like a storm delayed, not averted, the air thick with the scent of rain.

The River's Warning

That night, Temieno's scouts returned with troubling news, their wrappers damp from the river's edge, their voices hushed in the war room. Vasco's ship had met an Ijaw canoe under cover of darkness, the moon a pale witness, exchanging crates for whispers carried on the wind. Ebi's spies in the market, their ears sharp among the stalls, confirmed the crates held muskets, their barrels gleaming with Portuguese crests, likely bound for Ijaw raiders hungry for revenge. The plot was clear—Vasco aimed to destabilize Warri's coast, sowing chaos to justify a Portuguese fort as "protection," a wolf in sheep's clothing. Domingos, in the war room, felt the weight of his Portuguese years, the memory of Lisbon's courts where nobles stirred unrest to seize power a bitter lesson. Warri would not fall to the same trap, its river a fortress against such treachery.

He summoned Anomu, Olua, and Temieno, the map a bat-tlefield of ink and memory. "We'll fortify Ale Eko Iwere ourselves," he said, his voice a steady current. "Anomu, move a hundred warriors to the village, their spears a wall. Build watchtowers of wood and stone, not forts of foreign design. Temieno, your scouts will patrol the coast, their eyes on the sea. If Vasco's muskets reach the Ijaw, we'll know, and the river will judge." Ebi suggested diplomacy, his hand tracing the map's lines. "Send a letter to Lisbon, Ogiame. Remind Philip of your service—your years in Coimbra, your knight-hood in the Order of Christ. Demand he leash Vasco, his ambition a threat to our peace." Domingos agreed, drafting a letter with Father João's aid, the quill scratching on parch-ment, invoking his time in Portugal to appeal to Philip's honour, the wax seal a mark of resolve. Yet he knew Lisbon was far, its response a slow tide, and Vasco was near, his ship a shadow on the water.

The church, a beacon of faith, became a rallying point, its bells a call to unity. Sister Clara organized women to weave nets for the watchtowers, their fingers nimble despite the storm's threat, the rustle of palm fronds a song of defiance. Father João preached unity, blending Bible verses—"The Lord is my shepherd"—with Itsekiri proverbs, "The river flows with many voices," his voice a bridge between worlds. Oritseje, the converted fisherman, led prayers for the river's protection, his faith a thread between cross and coral, the air filled with the scent of kola nuts and incense.

The Miracle of the Nets

A week later, a storm struck Ale Eko Iwere, its winds tearing at the village's new watchtowers, the rain a curtain of silver, the sound a roar that shook the lagoon. An Ijaw raid, armed with Vasco's muskets, followed, their canoes slipping through the chaos like shadows, the crack of gunfire splitting the air. Olua, commanding the village, rallied his warriors, their spears clashing with musket fire, the lagoon stained with blood. The battle was fierce, with ten Itsekiri falling to bullets, their bodies a silent testament, their leather vests torn. But the nets, woven by Sister Clara's women with prayers woven into every knot, held firm, tangling the Ijaw canoes in a web of palm and hope, allowing Olua's archers to strike with arrows that sang through the rain. The raiders fled, leaving behind muskets marked with Portuguese crests, their retreat a broken wave.

The village hailed the nets as a miracle, crediting Sister Clara and the church, their voices rising in gratitude, the air filled with the scent of wet earth and triumph. The story spread like the river's current, drawing more converts, their baptisms a defiant stand against external threats, the water blessed with both cross and kola nut. Domingos, visiting Ale Eko Iwere with Anthonio cradled in his arms, saw the nets swaying in the breeze and praised the women, gifting them coral beads that clinked like music. "Maria's spirit weaves with you," he said, his voice thick with memory, her blue-tinged eyes reflected in his son's gaze, a bridge to her legacy.

The Confrontation

Vasco, summoned to the palace, denied arming the Ijaw, his velvet doublet stained with the journey, his voice smooth as he claimed the muskets were stolen, a thief's excuse. Domingos, flanked by Anomu and Temieno, held up a captured weapon, its Portuguese crest undeniable, the metal cold in his hands. "Portugal trades in truth or treachery, Vasco. Choose, and let the river witness your answer." Vasco, cornered, his smile faltering, promised to withdraw his ship and investigate, his words a retreat masked as honour. But Ebi's spies, their eyes keen in the market's shadows, reported he sent a letter to Lisbon, its wax seal a plea for reinforcements, the ink a promise of return. Domingos, wary, strengthened Warri's defences, tasking Anomu with training new warriors, their spears gleaming in the dawn, and Olua with guarding the river camp, its stakes reinforced with mangrove wood. Temieno's scouts kept watch, their canoes silent as shadows, the river's currents their ally.

Anthonio's Shadow

In the palace, Anthonio played with a wooden cross, a gift from Father João, its edges worn by his tiny hands, his laughter echoing Maria's, a sound that filled the courtyard with light. Domingos, watching him from the threshold, felt her absence keenly, a wound that time could not heal, but drew strength from her legacy—the church, the nets, the people's faith—these were her gifts, woven into Warri's heart. At a council beneath the Iroko tree, its branches swaying in the evening breeze, he spoke to his chiefs, Ikenna among them, his defiance softened by the church's miracles, his coral beads a quieter presence. "Warri stands not by swords alone, but by our river, its currents our life, our faith, a light in the dark, our unity, a shield against the storm. Vasco tests us, his ships a shadow on the sea, but we are stronger, our roots deep as the Iroko."

A young scout burst into the council, his wrapper torn from a run through the mangroves, his face flushed with urgency. "Ogiame, another Ijaw raid struck the northern creeks! They took yams and a trader's canoe, leaving a note— 'Vasco's promise.' His ship moves closer!" Domingos's heart sank, but he masked it with resolve, handing Anthonio to Temieno, her arms a fortress of strength. "Prepare the war room," he said, his voice a steady drumbeat. In the war room, Ebi, Chief Oton, and Omajuwa gathered, the map a battlefield of ink and memory, its lines blurred by the scout's damp footsteps. "Mendes' shadow lingers in Vasco," Ebi warned, his finger tracing the coast. "The Ijaw are his pawns, their canoes his blades." Chief Oton shook his staff, its cowries rattling like a river's song. "Oritse Udeji demands we protect our waters but seek wisdom in the storm." Omajuwa spoke softly, "A strike against the Ijaw might deter Vasco, cousin, but guard the church—it's our soul."

Domingos nodded, recalling a parable from his father, of the Tortoise and the Storm. Tortoise hid in its shell as the storm raged, emerging to rebuild when the winds ceased, teaching patience and resilience. "We'll send Anomu with seventy warriors to the creeks, recover the goods, and warn the Ijaw. Demand Vasco's ship withdraws, or we'll seize it. Protect the church—its people are Warri's heart." Anomu led the sortie, returning with yams and the canoe, the Ijaw fleeing before the warriors' spears, the air filled with the scent of victory and wet earth. Domingos sent a stern letter to Vasco, delivered by Olua, its words a command: "Leave our waters, or face our blades." Vasco complied, his ship retreating, but Ebi's spies noted a smaller vessel lingered, a shadow in the mist.

In the palace, Domingos held Anthonio, the boy's cross a talisman, the Iroko tree looming outside, its roots a promise of endurance. The Portuguese would return, their ambition as relentless as the tides, but with Temieno's fire, Anomu's iron, Olua's vigilance, and the church's light, Warri would endure, its river flowing unbroken through the shadow of the sea.

CHAPTER TWELVE

King of Kongo Visit to King Dom Domingos

T he Warri River shimmered gold under the setting sun, its surface alive with ripples that danced like the heartbeat of the Warri kingdom, the air thick with the scent of palm oil and the distant hum of cicadas. In 1632, the river welcomed King Garcia II of Kongo, his flotilla approaching Ode-Itsekiri with canoes carved with Bini spirals, their hulls gleaming with crimson cloaks worn by Kongolese warriors, their masters chanting Latin hymns that mingled with the river's gentle song. On the shore, Ogiame Dom Domingos, (Atuwatse I), stood regal in a Portuguese doublet adorned with coral beads that clinked softly, his council of Ojoyes— nobles in flowing wrappers of indigo and green—arrayed behind him like a tapestry of tradition. The palace grounds, framed by the modest Saint Anthony's monastery with its thatched roof, glowed with torchlight, palm fronds swaying in the evening breeze, as the Itsekiri prepared to host the Manikongo, a meeting of rivers and realms. "Welcome, Garcia Nkanga a Lukeni," Dom Domingos called, his voice honed by years at Coimbra's halls, its resonance carrying over the water. "May Oritse Udeji, our supreme god, bless this union of strength and spirit." Garcia, tall and stern, his presence commanding as he stepped ashore, his eyes sweeping the crowd with a warrior's gaze, replied, "By God's grace, Ogiame, let us forge strength against those who bind us with chains, our rivers flowing as one."

The Omoko dance erupted, Itsekiri women in vibrant wrappers gliding to the pulse of drums that echoed like thunder, their steps as fluid as the river, the air filled with the scent of roasted yam and the rhythm of celebration. The palace grounds, alive with the flicker of torches, hosted a feast under palm-thatched pavilions: Banga soup rich with palm oil, smoked crab glistening with spice, and frothing palm wine poured from carved gourds. Bawo, the Ife priestess, her coral beads clinking like ancestral voices, performed a divination, casting shells to invoke Oritse's guidance, the soft clatter a prayer for harmony. Nzinga, a young Kongolese noble with eyes bright with curiosity, watched her, entranced, ignoring the court's protocol, his crimson cloak brushing the ground. Suddenly, a Kongolese guard clutched his throat, collapsing amid the revelry, his cup spilling wine into the dust. Gasps rippled through the crowd, the air thick with shock. "Poison!" a master hissed, his voice sharp as a blade, as healers rushed forward, their hands trembling with urgency. Dom Domingos's smile faltered, his heart a drum of concern. "A mishap, nothing more," he assured Garcia, but his Iyatsere, the war chief, tightened the guard, his spear gleaming in the torchlight. Garcia's hand rested on his sword, his gaze locking on a shadowed figure slipping into the night, a phantom in the flickering glow. Whispers spread—a Jaga warrior, some said, a ghost from Kongo's past, its shadow stretching across the feast. That night, a messenger delivered a cryptic note to Dom Domingos, its parchment damp from the river: "The shadow of the Jaga follows the Manikongo." The Ogiame's fingers tightened around the paper, his mind racing with the weight of hospitality and hidden threats.

Day 2: Trade and Treachery

Morning broke with the Warri River aglow, its waters reflecting the dawn as canoes glided in a vibrant regatta to honour the guests, their paddles slicing the surface like a dance. Garcia and Dom Domingos met in the palace's coral-walled chamber, its walls cool to the touch, maps of trade routes spread before them, the ink lines a map of ambition and alliance. "The Portuguese choke our wealth with their tariffs and ships," Garcia said, his voice low, a river current of resolve. "A pact—Kongo's ivory and fine cloth for Warri's palm oil—could free us both from their grip, a bridge of trade." Dom Domingos nodded, his scholar's mind weighing the stakes, the scent of kola nuts from a nearby offering filling the air. "But we protect our freeborn, Garcia. No Itsekiri will be enslaved, their blood our river's life." Their talks, a delicate weave of diplomacy, were interrupted by a cry: the Ife oracle's staff, a sacred relic of Ginuwa's time, its wood etched with ancestral symbols, had vanished from its shrine, the shrine's silence a wound in the palace's heart. Suspicion fell on a Kongolese master, Afonso, seen near the shrine at dawn, his crimson cloak a mark of guilt.

Garcia's eyes darkened, his hand tightening on the map. "My men are loyal, Ogiame, their hearts bound to Kongo," he snapped, but doubt lingered like mist on the river. Outside, a Portuguese merchant, Diego de Sousa, lingered in Warri's market, his velvet cloaks a stark contrast to the earth tones of the stalls, whispering to Isan, a disgruntled Itsekiri noble with eyes full of resentment, of Kongo's Dutch alliances, his words a seed of discord. Nzinga, defying protocol, met Bawo by the riverbank, where the water lapped softly against the shore, and she revealed a troubling vision from the oracle: "A dual shadow threatens both kings, a serpent in the reeds." Their stolen glances sparked a forbidden attraction, the air charged with unspoken words, but

Bawo whispered of overhearing Isan's plot to frame Kongo for the theft, her voice a tremor of warning. As drums signalled the evening's feast, a boatman reported seeing a cloaked figure—a Jaga?—hiding the staff in a mangrove grove, its branches a maze of green, suspense thickening like the river's mist, the night alive with the hum of insects.

Day 3: The Festival of Oritse Udeji

The festival of Oritse Udeji, honouring the Itsekiri supreme god, filled Ode-Itsekiri with colour, the air fragrant with the smoke of roasted fish and the beat of drums. Men in white robes performed the Ogono dance, their chants echoing tales of Ginuwa's founding, the riverbank a stage of history, while women scattered flower petals, their laughter a song of faith. Garcia joined the rites, offering a Kongolese crucifix to the shrine, its silver gleaming beside the empty space where the staff once stood, a gesture of unity that bridged cross and coral. But Isan seized the moment, his voice rising above the drums, accusing Kongo of disrespecting Itsekiri gods, his words a spark in dry grass. The court bristled, divided, the air thick with tension, and a stranger emerged from the crowd—a scarred warrior with a face like weathered stone, claiming to be a Jaga, survivor of the 1568 invasion of Kongo. "I seek the Manikongo," he declared, his eyes glinting with menace, his spear a shadow in the torchlight. Was he an ally seeking redemption or an assassin cloaked in history? Dom Domingos ordered him watched, his Iyatsere's men shadowing the figure, but the warrior vanished into the night, a ghost swallowed by the darkness.

Bawo, trembling with the weight of her vision, told Nzinga that Diego had offered her gold to betray the Kongolese noble, his coins a temptation against her priestess vows, testing her loyalty like a river tests its banks. She refused, her coral beads a shield, but fear gnawed at her heart, her hands shaking as she cast another divination. That evening, the palace glowed with torches, seafood pepper soup steaming on tables, its aroma mingling with the scent of palm wine, but the missing staff cast a pall, its absence a wound in the festivities. Garcia whispered to Dom Domingos, "The Jaga's shadow stirs old wounds, a serpent in our midst. We must find the traitor, or this alliance bleeds before it begins."

Day 4: The River Hunt

A river hunt was organized to ease tensions, the mangroves a green cathedral under moonlight, their roots a labyrinth of secrets. Garcia and Dom Domingos tracked game—deer and wild boar—alongside Itsekiri fishermen, their nets cast with songs weaving tales of Olukunmi migrations, the water reflecting the stars. But danger struck: a spear whizzed past Garcia, embedding in a tree with a trunk, its shaft quivering, the air filled with the scent of sap and threat. The Jaga warrior was spotted nearby, his scarred face a flash in the reeds, fleeing into the shadows. "He's no ghost," Garcia growled, drawing his blade, its steel glinting, his voice a thunderclap of resolve. Nzinga and Bawo, searching for clues, found Diego's letters hidden in Isan's quarters, the parchment crumpled with haste, revealing a scheme to frame Kongo and seize Warri's trade routes, the ink a map of treachery. The letters hinted at a Kongolese traitor—possibly Afonso, the master—his loyalty a shadow cast by the Kimpanzu faction.

Dom Domingos confronted Isan, who denied all, his eyes darting nervously like a trapped fish, his hands trembling as he clutched his wrapper. The hunt returned with no game but mounting distrust, the mangroves silent witnesses, as Garcia vowed to unmask the betrayer within his ranks, his hand resting on his sword. That night, under the Iroko tree, Bawo shared a parable with Nzinga, of the Egret and the Flood: "Egret stood tall as the flood rose, its wings sheltering its young, teaching us to protect what we love." Their bond deepened, a light in the darkness, but the threat loomed larger.

Day 5: The Oracle's Warning

Bawo consulted the Ife oracle in a candlelit shrine, its walls adorned with faded paintings of Ginuwa, her prayers rising with incense that curled like river mist. The shells spoke with a clatter: "A dual shadow threatens both kings. Restore the staff, or blood will flow, a river red with loss." Isan sabotaged the ritual, spilling sacred oil with a sneer, the liquid pooling like a wound, and whispers of war spread like wildfire through the palace. The Jaga warrior reappeared, his scarred face a mask of intent, demanding a ransom in slaves for the staff, his voice a growl. Garcia refused, citing Kongo's laws against enslaving Christians, his hand firm on his crucifix.

"Then you'll lose more than a relic," the warrior sneered, vanishing again into the night, his footsteps a whisper on the wind.

Nzinga's secret meetings with Bawo drew suspicion, the air thick with whispers, with Afonso accusing him of disloyalty, his voice a blade of accusation. Hurt, Nzinga confided in Garcia, his heart heavy, who sensed a deeper plot, his eyes narrowing. Dom Domingos, torn between trust and caution, doubled the palace guard, their war chants echoing through the night, the sound a drumbeat of resolve, the Itsekiri's coral jewellery gleaming in torchlight, a symbol of resilience amid chaos. Bawo, her love for Nzinga a secret flame, prayed for guidance, her beads a shield against the storm.

Day 6: Betrayal Unmasked

Evidence mounted like a rising tide: Isan and Diego had stolen the staff to provoke war, hoping to weaken both kingdoms for Portuguese gain, their plot a serpent in the reeds. Garcia and Dom Domingos confronted Isan, who fled to a Portuguese ship moored off the coast, its sails a dark promise on the horizon. The Jaga warrior, revealing himself as a mercenary hired by Diego, switched sides, his scarred hands trembling as he exposed the merchant's plan to incite an invasion, handing over the staff with a bow. "I seek only justice," he said, his voice a gravel of regret, the relic's wood warm in Dom Domingos's hands. Bawo's love for Nzinga was exposed, her priestess robes glowing in the firelight, shocking the court, but she stood defiant, her voice a river's strength. "Our hearts bind our kingdoms, a thread of hope in this shadow." Dom Domingos, moved, blessed their union, a symbol of hope, the air filled with the scent of palm wine and reconciliation.

The palace erupted in song, the Ogono dance weaving through the night, its rhythm a heartbeat of triumph, but Garcia's face remained grim, his hand on his sword. A final clue pointed to Afonso as the Kongolese traitor, loyal to the Kimpanzu faction, his confession a whisper in the torch-light. Garcia, heart heavy, ordered his execution, the blade falling with a soft thud, a stark reminder of trust's fragility, the ground stained with blood.

Day 7: Unity Forged

Garcia and Dom Domingos pursued Isan to a coastal village, its huts shadowed by the Portuguese ship, where Diego's forces waited, their muskets glinting. The Jaga warrior's testimony turned Diego's men against him, their loyalty shifting like sand, and the merchant was seized, his velvet cloak torn, his face pale with defeat. The staff was restored to the shrine, its return marked by a grand ceremony, the air filled with the sound of Itsekiri drummers pounding rhythms of triumph, their beats a song of resilience. Dom

Domingos gifted Garcia a coral crown, its beads a river of light, sealing their alliance, the exchange a bridge between kingdoms. But a final twist cut deep: a letter from Afonso, read aloud, revealed Kimpanzu plans to ally with the Dutch, a shadow over Kongo's future.

As Garcia's flotilla prepared to depart, Nzinga and Bawo stood hand in hand, their union a bridge between Kongo and Warri, the river gleaming under dawn's light, carrying hopes of peace. A young Itsekiri scout approached, his wrapper stained with mangrove mud, whispering, "Ogiame, a Dutch ship was seen near the coast, its flag hidden." Domingos's heart sank, but he masked it with resolve, vowing to watch the horizon.

Epilogue

The trade alliance flourished, curbing Portuguese dominance, its markets alive with ivory and palm oil, the air filled with the scent of trade. The Jaga warrior vanished, leaving a carved fetish with a cryptic note: "Kongo's shadow rises, a storm on the wind." Dom Domingos prayed at Saint Anthony's monastery, his Portuguese Bible open, its pages rustling, while Itsekiri storytellers wove tales of the visit into legend, their voices rising with the river's song. At the final feast, the Ogono dance pulsed, palm wine flowed from gourds, and the Warri River sang of unity forged in fire, its currents a promise. Garcia, gazing from his canoe, murmured, "May God and Oritse Udeji hold this bond, a light against the shadows." Domingos, holding Anthonio, knew the Dutch threat loomed, but with Garcia's alliance and Warri's spirit, the kingdom would endure, its river flowing unbroken.

CHAPTER THIRTEEN
Tackling Pirates

The Warri River, a silver vein threading through the heart of Ode-Itsekiri, bore the lifeblood of the Itsekiri people—trade flourishing with the clink of coral beads, fish glistening in the nets, and tales of their Olukunmi ancestors whispered along its banks, the air rich with the scent of mangrove and salt. But in the autumn of 1632, its waters carried a darker current, a shadow beneath the surface, as Ijaw pirates, emboldened by the chaos of European rivalries, prowled the Niger Delta, their swift canoes striking like vipers in the mist. Merchants huddled in the market, their voices trembling with tales of villages razed, cargos of palm oil vanished into the night, and freeborn neighbouring tribe dragged into the mangrove's shadowy depths, their cries swallowed by the river's flow. Ogiame Dom Domingos, scholar-king clad in a Portuguese doublet adorned with coral beads that gleamed like stars, and a wrapper of scarlet Kemeje, stood on the palace jetty, his eyes scanning the horizon where the river met the sea, the wooden planks creaking under his weight. The river, once a song of prosperity, now hummed with menace, its gentle ripples a mask for danger.

The crisis struck close when Uwangue, Dom Domingos's cousin and a trusted Ojoye whose laughter filled feasts with warmth, vanished during a trading voyage to Escravos, his canoe a lifeline to the coast. His vessel, found adrift near the jetty, bore slashes of machetes that scarred its hull and a taunting fetish—a shark's tooth wrapped in red cloth, the mark of Ebiowei, an Ijaw pirate lord rumoured to wield charms that turned men to stone, its presence a chill in the air. The court reeled, the palace walls echoing with grief, Uwangue's loss a wound to the kingdom's pride, his absence a silence where once there was song. "We cannot bend to these river wolves," Dom Domingos declared, his voice honed by Coimbra's halls, its resonance a call to action. "Oritse Udeji will guide us, but we must act, our spears raised against this tide." The palace, its coral walls glowing under torchlight that flickered like hope, buzzed with urgency, the scent of palm oil from the kitchens mingling with the tension of war.

The Iyatsere, war chief with a scar tracing his jaw like a river's path, rallied the palace guard, their war chants echoing through the night, the sound a drumbeat of resolve. Bawo, the Ife priestess, her coral beads clinking like ancestral voices, cast shells in the shrine, its walls adorned with faded paintings of Ginuwa, her vision clouded by a dual shadow. "The shark's tooth hides a traitor's hand," she murmured, her fingers trembling as the shells fell, their pattern a map of peril.

Suspicion fell on Isan, a disgraced noble exiled after his treachery during the Kongolese visit, now rumoured to lurk in the Delta, colluding with pirates, his shadow a stain on the river's silver. Dom Domingos summoned Odion, a young Itsekiri warrior whose skill with a canoe rivalled the river's currents, his lean frame sharp-eyed with determination. Odion had once sailed with Portuguese traders, learning their maps and the crack of muskets, his father, a fisherman, fallen to pirates' years before, fuelling his resolve with a fire that burned in his chest. "Find Uwangue," Ogiame commanded, his hand resting on Odion's shoulder. "Bring him home, and let Ebiowei taste our steel, his charms broken by our will." Odion bowed, his coral amulet glinting in the torchlight, and slipped into the night, his canoe vanishing into the river's embrace, the water lapping softly against its sides.

The Delta's Labyrinth

The Delta's waterways, a maze of mangroves and mist where the air hung heavy with the scent of mud and salt, hid Ebiowei's lair, a fortress of stilt huts and shadowed intent. Odion navigated by starlight, his paddle silent as a heron's wing, guided by tales from fishwives of a pirate camp near Mein Creek, their voices a thread of memory in the dark. He was not alone—Bawo, defying tradition with a priestess's courage, joined him, her robes traded for a fisherman's wrapper dyed with indigo, its folds hiding her beads. "The oracle demands my presence," she insisted, her eyes fierce with purpose, the shells' prophecy a weight on her soul. Odion, wary but trusting her visions, agreed, their bond forged by shared peril, the river a witness to their pact.

Their journey was fraught with danger, the Delta a living maze. A pirate scout, his canoe painted with shark motifs that gleamed under the moon, nearly spotted them, his paddle a threat in the silence, but Odion's swift manoeuvre outwitted him, the water rippling with their escape. At a river shrine, its stones worn smooth by time, Bawo offered palm oil to Umale Okun, the sea goddess, praying for safe passage, the oil's sheen a plea on the water's surface, the air filled with the scent of ritual. The Delta's sounds—crabs scuttling along the banks, herons crying into the night—masked their approach, a symphony of nature, but danger loomed like a storm on the horizon. In a fishing village, its huts shadowed by mangroves, a widow with hands rough from nets whispered of Isan's presence, her voice trembling with fear. "He seeks Ogiame's throne, trading Itsekiri secrets for pirate gold, his heart a traitor's den," she warned, her eyes darting to the shadows.

Odion and Bawo reached Mein Creek, where Ebiowei's camp sprawled—a cluster of stilt huts guarded by canoes bristling with spears, the air thick with the smell of smoked fish and musk. Uwangue, bound and bruised, sat under a palm canopy, his wrapper torn, Ebiowei taunting him with a shark-tooth dagger that glinted like a predator's grin. "Ogiame will pay a king's ransom, or you'll feed the river, your blood its feast," the pirate growled, his charms rattling like bones in the wind. Odion, hidden in the reeds, counted thirty pirates, their muskets stolen from Dutch traders, their barrels a threat in the moonlight. A direct assault was suicide, the odds a river too deep to cross. Bawo's oracle vision guided their plan, a thread of hope in the dark. She slipped into the camp, posing as a wandering priestess, her charms disarming the guards with a priestess's grace. "The river gods demand a feast to appease their wrath," she declared, offering tainted palm wine laced with sleeping herbs from the shrine, the liquid a silent weapon.

As pirates drank, their laughter fading into stupor, Odion freed Uwangue, the ropes falling like shadows, but Ebiowei, immune to the wine, his charms a shield, raised the alarm, his voice a roar that split the night. A chase erupted, canoes slicing through the darkness, arrows hissing past like angry spirits, the water churning with pursuit. Odion's musket, a relic from his Portuguese days, felled a pursuer, the crack echoing, but Ebiowei's canoe closed in, his charms glinting like eyes in the dark, the shark-tooth dagger raised. Back in Ode-Itsekiri, Dom Domingos prepared a counterstrike, the palace a hive of activity, the scent of war paint mingling with the river's breath.

The River's Reckoning

The Iyatsere mobilized war canoes, their prows carved with Bini spirals that danced in the torchlight, their chants a call to arms, while Ogiame consulted Portuguese allies, the air thick with the sound of planning. Diego de Sousa, the merchant humbled by the Kongolese affair, offered a ship's cannon, its barrel gleaming with promise, seeking favour with a smile that masked his ambition. "The pirates threaten us all, Ogiame," he said, his eyes calculating, his voice smooth as oil. Dom Domingos accepted, wary of Diego's motives, the cannon a double-edged sword, and led a flotilla upriver, guided by a fisherman's map of Mein Creek, its lines a lifeline in the dark. The rescue converged with chaos, the river a battlefield of wills.

Odion's canoe capsized under Ebiowei's assault, the water swallowing them like a beast, but Bawo's prayer to Umale Okun stirred a sudden tide, its force a miracle that righted their craft, the wood groaning with relief. Uwangue, weakened but defiant, seized a pirate's machete, its blade slick with blood, wounding Ebiowei's arm, the pirate's roar a cry of pain. As dawn broke, painting the sky with gold, Dom Domingos's flotilla arrived, the cannon's roar scattering the pirates like leaves in a storm, the sound a thunderclap over the water. War canoes clashed, Itsekiri warriors chanting as they drove Ebiowei's men into the mangroves, their spears flashing, the air filled with the scent of gunpowder and sweat. Isan, unmasked as the traitor, fought beside Ebiowei, his dreams of power shattered by a warrior's spear that pierced his chest, his fall a silent end. Ebiowei, cornered, invoked his charms, his voice rising in a chant, but Bawo countered with an Ife incantation, her words a storm of power. "Oritse Udeji sees your greed, your heart a stone in the river," she declared, and the pirate's resolve faltered, his charms dimming. Odion's musket found its mark, the bullet striking true, and Ebiowei fell, his shark-tooth dagger sinking into the river, its ripples a farewell.

The Return and Triumph

The camp was razed, its stilt huts reduced to ash, its captives freed, their chains clanking as they stumbled into the light, and Uwangue, supported by Odion, embraced Dom Domingos on the shore, the water lapping at their feet. "Kin and kingdom endure, cousin," Ogiame said, his voice thick with emotion, his coral beads a testament to their bond. The return to Ode-Itsekiri was triumphant, the riverbank alive with the Omoko dance, women in vibrant wrappers swaying to drums that echoed Ginuwa's legacy, the air filled with the scent of roasted fish and celebration. A feast spilled across the palace grounds—banga soup rich with palm oil, smoked fish glistening with spice, and palm wine flowing from gourds, its froth a symbol of joy. Storytellers wove Odion's deed into legend, their voices rising with the river's song, the crowd cheering as the young warrior stood tall.

Bawo, her priestess status restored, led a rite at the Ife shrine, the oracle's shells proclaiming peace restored, their clatter a hymn of victory, the air thick with incense. Odion, gifted a coral sword by Ogiame, its blade etched with river motifs, stood tall, his father's memory honoured, the weapon a badge of pride. Yet shadows lingered, a current beneath the calm. Diego's cannon, a symbol of uneasy alliances, hinted at Portuguese ambitions, its barrel a silent threat on the shore. A fisherman found Ebiowei's fetish afloat, its red cloth untorn, whispering of unquiet spirits, its presence a chill in the dawn. Dom Domingos, praying at Saint Anthony's monastery, his Portuguese Bible open, its pages rustling in the breeze, vowed to guard the river's peace, the scent of candle wax a promise.

A young scout approached, his wrapper stained with mangrove mud, his voice breathless. "Ogiame, a Dutch trader was seen bartering with Ijaw survivors! They spoke of Ebiowei's kin seeking revenge." Domingos's heart sank, but he masked it with resolve, turning to the council. "Prepare the Iyatsere," he said, his voice steady. In the war room, Ebi, Chief Oton, and Odion gathered, the map a battlefield of ink. "The Dutch stir the pot," Ebi warned, his finger tracing the Delta. "Ebiowei's kin will strike again." Chief Oton shook his staff. "Umale Okun demands vigilance, a shield for our waters." Odion, his coral sword in hand, said, "Let me lead, Ogiame. The river taught me its secrets."

Domingos nodded, recalling a parable from his mother, of the Otter and the Current: "Otter swims with the current, yet turns it to its will, teaching us to flow with strength." He devised a plan: Odion would lead a patrol to track the Dutch, supported by fifty warriors, while Bawo consulted the oracle for guidance. The patrol set out, their canoes slicing the water, and returned with news of a Dutch ship retreating, its crew shaken by Odion's musket fire. Yet a captured sailor whispered of a larger fleet, a storm brewing on the horizon. Dom Domingos, holding Anthonio, vowed to fortify the Delta, the Warri River, gleaming under moonlight, sang of resilience, its currents carrying tales of pirates tamed and a kingdom unbroken, ready for the tides to come.

CHAPTER FOURTEEN

A Visit to Bini

T he Warri River gleamed under a midday sun, its waters alive with the rhythm of paddles as a flotilla of carved canoes bore Ogiame Dom Domingos and his entourage toward the Kingdom of Benin, the air filled with the scent of fresh mangrove and the distant call of herons. It was the spring of 1635, and Warri, tempered by wars with the Awori and Ako, and the church's gentle rise, stood strong under Domingos's reign, its spirit a river unbowed. His scarlet Kemeje, adorned with coral beads that clinked like a soft melody, fluttered in the breeze, a symbol of Itsekiri pride, while his European crown, a gift from his Portuguese years at Coimbra, rested in a carved box of Iroko wood, a nod to his dual heritage, its gold a quiet gleam. Beside him sat Anthonio Domingos, now seven, clutching a strip of Olori Maria's indigo wrapper, its fabric worn soft by his tiny hands, his blue-tinged eyes wide with wonder at the world unfolding before him. Princess Temieno, her dagger strapped to her thigh, its hilt worn smooth by her grip, stood at the prow, her gaze sharp as a hawk's as she scanned the horizon, the wind tugging at her braided hair. Chief

Anomu, the war-scarred captain whose face bore the map of Oke-Aro, and Olua, now a seasoned commander with a steady hand, flanked the royal canoe, their warriors alert, their spears glinting in the sunlight. Ebi, the ever-watchful advisor with a map clutched in his hands, and Chief Oton, the high priest with a cowrie-laden staff, carried offerings—coral glistening like river pearls, ivory tusks smooth as the Delta's flow, and pepper sacks fragrant with spice—for the Oba of Benin, whose realm, Edo, loomed as both kin and rival, its earthen walls a distant promise.

The visit was no mere courtesy, a voyage of diplomacy woven with history. Historical ties bound Warri and Benin, rooted in legend: Ogiame Ginuwa, Warri's first king, was a prince of Benin, sent by his father, Oba Nuwa the Great, in the 15th century to found a new kingdom, his canoe a seed cast into the river's heart. Yet centuries had strained this bond—Benin's empire, with its brass plaques and warrior kings, dwarfed Warri's riverine domain, and trade rivalries, especially over Portuguese commerce, sparked tensions like embers in dry grass. The Oba at this time, historically accurate, was Oba Ohuan, who ruled in the early 17th century, a period of relative stability before Benin's decline, known for consolidating trade with the Portuguese, his court a fortress of ritual and power. Ohuan had invited Domingos to Benin City to discuss shared threats: Ijaw pirates lurking in the Delta, Portuguese overreach with their ships and forts, and whispers of Dutch traders encroaching on their coasts, their sails a shadow on the horizon. The visit, a rare event, was a chance to reaffirm kinship, negotiate trade, and display the cultural splendour of both kingdoms, their rivers flowing as one.

The Journey to Edo

The journey upriver was a spectacle, a procession of pride and peril. Warri's canoes, painted with coral patterns that shimmered in the sun and mounted with blunderbusses from Jean-François Landolphe's accounts, cut through the water, their sails catching the wind like wings, the sound of wood against water a rhythmic pulse. Drummers beat rhythms of honour, blending Itsekiri war chants with Christian hymns, a nod to the church's growing influence, the air filled with the scent of roasted yam from the warriors' provisions. Temieno's scouts, led by a young woman named Adesuwa, her wrapper dyed with indigo, navigated the labyrinthine creeks, wary of Ijaw ambushes, their eyes scanning the mangroves for shadows. Anthonio, perched on Domingos's lap, pointed at egrets skimming the water, their white wings a flash of grace, his laughter easing the tension, a child's joy a balm for the king's heart. Ebi, clutching a map etched with the Delta's twists, murmured to Domingos, "Oba Ohuan will test us, Ogiame. His court is a maze of ritual, its walls a mirror of power, and his chiefs watch for weakness, their eyes sharp as spears." Domingos nodded, his mind drifting to his Portuguese education in Lisbon, where he had learned diplomacy's dance—smiles hiding steel, words a shield. "We go as kin, Ebi, but not as vassals," he replied, his coral beads clicking softly, a reminder of Umale Okun's strength and Olori Maria's love, her memory a current in his soul. "Warri's river flows free, its spirit unbroken."

At dusk, Benin City's earthen walls loomed, their moats reflecting the torchlight, a marvel described by Olfert Dapper in 1668, the air thick with the scent of earth and smoke. The Itsekiri flotilla docked at Gwato, Benin's bustling port, where Edo warriors in coral-adorned vests greeted them with cautious respect, their spears upright, the sound of their footsteps a steady drum. A herald, bearing an Eben ceremonial sword that gleamed with history, led them through wide streets lined with houses, their roofs topped with brass pythons, symbols of Oba Ohuan's divine power, their scales catching the fading light. The Itsekiri, in their woven wrappers and coral necklaces, drew stares, their European-influenced attire—Domingos's doublet beneath his Kemeje, Temieno's Portuguese-style boots with coral embroidery—a contrast to Edo's traditional regalia, the clash of cultures a silent dialogue. Anthonio, awed by the brass pythons, clung tighter to his father, his whisper a child's wonder, "Are they alive, Papa?"

The Court of Oba Ohuan

The Oba's palace, a sprawling complex of courtyards and bronze-decorated pillars that towered like ancient trees, was a testament to Benin's might, the air within heavy with incense and the murmur of courtiers. Oba Ohuan, a tall man with a commanding presence, his skin marked by ritual scars, sat on a throne draped in coral and leopard skins, his Akpa net shirt glittering with beads from Mediterranean trade, the fabric a map of wealth. His chiefs, including the Ezomo with his brass armlets and the Iyase with a Uhunmwu-Ẹkuẹ pendant mask, stood in ranks, their regalia a display of power, the scent of palm oil from their offerings mingling with the incense. Queen Mother Iyoba, Ohuan's mother, watched from a separate dais, her ivory pendants clinking softly, a nod to her regiment's power, her eyes sharp with wisdom. The air was thick with anticipation as a guild artisan presented a brass plaque depicting Ohuan's ancestors, its vivid detail a record of Benin's glory, the metal cool to the touch.

Domingos, entering with Anthonio in his arms, bowed but did not kneel, a gesture of equality that stirred a ripple among the chiefs, his coral beads a counterpoint to their brass. His chiefs followed, their Iroko-carved staffs mirroring Benin's artistry but distinct in Itsekiri style, the wood warm with tradition. Temieno, her hair braided with coral strands that caught the light, carried a carved ivory tusk, a gift from Warri's artisans, its surface smooth as the river's flow, while Anomu bore a basket of pepper, its fragrance a reminder of Warri's trade wealth, the spice a silent promise. Oton, chanting softly to Umale Okun, sprinkled kola nuts, their bitter taste a bridge between Itsekiri and Edo rituals, the sound of his voice a prayer in the vast hall. The crowd murmured, noting the Itsekiri's Christian cross alongside their ancestral offerings, a fusion that sparked both curiosity and unease. Ohuan rose, his voice resonant as a drum. "Ogiame, son of Ginuwa, welcome to Edo, city of my fathers. Our blood is one, yet the river divides us with its currents. Let us speak as brothers, our voices a song of unity." His words, warm but measured, echoed the historical affinity noted in 2018 when Oba Ewuare II visited Warri, calling it a bond "age-old," a thread unbroken by time.

Domingos replied, his Portuguese accent subtle but clear, a legacy of Coimbra. "Oba Ohuan, Warri honours Benin, our root and our strength. We come to strengthen what Ginuwa began, for the river and sea threaten us both, their tides a common foe." Anthonio, sensing the moment, clutched his father's beads, drawing smiles from the Edo court, his innocence a bridge between the kings, the crowd's murmur softening with affection.

The Feast of Kinship

The palace hosted a feast, a cultural tapestry of both kingdoms, the air filled with the scent of yam and spice. Edo drummers beat rhythms on Ogume drum, their carvings depicting Oba Omajuwa's victories, the wood resonant with history, while Itsekiri drummers answered with Christian-influenced chants, their canoes' blunderbuss mounts displayed as trophies, the metal a gleam of pride. Benin's guilds served yam pounded with palm oil, its texture a comfort, goat stew rich with herbs, and kola nuts sacred to Osanobua, the creator god, their bitterness a ritual taste. Warri's women, led by Mama Ose, offered fish smoked with pepper, a nod to their riverine life, the aroma a song of the Delta. Anthonio, seated between Domingos and Temieno, nibbled yam, his presence softening the Edo chiefs' stern gazes, his laughter a ripple of joy.

A plot simmered beneath the feast's harmony, a shadow in the light. Chief Ikenna, still smarting from his failed church plot, whispered to an Edo chief, Obasogie, a blacksmith-sculptor known for his loyalty to Ohuan, his house bearing intricate brass designs that gleamed in the torchlight. Ikenna, resentful of Domingos's Christian leanings, suggested Warri's church weakened its Itsekiri roots, hoping to sway Obasogie against the alliance, his voice a serpent's hiss. Obasogie, his hands rough from forging, listened but said little, his loyalty to Ohuan outweighing Ikenna's intrigue, his silence a wall of resolve. Temieno, ever alert, overheard Ikenna's murmurs and signalled Ebi, her hand brushing her dagger. "He stirs trouble again, a thorn in our side," she whispered, her voice low. Ebi, slipping through the crowd with the grace of a river otter, warned Domingos, who kept his composure, engaging Ohuan in talk of trade, the air thick with the scent of feast and strategy. "The Portuguese push for forts, their ships a shadow on our waters," Domingos said, "but Warri and Benin can guard our coasts together, our rivers a united front." Ohuan nodded, his eyes flicking to Ikenna, sensing the undercurrent, his hand resting on his throne.

The Ritual of Unity

The next day, a ceremony at Benin's royal shrine showcased both kingdoms' spiritual depth, the air fragrant with incense and the sound of chanting. Ohuan led a procession to honour Osanobua, warriors performing an acrobatic dance for Drum, the god of iron, recalling a mythical war against the sky, their leaps a story in motion. A brass Uhunmwum elao head of an Oba, placed on an altar, gleamed, its stylized features a testament to Edo artistry, the metal cool against the warm stone. Oton, representing Warri, offered kola nuts to the river spirits, their bitter taste a prayer, while Father João, invited at Domingos's insistence, sprinkled holy water, blending Christian and Itsekiri rites, the water a shimmer of unity. The Edo crowd, unused to such fusion, watched in silence, the tension palpable, but Iyoba, her ivory pendants clinking softly, nodded approval, her role as advisor mirroring Temieno's in Warri, her wisdom a quiet strength.

A second plot emerged during the rite, a ripple in the calm. An Ijaw spy, posing as a trader with a basket of yams, infiltrated the crowd, sent by a rogue Portuguese captain, Diogo, who had replaced Vasco after the pirate affair. Diogo, learning of the visit, aimed to disrupt the alliance, fearing a united Warri-Benin front would thwart Portuguese ambitions, his ships a threat on the coast. The spy, armed with a poisoned dart hidden in his sleeve, targeted Anomu, whose war prowess threatened Ijaw raids, the dart's tip glinting with venom. Adesuwa, Temieno's scout, her wrapper fluttering in the breeze, spotted the spy's furtive movements and tackled him, her dagger pinning his sleeve to the ground with a thud, the crowd gasping as the dart fell. Anomu, unharmed, seized the weapon, its tip reeking of death, his scar a badge of survival. The crowd's murmur rose, and Ohuan's warriors bound the spy, his Portuguese coin pouch spilling onto the stone, revealing Diogo's hand, the metal a traitor's mark. Ohuan, enraged, his voice a thunderclap, declared, "The sea wolves test us, their fangs bared, but Benin and Warri stand as one, our rivers a shield." He gifted Domingos a brass plaque depicting Ginuwa's departure, its detail a bridge of history, and Domingos reciprocated with an Iroko-carved cross, its coral inlays blending faiths, the wood warm with

Warri's spirit. The ceremony ended with a chant, Edo and Itsekiri voices rising together, a rare unity, the air filled with the scent of kola nuts and hope.

The Trade Pact

The visit's heart was a council in the palace's central hall, its pillars adorned with brass plaques showing Portuguese merchants and Edo warriors, the metal a chronicle of trade. Ohuan proposed a pact: Warri and Benin would jointly patrol the coast, their canoes a united fleet, sharing pepper and ivory profits while rejecting Portuguese forts, their walls a foreign chain. Domingos, drawing on his Lisbon years, suggested a school in Gwato, modelled on Warri's, to teach Portuguese and Edo literacy, strengthening trade without bending to European will, the quills a tool of empowerment. Ohuan agreed, appointing Obasogie to oversee it, his blacksmith hands a promise of craft, quashing Ikenna's hopes of discord, the chief's silence a victory. A third plot surfaced here, a whisper in the hall. A Benin chief, Ezomo, wary of Warri's growing church, its cross a foreign star, proposed to Ohuan that the pact exclude Christian missionaries, fearing they diluted Edo's spiritual purity, his voice a current of tradition. Ebi, catching wind through a palace servant, his ears sharp as a river bird, alerted Domingos, who countered subtly, the air thick with strategy.

At the council, Domingos invited Sister Clara to speak, her healing tent a beacon in Warri, offering herbs to Iyoba, the bundles fragrant with mint and root. "Faith heals, not divides," she said, her voice a gentle stream, and Iyoba accepted with a smile, her ivory pendants a nod of approval. Ezomo, outmanoeuvred, relented, his protest a fading echo, and the pact was sealed with kola nuts and palm wine, the bitter taste a bond, the liquid a toast to unity.

The Return and Legacy

As the flotilla prepared to depart, Ohuan hosted a final procession, warriors bearing Ogume drum carved with victory tales and coral Ikoro bands, symbols of Benin's might, the wood resonant with history. Warri's drummers answered, their blunderbusses firing salutes that echoed over the river, a fusion of Itsekiri and European flair, the smoke a fleeting cloud. Anthonio, riding on Olua's shoulders, waved a coral bead gifted by Iyoba, its surface smooth as a river stone, a token of kinship, his laughter a bridge between realms. The Ijaw spy's fate was grim—Ohuan sent him to Diogo's ship, bound with ropes, with a warning carved on a wooden tablet: "The river bows to no sea, its current our strength." The ship's sails vanished into the horizon, a shadow retreating.

Back in Warri, Domingos stood beneath the Iroko tree, its gnarled branches a canopy of resilience, Anthonio asleep in his arms, the boy's breath a soft rhythm. The visit had forged a pact, strengthened by shared blood and culture, the brass plaque from Ohuan a testament, but Diogo's shadow loomed, a storm on the sea. Temieno, her wound from the spy's scuffle bandaged by Sister Clara's skilled hands, vowed to patrol the coast, her dagger a promise. Anomu trained new warriors, their spears gleaming in the dawn, and Father João preached of unity, the church's cross now joined by the Benin plaque, its metal a bridge of faiths. Ikenna, chastened, swore loyalty, his plot undone by Warri's strength, his coral beads a quieter presence.

A young scout approached, his wrapper torn from a run through the mangroves, his voice urgent. "Ogiame, a Dutch ship was sighted off Escravos, its crew bartering with Ijaw! They spoke of Diogo's return." Domingos's heart sank, but he masked it with resolve, turning to the council. "Summon the Iyatsere," he said, his voice a steady current. In the war room, Ebi, Chief Oton, and Adesuwa gathered, the map a battlefield of ink. "The Dutch stir the Ijaw," Ebi warned, his finger tracing the coast. "Diogo's shadow grows." Chief Oton shook his staff. "Umale Okun demands we guard our waters, a prayer in the storm." Adesuwa, her eyes fierce, said, "Let me lead a scout, Ogiame. The creeks know me."

Domingos nodded, recalling a parable from his father, of the Ibis and the Tide: "Ibis stands firm as the tide rises, its beak turning the water to its will, teaching us to rise with strength." He devised a plan: Adesuwa would lead a scout party to track the Dutch, supported by thirty warriors, while Oton consulted the oracle for guidance. The party set out, their canoes silent as shadows, and returned with news of a Dutch ship retreating, its crew shaken by Adesuwa's arrows, the air filled with the scent of victory. Yet a captured sailor whispered of a larger fleet, a storm brewing on the horizon, his words a chill in the dawn. Dom Domingos, holding Anthonio, vowed to fortify the coast, the Warri River, gleaming under moonlight, sang of resilience, its currents carrying tales of Benin's alliance and Warri's spirit, ready for the tides to come.

CHAPTER FIFTEEN

Emagin,
The King's Brother

T he Warri River sparkled under a late afternoon sun, its waters still rippling from the return of Ogiame Dom Domingos's flotilla from Benin, the air alive with the scent of fresh mangrove and the distant hum of cicadas celebrating their safe passage. The visit to Oba Ohuan had forged a pact of unity, its echoes lingering in the brass plaque now displayed in the palace courtyard, a gift from Benin symbolizing the shared blood of Ginuwa, its surface cool and gleaming under the torchlight. Warri buzzed with renewed Vigor—drummers played rhythms of triumph that pulsed through the streets, fishermen hauled bountiful catches of silver fish from the river, their nets heavy with promise, and the church, under Father João and Sister Clara, drew crowds with tales of miracles, the scent of incense mingling with the salt air. Yet beneath this harmony, a new shadow crept into the kingdom, carried not by Portuguese ships or Ijaw raiders but by a figure from Domingos's past: his younger brother, Emagin, sent from Ile-Ife, the sacred Yoruba city, with a plea that masked a darker intent, its whisper a chill in the warm breeze.

Domingos stood in the palace's inner chamber, its coral walls glowing softly in the fading light, his scarlet Kemeje vibrant against his coral beads that clinked with each step, a testament to Itsekiri pride, though his European crown remained in its Iroko-carved box, a nod to his roots after Benin's grandeur, its gold a quiet memory. Anthonio, now eight, played nearby, stacking coral beads into a small tower under Princess Temieno's watchful eye, her dagger glinting at her thigh, his laughter echoing Olori Maria's, a balm to Domingos's heart still tenders from her loss, the sound a ripple of joy in the chamber. Ebi, his advisor with a mind as sharp as the river's edge, sorted reports from the river clans, the parchment rustling with news, while Chief Anomu, fresh from fortifying Ale Eko Iwere, sharpened his spear, its blade catching the light, ever ready for threats that lurked beyond the horizon. Chief Oton, the high priest, prepared offerings for the river spirits—kola nuts and palm oil—grateful for the safe return, the air thick with the scent of ritual and peace. But a messenger's arrival, his wrapper stained with the dust of travel, shattered the calm, his breath heavy as he bowed. "Ogiame," he said, his voice low, "Emagin, your brother, comes from Ile-Ife. He seeks audience, sent by the Ooni with a plea for mercy, his canoe nearing our shores." Domingos's brow furrowed, a shadow crossing his face. Emagin, his illegitimate younger brother, born to a concubine of King Sebastian, had been sent to Ile-Ife years ago to study under the Ooni's priests, a gesture to strengthen Warri's ties with the Yoruba heartland, his name whispered in Warri as a distant figure, neither heir nor outcast, a ghost of family ties. "What plea?" Domingos asked, his voice steady but wary, the weight of kinship heavy in his tone. "An Ife native doctor, Ojo, faces death by hanging," the messenger replied, his eyes downcast. "He was caught in Warri, brewing potions to curse a chief's rival, a brew that killed a child. Emagin begs you spare his life, a mercy from the Ogiame's hand." Temieno's eyes narrowed, her hand brushing her dagger, its hilt warm from her grip. "Ojo's potions killed a child, her laughter silenced," she said, her voice a blade of justice. "The chiefs demand justice, and the church calls it sorcery, a sin against God. Why does the Ooni care for a poisoner, his hands stained with blood?" Ebi, ever cautious, his fingers tracing the map, added, "The Ooni's plea may hide more, Ogiame. Emagin's return after years is no coincidence, a shadow cast by Ile-Ife. They watch our alliance with Benin, their eyes on our river's wealth." Domingos nodded, his Portuguese education sharpening his instincts, memories of Lisbon's courts where nobles masked ambition with diplomacy flooding back. "Let Emagin come," he said, his voice a steady current. "We'll hear him in the courtyard, before the people, the river as our witness. Justice will speak, but so will Warri's heart, its pulse unbroken."

The Arrival of Emagin

At dusk, Emagin's entourage arrived, a procession of Yoruba splendour that cut through the twilight, his canoe carved with Ife's sacred orisha motifs—Drum's axe, Oshun's river—docking amid Warri's drummers, their rhythms blending Itsekiri chants with Yoruba cadences, the sound a bridge of cultures. Emagin, tall and lean, stepped ashore, his wrapper dyed in indigo and adorned with cowrie shells that rattled like ancestral voices, a bronze pendant of Orunmila, the orisha of wisdom, hanging at his chest, its weight a symbol of his Ife training. His eyes, dark and piercing, mirrored Domingos's but held a flicker of something else envy, perhaps, or a deeper intent, a current beneath his calm. Behind him followed Ife priests, their staffs topped with brass that gleamed in the torchlight, and a young woman, Yemi, introduced as his aide, her gaze sharp and elusive, her wrapper hiding secrets in its folds. The palace courtyard, lined with palm mats and lit by oil lamps that cast a warm glow, filled with Itsekiri—chiefs with coral necklaces, fishermen with nets slung over shoulders, and converts from the church clutching wooden crosses—their voices a murmur of anticipation.

Anthonio sat on a small stool beside Domingos, clutching his mother's indigo wrapper strip, its fabric a talisman, while Temieno and Anomu stood vigilant, their presence a wall of strength. Emagin bowed, his gesture graceful but not subservient, a prince's pride in his stance. "Brother, Ogiame," he said, his voice smooth as river water, flowing with intent, "Ife greets Warri, its sacred soil reaching to your shores. The Ooni, guardian of our motherland, sends me to plead for Ojo, a healer misguided but not evil, his hands skilled in herbs. Spare him, and strengthen our Yoruba bond, a thread to bind us." Domingos's gaze held Emagin's, searching for truth beneath the words, the air thick with the scent of palm oil from the nearby feast. "Ojo's potions brought death, Emagin," he replied, his voice firm as the riverbed. "A child lies cold, her mother broken, her cries a wound in our land. Warri's justice is clear hanging for murder, its river unyielding. Why does the Ooni defend him, a poisoner's shadow?" Emagin's smile was measured, a mask over his intent. "Ojo is Ife's son, trained in herbs to heal, not harm, his error a misstep in wisdom. Mercy shows strength, brother. The Ooni offers gold and priests to teach Warri's healers, a gesture of kinship to weave our fates." The crowd murmured, some swayed by the promise of wealth, others wary of Ife's reach, their voices a wave of doubt. Ikenna, ever the sceptics, whispered to a chief, "Ife meddles, and this brother reeks of ambition, his cowries a chain," his words a ripple of dissent.

Temieno, catching the words, signalled Ebi, who slipped into the crowd to listen, his steps silent as a shadow.

Domingos rose, Anthonio in his arms, the boy's weight a reminder of his duty. "Warri honours Ife, our motherland, its soil our root, but justice flows like our river—unbending, its current true. I'll hear Ojo's case tomorrow, before the chiefs and church, the cross and coral as witnesses. Stay, brother, and feast with us, let the river judge our hearts." The feast was a cultural tapestry, the air filled with the scent of smoked fish and yams from Itsekiri women, their coral beads clinking, while Ife priests offered Obe Ata stew, its peppers a nod to Yoruba fire, the spice a dance on the tongue. Drummers from both kingdoms played, their rhythms weaving a fragile unity, the sound a heartbeat of hope. Anthonio, charmed by Yemi's bronze bangles that jingled with her movements, giggled as she danced with him, a child's joy breaking the tension, but Temieno's eyes followed her, sensing a shadow in her grace, her hand resting on her dagger.

The First Plot: Whispers of Poison

That night, in the palace's guest quarters, its walls draped with palm mats, Emagin met Yemi in secret, their voices hushed beneath the hum of cicadas that filled the air with their song. Ebi's spy, a young fisherman named **Oritse** with hands rough from nets, hid in the mangroves, the water lapping at his feet, catching fragments of their talk, the scent of damp earth his cloak. "The Ogiame is strong," Emagin said, his voice a low current, "but his Christian ways weaken Warri, his cross a foreign yoke. Ojo's death would anger Ife, giving the Ooni cause to challenge him, a storm to sweep him away. A potion, subtle, in his palm wine, a sip to end his reign..." Yemi hesitated, her loyalty to Ife warring with her unease, her fingers tracing the bronze bangles. "Poison risks war, Emagin, its shadow a blade on both lands. The Ooni seeks alliance, not blood, his heart set on peace." Emagin's voice hardened, a rock in the stream. "Domingos's crown should be mine, its weight my right. Father sent me to Ife to be forgotten, a shadow cast aside, while he studied in Portugal's halls. If he falls, I rule, and Ife's priests guide Warri, their wisdom our law." Oritse, heart pounding like the drums of war, slipped away, the mangrove branches brushing his face, reporting to Ebi, who woke Domingos, the vial of powder Oritse had seen Yemi hide clutched in his hand. "Your brother plots treachery, Ogiame," Ebi said, his voice a whisper of urgency, the powder's grains glinting in the lamplight. "This is Ojo's craft—odourless, deadly in drink, a serpent's bite." Domingos's face darkened, his Portuguese diplomacy clashing with Itsekiri rage, his heart a battlefield of kinship and duty. "My brother betrays our blood, a wound deeper than the river's cut. But we'll unmask him carefully, a net cast with skill. Temieno, watch Yemi, her bangles a clue. Anomu, guard the palace kitchens, their fires our shield. Ebi, summon Father João. The church will witness justice, its cross a light in this shadow."

The Trial of Ojo

The next morning, the courtyard hosted Ojo's trial, a spectacle of Itsekiri justice, the air thick with the scent of kola nuts and the murmur of the crowd. Ojo, a wiry man with haunted eyes shadowed by guilt, stood bound, his herbs confiscated, their bundles a silent confession. Chiefs, led by Anomu, recounted his crime: a potion meant to curse a rival chief had poisoned a child, her death tearing a village apart, the mother's wails a memory in the air. Father João, citing Christian mercy, urged reform, his cross held high, "Let him repent, his soul saved," while Oton, invoking Umale Okun, demanded death for blood spilled, his staff rattling with cowries. The crowd, torn between faith and tradition, looked to Domingos, their voices a wave of tension. Emagin spoke, his voice honeyed as a river's flow. "Ojo erred, but his heart is Ife's, its wisdom deep. Spare him, Ogiame, and let him serve the church, healing as Sister Clara does, a bridge between our lands." Domingos, knowing Emagin's plot, played his part, his eyes steady. "Mercy is noble, brother, its grace a gift, but justice is Warri's root, its tree unyielding. Ojo will hang, unless proof clears him, the river's truth revealed." As the crowd debated, Temieno signalled Adesuwa, her scout with eyes like the Delta's depths, who had trailed Yemi to the palace kitchens, the scent of yam flour lingering.

Adesuwa found the vial, swapped with harmless yam flour by Ebi's order, a ruse to trap the plotter. During the trial's recess, Domingos drank palm wine publicly, his eyes on Emagin, who paled, expecting collapse, the crowd holding its breath. When Domingos stood firm, the crowd cheered, unaware of the deception, their faith in his strength renewed, the air filled with the sound of ululations.

The Twist: Emagin's Betrayal Unmasked

That evening, Domingos summoned Emagin to the Iroko tree, its gnarled branches a canopy of judgment, the court gathered under its shade, the scent of damp earth rising from the roots. Anomu's warriors surrounded the clearing, their spears glinting like stars, a ring of steel. "Brother," Domingos said, holding the vial, its powder a silent accusation, "you sought my death, a shadow cast on our blood. This poison, Ojo's craft, was meant for me, its taste in my wine. Yemi confessed, fearing Ife's wrath, her heart turned by truth." Emagin's composure cracked, his eyes darting to Yemi, now guarded by Temieno, her bronze bangles still. "Lies, Ogiame! I came for peace, not blood, my hands clean of this!" Yemi, trembling, her wrapper trembling with her breath, spoke, her voice a river breaking its banks. "Emagin ordered the poison, Ogiame, its vial in my care. He sought your throne, believing Ife would crown him, his ambition a storm on our peace." The crowd gasped, Ikenna's whispers silenced by shame, his coral beads a quiet weight. Oton, raising his staff, declared, "The river gods see treachery, its current clear. Oritse-Udeji demands truth, its justice swift." Father João, holding a cross that gleamed in the lamplight, added, "God's justice spares no betrayer, even a brother, its light unyielding."

Domingos's heart ached—Emagin was blood, a tie to their father, Sebastian, whose shadow lingered in the palace—but Warri's safety came first, its river a priority over kin. "Emagin, you are banished, your canoe cast to the sea," he said, his voice a steady drum. "Leave Warri by dawn, never to return, your name a whisper in exile. The Ooni will hear of your shame, and Ojo hangs for his crime, his potion's debt paid." Emagin, stripped of his Orunmila pendant, its bronze clattering to the ground, was escorted to his canoe, his priests silent, their staffs lowered in defeat. Yemi, spared for her confession, her loyalty turned by fear, was sent to serve Sister Clara, her skills turned to healing, the air filled with the scent of reconciliation. The crowd, stunned by the betrayal, rallied behind Domingos, their faith in his justice renewed, their voices rising in a chant of unity.

The Aftermath

The palace mourned the brotherly bond broken, its chambers echoing with the silence of lost kinship, but Warri stood stronger, its roots deep as the Iroko's. Anthonio, unaware of the drama, played with his cross, chanting a hymn Father João taught him, "The Lord is my shepherd," his innocence a light in the shadow. Temieno, her trust in outsiders shaken, doubled her scouts' patrols, their canoes slicing the river with vigilance, the scent of mangrove guiding their path. Anomu fortified the river, wary of Ife's response, his warriors' spears a wall against the horizon. Ebi drafted a letter to the Ooni, explaining Emagin's banishment with respect, preserving the Yoruba bond, the parchment sealed with coral wax. At dusk, Domingos stood by the Iroko tree, its branches swaying in the evening breeze, Anthonio asleep in his arms, the boy's breath a soft rhythm against his chest.

A young scout approached, his wrapper torn from a run through the mangroves, his face flushed with urgency. "Ogiame, a canoe from Ife lingers off Escravos! They carry a banner of the Ooni, but their intent is veiled." Domingos's heart sank, but he masked it with resolve, turning to the council. "Summon the Iyatsere," he said, his voice a steady current. In the war room, Ebi, Chief Oton, and Odion gathered, the map a battlefield of ink, its lines blurred by the scout's damp footsteps. "Ife tests us," Ebi warned, his finger tracing the coast. "The Ooni may retaliate." Chief Oton shook his staff, its cowries rattling like a river's song. "Umale Okun demands we guard our waters, a prayer in the storm." Odion, his coral amulet glinting, said, "Let me lead a patrol, Ogiame. The river taught me its secrets."

Domingos nodded, recalling a parable from his mother, of the Heron and the Reeds: "Heron stands tall among the reeds, its patience turning danger to flight, teaching us to wait with strength." He devised a plan: Odion would lead a patrol to monitor the Ife canoe, supported by forty warriors, while Oton consulted the oracle for guidance, its shells a compass. The patrol set out, their canoes silent as shadows, the water lapping softly, and returned with news of the Ife canoe retreating, its banner lowered, the air filled with the scent of relief. Yet a captured priest whispered of the Ooni's anger, his words a chill: "Ife will not forget Emagin's shame, a storm brews beyond the river." Domingos, holding Anthonio, vowed to fortify Warri's defences, the Warri River, gleaming under moonlight, sang of resilience, its currents carrying tales of treachery tamed and a kingdom unbroken, ready for the shadows to come.

CHAPTER SIXTEEN
Falling in Love

T he Warri River flowed like a lover's sigh under a crescent moon, its waters catching the silver light as they
wove through the mangroves, whispering secrets to the
night, the air thick with the scent of damp earth and the distant call of night birds. Ogiame Dom Domingos stood at the
palace's edge, his scarlet Kemeje loosened, its fabric soft
against his skin, coral beads warm against his chest, their
clink a quiet rhythm, the weight of his European crown set
aside in its Iroko-carved box, a nod to his Itsekiri roots re-
claimed after the turmoil of Emagin's banishment. The exile
of his brother had left a scar, a reminder that even blood
could betray, its wound a silent ache in his heart, yet Warri
stood resilient, its church thriving with Father João's sermons and Sister Clara's healing, its trade routes secure with
Benin's alliance, and its spirit a beacon of hope under the
Iroko tree's watchful boughs. Anthonio, his eight-year-old
son, slept in the palace, his dreams cradling the memory of
Maria, whose indigo wrapper still hung in Domingos's
chamber, its fabric a ghost of love lost, its scent a faint echo
of her presence. But tonight, under the moon's gentle gaze,

Domingos's heart stirred with a new rhythm, one that echoed the river's song—a longing for love, tender and unbidden, sparked by tales of a woman from Ugborodo, an Itsekiri village where the river kissed the sea, its waters a mirror to his soul. Her name was Tuaso, a weaver of nets and dreams, whose beauty was said to rival the dawn, her presence a legend among the fishermen. Whispers of her had reached Warri through their songs, their voices painting her as a daughter of the river, her eyes like polished coral glinting in sunlight, her laughter a melody that tamed the tides, a sound to soothe the storms of his reign. Domingos, hardened by wars with the Awori, betrayal by Emagin, and the loss of Maria, felt his soul soften at these tales, his heart yearning for a companion to share Warri's burdens and joys, a flame to warm the nights left cold by her absence. The church, with its hymns and crosses, had filled his spirit with faith, but the river called for a love rooted in Itsekiri soil, a bond to anchor his future.

The Spark of Ugborodo

The story of Tuaso began with Eloko, a grizzled fisherman from Ugborodo, whose nets had hauled treasures from the river—fish, pearls, and tales—for decades, his hands rough as the mangrove roots. Known for his stories spun under palm wine's warm glow, Eloko was a friend to Ebi, Domingos's advisor, their bond forged in the Eko Travails when Eloko's boat carried wounded warriors' home, its hull scarred by battle. One evening, in Warri's bustling market, its stalls alive with the scent of smoked fish and the clatter of trade, Eloko regaled Ebi with a tale of Tuaso, daughter of a Ugborodo elder, whose skill with nets rivalled her beauty, her fingers weaving magic into every thread. "She weaves as if the river gods guide her hands," Eloko said, his eyes alight with pride, the lantern casting shadows on his weathered face. "Her smile calms storms, and her heart is fierce as Umale Okun's fire, a flame to light Warri's nights. Ogiame should know her, Ebi, for Warri needs a Olori to bind its soul." Ebi, ever the strategist, saw more than romance—a Olori from Ugborodo, a coastal village vital to Warri's trade with its sandy shores and fishing fleets, could bind the kingdom's fringes closer, especially with Portuguese ships like Diogo's lurking like sharks on the horizon. He shared Eloko's tale with Temieno, expecting her scepticism, her warrior's heart wary of softness, but the princess, softened by Anthonio's growth and the Benin alliance, smiled, her dagger resting at her side. "If this Tuaso is as Eloko claims, she might heal brother's heart, a balm for his grief," she said, her voice a gentle current. "But let her prove her worth— Warri's Olori must be iron and silk, strength and grace." Ebi tasked Eloko with a mission: bring Tuaso to Warri, under the guise of a weaving contest to honour the church's hospital tent, where Sister Clara's healing drew crowds, its canvas a haven of hope. Eloko, eager to serve, returned to

Ugborodo, his canoe slicing through the dawn, the water rippling with purpose.

Ugborodo, a village of stilted huts where mangroves met sandy shores, buzzed with life—the scent of drying fish hung in the air, fishermen mending nets with calloused hands, women dyeing cloth with indigo that stained the breeze, children chasing crabs along the tide. Tuaso, twenty-two, stood at her loom, its wooden frame a gift from her mother, her fingers dancing over threads, weaving nets that shimmered like the sea, their patterns a map of her soul. Her wrapper, dyed coral-red, hugged her form, its fabric a celebration of her heritage, and her eyes, deep as the river's heart, held a quiet fire, a spark of destiny. Eloko approached, bowing low, his voice rough with respect. "Tuaso, daughter of Ugborodo, Warri calls. Ogiame seeks weavers for the church's work, a contest to honor its healing. Come, show your skill, and let the river sing your name, its current your guide." Tuaso's smile was wary but warm, her hands pausing on the loom. "The river carries many tales, Eloko, its waters deep with secrets. Why me, a weaver from the coast?" Her father, Elder Omatsola, a stern man with coral armlets that gleamed in the sun, frowned, fearing Warri's politics, his voice a rumble of caution. "Warri's court is a nest of vipers, daughter. Stay, tend your nets." But Tuaso, curious and bold, her spirit a match for the river's flow, agreed, sensing destiny in the invitation, her heart fluttering like egret wings.

She packed her loom, its wood worn smooth by her touch, and boarded Eloko's canoe, the water lapping at its sides, her journey a thread in the tapestry of fate.

The Weaving Contest

Warri's palace courtyard bloomed with colour as the contest began, a festival to celebrate the church's growth and honour Maria's memory, its mud walls adorned with coral patterns, the air filled with the scent of roasted yam and the sound of laughter. Women from across the kingdom gathered, their looms a forest of wood and thread, their wrappers vibrant—indigo, coral, and green—against the earthy tones, their voices a chorus of pride. Drummers played, blending Itsekiri rhythms with Christian hymns, the beat a heartbeat of unity, while Father João blessed the event, his cross raised beside Oton's cowrie staff, the clash of faiths a harmony. Anthonio, perched on a stool carved with river motifs, clapped as dancers swirled, their coral beads clinking like rain, his joy a light in the gathering. Domingos, seated on a throne of Iroko wood, his Kemeje resplendent, watched the weavers, his eyes seeking the woman Eloko had described the anticipation a current in his chest. Tuaso stepped forward, her loom set by the Iroko tree, its shade a quiet embrace, the bark rough against her hands. Her fingers moved with grace, weaving a net of indigo and coral threads, its patterns echoing the river's flow, the threads a dance of skill and soul. The crowd hushed, captivated by her artistry, her beauty a flame that drew every gaze, the air thick with awe. Domingos's breath caught—her eyes, meeting his across the courtyard, held a depth that stirred memories of Maria yet burned with a new light, a promise of renewal. Temieno, at his side, whispered, her voice a gentle prod, "She's more than Eloko promised, brother, a river's daughter. But test her heart, not just her hands—Warri's Olori must weave more than nets." The contest ended with Tuaso's net declared the finest, its weave strong enough for fishermen yet delicate as a Olori's veil, the crowd's cheers a wave of approval. Domingos presented her a coral necklace, his fingers brushing hers, a spark passing between them like lightning on water. "Ugborodo's daughter," he said, his voice low, a river's murmur, "your hands weave Warri's future, its threads strong and true. Stay, and let us know you, your spirit our guide." Tuaso's smile was a dawn breaking, her eyes reflecting the moon. "Ogiame, the river brought me here, its current my path. I'll stay, if Warri wills it, my heart open to its call." The crowd cheered, their voices rising like the tide, but Ikenna, ever the shadow, muttered to a chief, "Another foreign heart, even if Itsekiri, its roots too new. The church blinds him, its cross a chain," his words a ripple of dissent.

A Plot in the Shadows

As Tuaso settled in Warri, housed with Mama Ose's family, her loom a quiet presence in their hut, a plot simmered beneath the surface, a shadow cast by jealousy. Chief Ikenna, his influence waning since Emagin's banishment and the Benin alliance, saw Tuaso's rise as a threat, her beauty and skill a beacon that could sway coastal clans, diminishing his creek-bound power, his coral armlets a fading symbol. He enlisted Uwala, the young warrior pardoned after the Omeyin conspiracy, now bitter and eager for status, his spear idle in his hands. "Tuaso's beauty clouds Ogiame's judgment," Ikenna whispered in a mangrove-shaded hut, the air heavy with the scent of damp wood, "its light a distraction from our ways. A potion, not to kill but to sicken her, will drive her back to Ugborodo, her nets abandoned. The Ogiame will turn to us, not the church or coastal dreams, his heart ours to guide." Uwala, hesitant but loyal, his eyes shadowed by regret, procured a herb from a disgraced healer, Ojo's apprentice, meant to induce fever, its leaves a bitter green. He slipped it into a basket of yams gifted to Tuaso, disguised as a village offering, the basket's weave a mask for treachery. But Adesuwa, Temieno's scout with eyes like the Delta's depths, noticed Uwala's furtive movements in the market, her instincts honed by the Benin visit, the clatter of trade her guide. She trailed him, her wrapper blending with the shadows, finding the healer's hut, its walls stained with failed potions, and alerted Ebi, who tested the yams on a goat, the animal falling ill by nightfall, its bleat a cry of warning. Ebi, enraged, his voice a river's edge, reported to Domingos, who felt a chill—not just at the plot, but at the risk to Tuaso, whose laughter had begun to warm his days, her presence a light in his shadowed heart.

The Bloom of Love

Domingos and Tuaso's bond grew in stolen moments, a love budding like a river lotus. By the river, under moonlight that painted the water silver, they walked, her bare feet brushing the sand, his sandals soft against the earth, her stories of Ugborodo's tides blending with his tales of Lisbon's spires, the air filled with the scent of night blooms. "The sea is vast, its waves a challenge," she said, her voice a melody, "but the river holds my heart, its flow my home." Domingos, his hand grazing hers, the touch a spark, replied, "And you hold mine, Tuaso, your spirit a current in my soul. Warri needs a Olori, its throne steady, but I need you, your love a bridge to my future." Their first kiss, beneath the Iroko tree, its branches a canopy of stars, was a vow unspoken, its roots witnessing a love as deep as the river's flow, the bark rough against their hands. Tuaso joined Sister Clara's hospital tent, her healing skills—learned from Ugborodo's elders with herbs and chants—blending with Christian charity, the canvas a haven of hope. She tended Anthonio's scraped knee, her gentleness winning his heart, his giggle a gift, and taught weavers to craft nets for the church, her loom a bridge between tradition and faith, the threads a tapestry of unity. The people, seeing her devotion, began to call her "Olori

Tuaso," a Olori in spirit before title, their voices a chorus of acceptance.

Yet Ikenna's plot cast a shadow, a cloud over their joy. Ebi, with Adesuwa's aid, confronted Uwala in the market, the young warrior's spear trembling, his confession spilling like a broken dam under Anomu's stern gaze. "Ikenna's orders," Uwala stammered, his voice a whisper of shame, "to sicken Tuaso, not kill, her fever a return to Ugborodo, her absence our gain." Domingos, his heart torn between love and justice, summoned Ikenna to the palace, the chief's coral armlets dull with defeat. The chief, cornered, denied all, his eyes darting like a trapped fish, but the evidence—yam basket stained with herb, healer's testimony of the apprentice's craft, and Uwala's confession—was damning, a net cast tight.

The Twist: A Test of Mercy

In the courtyard, under the Iroko's shade, its leaves rustling with the night breeze, Domingos held court, Tuaso at his side, her coral necklace gleaming like a river's heart. Anthonio sat with Temieno, his eyes wide with wonder, his tiny hand clutching her dagger's hilt. "Ikenna," Domingos said, his voice a river's calm before a storm, its depth unwavering, "you sought to harm Tuaso, to break Warri's heart with your shadow. Speak your truth, let the river hear." Ikenna, his coral armlets dull with shame, knelt, his voice a plea.

"Ogiame, I feared the church, its cross a foreign star, the coast, its tides too strong, would eclipse our ways, our roots forgotten. I was wrong, my heart misled. Spare me, for Warri's sake, its people my home." Tuaso, her voice soft as dawn breaking over the river, spoke, her words a thread of compassion. "Ogiame, mercy heals where justice cuts, its balm a gift. Let Ikenna serve the church, not the gallows, his hands turned to good." Her words, echoing Maria's compassion, swayed Domingos, his heart a bridge between love and duty. He banished Ikenna to labour in the hospital tent, his status stripped, a warning to dissenters, the chief's coral a faded echo. Uwala was sent to fish in Ugborodo, under Elder Omatsola's stern watch, his spear a tool of redemption.

The River's Embrace

That night, Domingos proposed to Tuaso by the river, its waters reflecting the crescent moon, a coral ring in his hand, crafted by Mama Ose with threads of love, its surface smooth as her nets. "Be my Olori, Tuaso," he said, his voice a poem, "let our love weave Warri's future, its threads strong and true, as your nets weave the sea, a bond to last. Let me share your laughter, your strength, my heart yours." Tuaso, tears like river pearls glistening in the moonlight, accepted, her kiss a tide that swept away his grief, her lips a promise against his, the water lapping at their feet. The palace prepared for a wedding, drummers blending hymns with Itsekiri songs, the beat a heartbeat of joy, weavers crafting a veil from Tuaso's nets, its indigo a tribute to her roots. Anthonio, calling her "Mama," wove a tiny net with Mama Ose's guidance, a child's gift of love, his fingers clumsy but earnest. Temieno, smiling, her wound from past battles a memory, planned the feast, her voice a command of celebration, while Anomu fortified the river, wary of Diogo's ships, their sails a shadow on the horizon.

The church, with Father João's blessing, would host the vows, a union of cross and coral, its bells ringing with hope. A young scout approached, his wrapper torn from a patrol, his voice breathless. "Ogiame, a Portuguese ship, Diogo's banner, was seen off Escravos! They parley with Ijaw, their intent unclear." Domingos's heart sank, but he masked it with resolve, turning to the council. "Summon the Iyatsere," he said, his voice a steady drum. In the war room, Ebi, Chief Oton, and Adesuwa gathered, the map a battlefield of ink, its lines blurred by the scout's haste. "Diogo stirs the Ijaw," Ebi warned, his finger tracing the coast. "A storm brews." Chief Oton shook his staff, its cowries a river's song. "Oritse Udeji demands we guard our waters, a prayer against the sea." Adesuwa, her eyes fierce, said, "Let me lead a scout, Ogiame. The river knows my path."

Domingos nodded, recalling a parable from his mother, of the Egret and the Horizon: "Egret flies far to seek its mate, its patience turning distance to love, teaching us to wait with hope." He devised a plan: Adesuwa would lead a scout party to monitor Diogo's ship, supported by fifty warriors, while Oton consulted the oracle, its shells a guide. The party set out, their canoes silent as night, the water a mirror to the stars, and returned with news of the Portuguese retreating, their crew shaken by Adesuwa's arrows, the air filled with the scent of victory. Yet a captured sailor whispered of Diogo's vow, his words a chill: "We'll return with cannon, a war on your river." Domingos, holding Tuaso's hand, vowed to fortify the coast, the Warri River, gleaming under moonlight, sang of resilience, its currents carrying tales of love reborn and a kingdom unbroken, ready for the storms to come.

CHAPTER SEVENTEEN

The Oracle's Whisper

The Warri River flowed with a restless murmur under a sky bruised with storm clouds, as if the gods themselves sensed the unease settling over the kingdom, the air heavy with the scent of rain and the distant rumble of thunder. Ogiame Dom Domingos stood at the palace's edge, his scarlet Kemeje vibrant against the gathering dusk, its fabric a flag of resilience, coral beads heavy with the weight of his reign, their clink a soft prayer against his chest. Beside him, Tuaso, his betrothed, her coral-red wrapper glowing like embers in the fading light, wove a net with deft fingers, the threads a quiet anchor to his heart, her presence a balm against the storm. Anthonio, now nine, played nearby, his laughter mingling with the river's song, a strip of Maria's indigo cloth tied around his wrist, its fabric a talisman of memory, his small hands shaping mud into castles. The alliance with Benin, forged under Oba Ohuan's brass plaques, held firm, its echo a steady pulse in Warri's trade, and the church's cross cast a steady light over the kingdom's growing faith, its bells ringing with hope. Yet a shadow loomed, not from Portuguese ships or Ijaw raiders with their swift canoes, but from within—a whisper of unrest among the river clans, stirred by dreams of famine and whispers of a curse, the air thick with the scent of fear. The peace that followed Emagin's banishment and Tuaso's arrival was fragile, like a canoe caught in a sudden current, its hull trembling with uncertainty.

Reports from the creeks spoke of failing crops in Ode-Itsekiri, their fields a patchwork of withered stalks, fish vanishing from nets that hung empty in the dawn, and children falling ill with fevers no herbs could break, their cries a haunting melody. The chiefs, led by a humbled Ikenna now labouring in the church's hospital tent, his coral armlets dulled by humility, blamed the gods' anger, pointing to Domingos's Christian leanings—his cross a foreign star—and his love for Tuaso, an Ugborodo woman with coastal blood, as a slight to tradition, their voices a chorus of discontent. Even the church's converts, loyal to Father João and Sister Clara, murmured of divine displeasure, their faith shaken by empty baskets and silent prayers, the scent of incense unable to mask their doubt. Ebi, the ever-watchful advisor, brought the news to Domingos, his voice low as the river's flow, the parchment in his hands creased with urgency. "Ogiame, the people fear a curse, its shadow deep. They demand answers, not from the cross, but from the oracle, its wisdom older than our walls." Domingos's heart tightened, a knot of duty and doubt. His years in Portugal had taught him the power of reason, its logic a shield, but Warri's soul was tied to the river gods—Umale Okun, the river spirits, the ancestors whose voices lingered in the breeze. Tuaso, her eyes like coral under moonlight, touched his arm, her fingers warm against his skin. "The river speaks, my love, its current a guide," she said, her voice a gentle tide. "Seek the oracle, not to appease Ikenna, but to hear its truth, its heart our own. Our wedding waits, its joy a promise, but Warri's heart cannot endure this silence." Temieno, her dagger gleaming at her thigh, nodded, her warrior's stance unyielding. "The people trust you, brother, their faith a river's strength, but they trust the gods more, their roots deep. Consult the oracle, its voice a light, but guard your back—Ikenna may see this as a chance to stir trouble, his hands still restless." Domingos agreed, his mind turning to Ile-Ife, the Yoruba heartland where his brother Emagin had trained, its oracles revered across the region, their wisdom older than Warri's Iroko tree. "Send for an oracle man from Ife," he told Ebi, his voice a steady drum. "Let him be old, untouched by Emagin's schemes, his hands clean of treachery. We'll hear the gods' will under the Iroko, before all Warri, the river as our witness."

The Oracle's Arrival

Days later, a canoe from Ile-Ife docked at the river's edge, its prow carved with Orunmila's sacred symbols—axe and river—its wood weathered by the journey, the air filled with the scent of sacred oil. The oracle man, Obawole, was ancient, his frame stooped but his eyes sharp as a hawk's, piercing the dusk, his wrapper dyed deep indigo and adorned with cowrie shells that rattled like ancestral voices. His staff, topped with a brass orisha that gleamed in the torchlight, clinked as he stepped ashore, escorted by two Ife priests, their faces solemn, their robes a contrast to Warri's coral hues. Obawole, a priest of Ifa, was renowned for divining truth through palm nuts, his visions guiding kings from Ife to Oyo, his presence a bridge between past and present. Ebi greeted him with kola nuts, a gesture of respect, the bitter taste a ritual bond, but Temieno's scouts, led by Adesuwa, her wrapper blending with the shadows, watched the priests, wary of Ife's ties to Emagin, the banished brother's shadow a lingering chill. The palace courtyard, lit by oil lamps that cast a warm glow, buzzed with anticipation, its palm mats a sea of colour. Chiefs with coral necklaces, fishermen with nets slung over shoulders, and converts clutching wooden crosses gathered, their wrappers a tapestry of indigo and coral, their voices a murmur of hope and fear. Anthonio sat on Tuaso's lap, his cross-necklace glinting beside his mother's cloth, his small hand tracing its pattern. Father João and Sister Clara stood at the church's edge, their presence a quiet bridge between faiths, the scent of herbs from the hospital tent mingling with the air. Oton, Warri's high priest, sprinkled river water, honouring Umale Okun the god of the sea and river, his staff a beacon, while Ikenna, his labour in the hospital tent humbling his pride, watched silently, his eyes flickering with hope of discord, his coral beads a faded crown.

Obawole sat beneath the Iroko tree, its roots sprawling like veins of the earth, the bark rough against his mat. He spread a woven mat, its threads worn by time, scattering sixteen palm nuts, their fall a rhythm of destiny, his chants low and rhythmic, invoking Ifa's wisdom, the sound a prayer carried on the wind. The crowd hushed, the air thick with incense and expectation, the scent of kola nuts rising from Oton's offering. Domingos, his Kemeje regal, stood before the oracle, his coral beads a prayer against his chest, the weight a reminder of his duty. "Obawole, voice of Ifa, keeper of truth," he said, his voice steady as the river's flow, "Warri's crops fail, their stalks withered, our nets empty, our children sicken with fevers no herbs can break, their cries a wound. Is this a curse, its shadow deep? Speak, and let the river hear, its current our guide." Obawole's hands moved, the nuts falling in patterns only he could read, their clatter a language of the gods. His voice, weathered as driftwood, rose, a tide of revelation. "The river weeps, Ogiame, its tears a flood. A shadow clings to Warri, born of blood spilled and trust broken, its roots in the past. The gods see your heart, torn between cross and coral, its halves at war, but they demand balance, a harmony of faiths. A sacrifice—kola, ram, and river water—must cleanse the land, its waters purified. Yet beware: a hand within seeks to deepen the shadow, its fingers stained with greed. Seek him where the creeks hide their secrets, their waters dark." The crowd gasped, whispers rippling like waves, the air charged with tension. Ikenna shifted, his face taut with unease, while Temieno's hand rested on her dagger, its hilt a promise of protection. Domingos's gaze met Obawole's, searching for clarity, his voice a quiet plea. "Whose hand, oracle? Name the shadow, its face revealed." Obawole cast the nuts again, his eyes narrowing, the patterns a map of fate. "The shadow wears a chief's beads, its gleam a lie, but his heart is a coiled snake, its venom hidden. Seek him in the creeks, where secrets fester, their silence a shroud."

A Plot in the Creeks

The oracle's words ignited a storm, its thunder a call to action. Ikenna, sensing suspicion, protested, his voice rising above the crowd, "I serve the church, Ogiame! My hands are clean, my labour a penance!" But Temieno, her instincts sharp as a river's edge, dispatched Adesuwa to the creeks, where Ojo's apprentice, a healer named Eghosa, had fled after the trial, his shadow a lingering threat. Eghosa, bitter at Ojo's hanging, his hands stained with failed potions, had allies among the river clans, where traditionalists resented the church's rise, their voices a chorus of dissent. Adesuwa, disguised as a fish trader, her wrapper dyed with indigo to blend with the shadows, overheard Eghosa in a mangrove hut, its walls damp with the river's breath, plotting with a minor chief, Obaro, a man with coral armlets dulled by greed. "Ikenna will lead us when the Ogiame falters," Eghosa hissed, his voice a serpent's whisper, "his hand guiding our poison. We'll taint Warri's wells, blaming the church for the curse, its cross a scapegoat." Adesuwa, her heart pounding, slipped away, the mangrove branches brushing her face, reporting to Ebi, who rallied Anomu's warriors, their spears gleaming in the torchlight. Under cover of night, the air thick with the scent of mud and secrecy, they raided the hut, the sound of their footsteps a drumbeat of justice, capturing Eghosa and Obaro, their vials of poison—derived from mangrove roots, their green a mockery of life—seized, the glass clinking in the dark. Ikenna, summoned to the palace, denied involvement, his voice a trembling reed, but Eghosa, under Anomu's stern glare, his scar a map of battles, confessed, his words a flood. "Ikenna sent word to deepen the famine, its shadow his gain, to turn the people against the church, its bells silenced."

The Trial and Sacrifice

The next dawn, the courtyard hosted a trial, the Iroko tree a silent judge, its leaves rustling with the morning breeze, the air filled with the scent of kola nuts and the murmur of the crowd. Ikenna, bound, faced Domingos, his defiance crumbling like dry earth, his coral beads a faded crown. "Ogiame, I sought to save our ways, their roots deep," he pleaded, his voice a broken wave, "not destroy Warri, its heart my home.

The church blinds us, its light too bright, and Tuaso's coastal blood dilutes our river, its current lost." Tuaso, her eyes fierce as the river's fire, stepped forward, her coral-red wrapper a flag of pride. "My blood is Itsekiri, Ikenna, its pulse strong," she said, her voice a steady tide. "The river flows through me, as it does Ogiame, its spirit unbroken. Your poison harms us all, its venom a wound." Domingos, his heart heavy with the weight of judgment, spoke, his voice a river's calm. "Ikenna, you've betrayed Warri thrice—Omeyin's shadow, Tuaso's harm, now this curse. Death is just, its blade sharp, but mercy is our strength, its root deeper. You're banished to the farthest creeks, your title stripped, your beads a memory. Eghosa and Obaro hang for their poison, its debt paid." The crowd, torn between anger and relief, cheered as Ikenna was led away, his coral beads confiscated, the sound of their footsteps a fading echo. Oton led the sacrifice Obawole prescribed—a ram, its bleat a final cry, kola nuts bitter with promise, and river water drawn from the shrine's depths—offered at the sacred site, with Father João's prayers blending Christian and Itsekiri rites, the water a shimmer of unity. The clouds parted, a soft rain falling, its drops a blessing, seen as a sign of the gods' approval, the air fresh with renewal.

The Twist: A Hidden Ally

As the kingdom cleansed itself, a twist emerged, a current beneath the calm. Obawole, in a private audience with

Domingos in the inner chamber, its coral walls a cocoon of trust, revealed a secret, his voice a whisper of wisdom. "Ogiame, I knew Emagin in Ife, his shadow long," he said, his eyes gleaming with memory, "his banishment left a wound, its scar deep, but he sent me, not to betray, but to warn, a thread of redemption. The Ooni feared his shadow lingered in Warri, stirring men like Ikenna, its poison his legacy. I came to unmask it, my staff a guide." Domingos, stunned, gripped Obawole's hand, the old man's skin rough as the river's edge. "You risked Ife's wrath to save us, its gods your judge," he said, his voice thick with gratitude. "Why, oracle, your heart so bold?" Obawole's eyes gleamed, a light in the dusk. "Warri is Ife's child, as Benin is, its river a shared vein. Your love for Tuaso, your son Anthonio, your rule over this land—it's the gods' will, their breath in your reign. Balance the cross and coral, their harmony your strength, and Warri endures, its roots unyielding." The oracle's words healed a rift Domingos hadn't seen, a bridge between past and present, his heart a tapestry of faith and tradition. He gifted Obawole a coral staff, its beads a river's song, sending him back to Ife with gold and a letter to the Ooni, affirming kinship, the parchment sealed with wax and hope. Tuaso, at his side, wove a net for Anthonio, her love a beacon, the threads a promise of family.

The River's Renewal

Weeks later, the crops in Ode-Itsekiri sprouted, their green a hymn of life, fish filled the nets with silver abundance, and fevers eased, the hospital tent bustling under Sister Clara and Tuaso's care, the scent of herbs a healing breeze. The church, its cross joined by Oton's shrine with its cowrie-laden altar, thrived, converts chanting hymns with river songs, the air filled with the sound of unity. Anthonio, wearing a tiny Kemeje crafted by Tuaso, ran to Domingos, who lifted him, his heart full, the boy's laughter a melody of joy. The wedding loomed, its preparations a celebration of love and unity, drummers blending hymns with Itsekiri songs, their beat a heartbeat, weavers crafting a veil from Tuaso's nets, its indigo a tribute to her roots, the fabric soft against the light.

But a shadow lingered on the horizon. A young scout approached, his wrapper torn from a patrol through the mangroves, his face flushed with urgency, the scent of salt on his skin. "Ogiame, a Portuguese ship, Diogo's banner bold, was seen off Escravos!" he gasped. "They parley with Ijaw, their muskets gleaming, their intent a storm!" Domingos's heart sank, but he masked it with resolve, turning to the council. "Summon the Iyatsere," he said, his voice a steady drum, the room tense with purpose. In the war room, its walls lined with maps, Ebi, Chief Oton, and Odion gathered, the map a battlefield of ink, its lines blurred by the scout's damp footsteps. "Diogo stirs the Ijaw," Ebi warned, his finger tracing the coast, "their alliance a blade on our peace." Chief Oton shook his staff, its cowries a river's song. "Umale Okun demands we guard our waters, a prayer against the sea's wrath." Odion, his coral amulet glinting, said, "Let me lead a patrol, Ogiame. The river taught me its secrets, its currents my guide."

Domingos nodded, recalling a parable from his father, of the Crocodile and the Flood: "Crocodile waits as the flood rises, its patience turning danger to strength, teaching us to endure with wisdom." He devised a plan: Odion would lead a patrol to monitor Diogo's ship, supported by sixty warriors, their canoes armed with blunderbusses, while Oton consulted the oracle again, its shells a compass in the storm. The patrol set out, their canoes silent as shadows, the water a mirror to the stars, the night air thick with tension. They returned at dawn, the sky painted with gold, with news of the Portuguese retreating, their crew shaken by Odion's musket fire, the air filled with the scent of gunpowder and victory. Yet a captured sailor, his face pale with fear, whispered a chilling vow, his words a shiver: "Diogo plans a fleet, its cannons a war on your river, its tide unstoppable." Domingos, holding Tuaso's hand, her fingers warm against his, vowed to fortify the coast, the Warri River, gleaming under the morning sun, sang of resilience, its currents carrying tales of curses lifted and a kingdom unbroken, ready for the storms to come, its king guided by love, faith, and the oracle's truth.

CHAPTER EIGHTEEN

The Rightful Heir

The Warri River flowed with a restless undercurrent, its waters catching the flicker of a waning moon as storm clouds gathered on the horizon, mirroring the tension that gripped the kingdom, the air thick with the scent of rain and the distant cry of night herons. It was 1637, and Ogiame Dom Domingos, now in his late forties, stood at the palace's edge, his scarlet Kemeje weathered but proud, its fabric a testament to battles fought and won, coral beads heavy with the weight of a reign marked by wars with the Awori, faith in the church's rise, and love for Tuaso. Beside him, Olori Tuaso, his betrothed, her coral-red wrapper a beacon of grace against the dusk, wove a net for the church's hospital tent, her fingers steady despite the whispers of unrest, the threads a quiet rhythm of hope. Anthonio Domingos, their sixteen-year-old son, stood tall nearby, his features a striking blend of Olori Maria's sea-blue eyes—deep as the river's heart—and Domingos's bronze skin, his Kemeje adorned with a cross that gleamed in the lamplight and coral beads that clinked with each step, a symbol of Warri's dual soul, its heritage a tapestry of tradition and faith. The kingdom, strengthened by the Benin alliance forged under Oba Ohuan's brass plaques, its trade routes pulsing with life, and the church's growth under Father João and Sister Clara, thrived, its spirit a river unbowed. Yet a shadow loomed within—a question of succession that threatened to fracture the unity Domingos had fought to forge, its roots deep in the soil of tradition.

Anthonio, trained in Warri's ways under Chief Anomu's stern hand and the church's teachings with Father João's guidance, was the heir apparent, his intelligence evident in his mastery of the river's currents, his courage shining in his skill with a spear that pierced the air with precision. Yet his mixed heritage, a first in Warri's history—born of Maria's Portuguese blood and Domingos's Itsekiri lineage—stirred unease among the traditionalists, their voices a murmur of doubt. The chiefs, led by Iyatsere, the voice of the council, his broad shoulders a pillar of strength, and Olekun, the keeper of ancestral rites, his wrapper adorned with bronze pendants that gleamed like the river at dawn, feared a half-Portuguese Ogiame would erode Itsekiri identity, tilting the kingdom toward European shores, its river a bridge to foreign rule. Their concern, born of loyalty rather than malice, had simmered since Anthonio's birth, a quiet undercurrent, but now, with Domingos's health strained by years of battle and grief—his breath shorter, his frame less steady—it erupted into a confrontation that would test Warri's heart, its pulse a drumbeat of uncertainty.

The Chiefs' Petition

The palace courtyard, lit by oil lamps that cast a warm glow, buzzed with anticipation as the chiefs gathered beneath the Iroko tree, its roots sprawling like the kingdom's lineage, the bark rough with history, the air thick with incense and the scent of smoked fish, a feast prepared to honour the harvest but now overshadowed by the council's purpose. Domingos sat on a carved throne of Iroko wood, its surface worn smooth by time, Tuaso at his side, her coral necklace glinting like a river's heart. Anthonio, summoned from his training with Chief Anomu, his spear still in hand, stood beside Temieno, now a seasoned advisor with wisdom in her eyes, her dagger ever-present at her thigh, its hilt a promise of protection. Ebi, his hair greying with the years, watched the crowd, his map of the Delta creased with thought, while Chief Oton, the high priest, clutched his cowrie staff, its rattle a prayer, sensing the gods' unease, the scent of palm oil from his offering rising in the air. Iyatsere, a broad-shouldered man with coral armlets that gleamed faintly, stepped forward, his voice steady but heavy with the weight of tradition. "Ogiame, Warri's river flows strong under your hand, its current a testament to your reign, but the future stirs our hearts, its path unclear. Anthonio, your son, is brave, wise, his spear true, but his blood—half white, half Itsekiri—has no precedent in our history, its mix a shadow on our lineage. The ancestors chose Ogiame of pure river blood, their voices in the wind. We seek clarity: who is the rightful heir, his claim unbroken?" Olekun, his wrapper adorned with bronze pendants that clinked softly, nodded, his voice a rumble of ritual. "The gods speak through lineage, Ogiame, their will in our roots. Anthonio's cross is noble, a light of faith, but Warri's throne is Oritse-Udeji's, its spirit pure. We fear the river's soul weakens if a mixed-blood Ogiame sits, its current turned to foreign shores." The crowd murmured, some nodding in agreement, their coral beads a quiet echo, others glancing at Anthonio, whose jaw tightened but whose eyes held steady, a river's resolve in his gaze. Tuaso's hand gripped Domingos's, her breath catching, a silent plea, while Temieno's hand rested on her dagger, her gaze piercing Iyatsere, her voice a whisper of warning. Domingos rose, his Kemeje a flame in the lamplight, its scarlet a banner of strength, his voice calm but edged with steel, a river's edge. "Iyatsere, Olekun, you speak for Warri's heart, its pulse deep, and I honour your truth, its roots in our past. Anthonio is my son, born of Maria, blessed by Oritse-Udeji and the cross, his spirit Warri's own. But the throne is not mine to claim—it is the ancestors', their voices our guide. I will consult them, and the river will speak, its current our judge." The chiefs bowed, their faces unreadable, their coral armlets a silent weight, but the tension lingered, a storm waiting to break, its thunder a heartbeat away. Ebi whispered to

Domingos, his voice low as the night tide, "They mean no treason, Ogiame, their hearts loyal, but their words stir others, a ripple in the creeks. Ikenna's old allies may see this as a spark, their hands restless." Anthonio, overhearing, met his father's gaze, his voice a steady current. "Father, I am Itsekiri, whatever my blood, its river in my veins. Let me prove it, my spear my oath." Domingos's heart ached—Anthonio's courage echoed Maria's, her blue eyes a memory in his son's face, but the chiefs' fears were rooted in tradition, not malice, a current he could not ignore. "You will, my son," he said, his hand on Anthonio's shoulder, "its test your strength. But first, the ancestors will guide us, their wisdom our light."

The Oracle's Call

Domingos summoned Obawole, the ancient Ife oracle who had unmasked Emagin's treachery years ago, now revered in Warri for his wisdom, his presence a bridge to the past. Obawole, his indigo wrapper frayed by time, its edges worn like the river's banks, his brass-topped staff trembling in his hands, arrived by canoe, the water lapping at its sides, his eyes still sharp as a falcon's, piercing the dawn. The palace shrine, nestled by the river, its mud walls adorned with faded paintings of Ginuwa, was prepared for the ritual, its altar adorned with kola nuts bitter with promise, palm wine fragrant with harvest, and a ram's blood dark with sacrifice, offerings to Umale Okun and the ancestors, the air thick with the scent of ritual. The crowd gathered, their wrappers muted in respect—indigo, coral, and green—a tapestry of unity, as Oton chanted, blending Itsekiri rites with Obawole's Ifa chants, the sound a prayer carried on the wind. Father João, present at Domingos's insistence, sprinkled holy water, his cross a quiet bridge to the church, its droplets a shimmer of faith, while Sister Clara tended the sick nearby, her herbs a scent of hope. Obawole cast his sixteen palm nuts on a woven mat, its threads worn by generations, his voice a low hum, invoking Orunmila, the orisha of wisdom, the nuts' fall a rhythm of destiny. The nuts fell, their patterns a cryptic map, the air hushed with anticipation. "Ogiame," he said, his eyes piercing through the dusk, "the ancestors see your son, Anthonio, born of river and sea, its currents a new song. His blood is new, its mix uncharted, but his heart is Warri's, its pulse strong. The river accepts him, its spirit in his veins, but a shadow doubt—chiefs whisper, and a hand plots to sway the throne, its greed a stain." Domingos's pulse quickened, a river's rush in his chest. "Name the shadow, Obawole, its face revealed," he said, his voice a plea. The oracle cast again, his hands trembling with age, the patterns a map of fate. "The hand is not Iyatsere or Olekun, their hearts true, but one who hides in their wake, a shadow cast by ambition. A chief's kin, in the creeks, seeks to crown another, his blood pure but his soul dark. Seek them where the mangroves twist, their secrets a shroud." Temieno's eyes flashed, her mind on Ikenna's old allies, their whispers a memory, while Anomu, gripping his spear, growled, "The creeks again, their waters a nest of vipers. We'll root them out, their roots torn." Tuaso, her voice soft but firm, added, "Ogiame, trust the oracle, its wisdom deep. Anthonio is our future, his light our guide, but we must unmask this plot, its shadow lifted."

A Plot in the Mangroves

Temieno, with Adesuwa's scouts, ventured into the creeks, their canoes gliding through mangrove shadows, the water dark and still, the air thick with the scent of mud and salt. Ebi's spies, their eyes sharp as the river's edge, had traced whispers to a minor chief, Oyen, a cousin of Ikenna's, his hut a maze of intrigue, who harboured dreams of placing his son, a pure Itsekiri youth named Bawo, on the throne, his ambition a current beneath the calm. Oyen, resentful of Anthonio's mixed blood, its blue eyes a foreign mark, had rallied creek traditionalists, promising to restore Warri's "true" lineage, their voices a chorus of dissent. His plan was subtle—not poison to kill, but a campaign of fear, spreading tales of omens: a fish with two heads caught in a net, a river turning red at dawn, signs the gods rejected Anthonio, their wrath a shadow on the land. Adesuwa, disguised as a fish trader, her wrapper dyed with indigo to blend with the dusk, infiltrated Oyen's village, its stilted huts a silhouette against the sky, overhearing him bribe a fisherman to plant a carved idol, painted with blood from a sacrificed goat, in Warri's market to fuel panic, its wood a lie carved deep. She signalled

Anomu, who led a night raid, the sound of their footsteps a drumbeat of justice, the torches casting shadows on the mangroves, capturing Oyen and his conspirators, their idol seized before it could spread fear, its blood a stain on the ground. The fisherman, trembling, his net abandoned, confessed, his voice a whisper of shame, "Oyen said Anthonio's blood would curse Warri, its river turned to ash. He planned a council to sway Iyatsere, their voices his tool." Adesuwa, her heart pounding, returned with the proof, the air thick with the scent of victory.

The Confrontation

The palace courtyard, now a crucible of suspense, hosted a trial under the Iroko tree, its leaves rustling with the morning breeze, the air filled with the scent of kola nuts and the murmur of the crowd, their wrappers a sea of colour. Oyen, bound, faced Domingos, his defiance fading under the crowd's gaze, his coral beads stripped, a faded crown. Iyatsere and Olekun, summoned, stood shocked, their petition for clarity twisted by Oyen's ambition, their faces a map of regret. Anthonio, his Kemeje proud, its cross glinting in the sun, stood beside Tuaso, her coral necklace a beacon, his blue eyes steady, a silent claim to his birthright. "Oyen," Domingos said, his voice a river's roar, its depth unwavering, "you sought to tear Warri's heart, using the chiefs' honest fears as a shield, your ambition a shadow on our unity. The oracle named you, its voice clear, and the river condemns you, its current true. Speak, let your truth be heard." Oyen, his coral armlets gone, knelt, his voice a broken wave. "Ogiame, I feared for our ways, their roots deep, their spirit pure. Anthonio's blood is foreign, its blue a mark of the sea, not the river. Bawo is pure, born of the creeks, his lineage unbroken." Anthonio stepped forward, his voice steady as the Iroko's roots, his spear a symbol of strength. "My blood is Warri's, Oyen, its river in my veins. My mother gave her life for me, her love my anchor, my father fought for this throne, his spear my guide. I serve Oritse-Udeji, its iron strong, the river, its flow my home, and the cross, its light my faith. Test me, and I'll prove it, my heart your proof." The crowd roared, their loyalty shifting like the tide, their coral beads a chorus of approval. Iyatsere, his face softening, his coral armlets a quiet weight, spoke, his voice a bridge. "Ogiame, we sought truth, its light our goal, not treachery, its shadow dark. Anthonio's heart is ours, his spirit the river's own. We stand with him, our voices one." Olekun nodded, his bronze pendants clinking, his voice a rumble of reconciliation. "The ancestors spoke through Obawole, their wisdom deep. We were wrong to doubt, our fears a mist. Anthonio is Warri's son." Domingos, his heart swelling with pride, raised a hand, his Kemeje a flame in the dawn. "Oyen, your plot ends here, its roots torn. You're confined to your village, your exile a lesson, your son Bawo spared but watched, his future a thread to mend. Warri's throne is Anthonio's, by the ancestors' will, its current his claim."

The Twist: Anthonio's Trial

To seal the succession, Domingos devised a test, a twist to silence doubters and unite the kingdom, its roots deep in ritual. He announced a ritual challenge for Anthonio, open to all Warri's youth, to prove the heir's worth, its waters a mirror of fate. In the river, under Oton's and Obawole's gaze, Anthonio would navigate a canoe through treacherous currents, their roar a challenge, retrieve a sacred coral from the riverbed, its depths a test, and offer it at the shrine, its altar a judgment. Bawo, Oyen's son, joined, his eyes burning with rivalry, his Kemeje a rival flame, his pure blood a banner. The river roared, its rapids fierce, the water churning with power, but Anthonio, trained by Anomu, paddled with skill, his cross and coral beads gleaming in the sunlight, his blue eyes a beacon of resolve. Bawo, strong but reckless, his canoe a mirror of his ambition, faltered, the current tipping his craft, its wood a cry in the waves. Anthonio, risking his own challenge, his heart a river's pulse, pulled Bawo to safety, his hands steady, earning gasps from the crowd, the air filled with the scent of wet wood and triumph. At the shrine, Anthonio offered the coral, its surface smooth as a promise, his prayer blending Umale Okun's strength with Christian grace, his voice a hymn of unity. Obawole, casting nuts, declared, his voice a tide of truth, "The river chooses Anthonio, its current clear. His blood is Warri's, its mix a strength, his heart the throne's, its pulse unbroken." The crowd erupted, their cheers a wave, Iyatsere and Olekun kneeling to Anthonio, their doubts erased, their coral armlets a salute. Tuaso, tears in her eyes like river pearls, embraced her stepson, whispering, "You are Maria's pride, her spirit in you," her voice a mother's love. Temieno, grinning, clapped his shoulder, her dagger a silent vow, while Anomu nodded, his spear raised in salute, his scar a map of battles shared.

The Kingdom's Resolve

That night, Warri feasted, drums blending hymns with Itsekiri chants, their beat a heartbeat of joy, palm wine flowing under the Iroko's shade, its roots a witness, the air filled with the scent of roasted yam and unity. Domingos, Tuaso at his side, her coral necklace a river's gleam, addressed the people, his voice a steady current. "Anthonio is Warri's heir, chosen by the river, its flow his guide, the gods, their will our strength, and the cross, its light our faith. Let no shadow doubt him, its darkness lifted." The crowd cheered, their coral beads a chorus, but a shadow lingered on the horizon, its breath a chill. A young scout approached, his wrapper torn from a patrol through the mangroves, his face flushed with urgency, the scent of salt on his skin. "Ogiame, a Portuguese ship, Diogo's banner bold, was seen off Escravos!" he gasped, his voice a wave of warning. "They parley with Ijaw, their muskets gleaming, their intent a storm on our peace!" Domingos's heart sank, but he masked it with resolve, turning to the council, the war room's walls a map of fate. "Summon the Iyatsere," he said, his voice a steady drum, the tension thick.

In the war room, its walls lined with maps stained by time, Ebi, Chief Oton, and Odion gathered, the map a battlefield of ink, its lines blurred by the scout's damp footsteps. "Diogo stirs the Ijaw," Ebi warned, his finger tracing the coast, "their alliance a blade on our river, its edge sharp." Chief Oton shook his staff, its cowries a river's song, its rattle a prayer. "Oritse Udeji demands we guard our waters, its spirit our shield, a prayer against the sea's wrath." Odion, his coral amulet glinting, said, "Let me lead a patrol, Ogiame. The river taught me its secrets, its currents my path." Domingos nodded, recalling a parable from his mother, of the Tortoise and the Storm: "Tortoise hides as the storm rages, its patience turning danger to safety, teaching us to endure with wisdom." He devised a plan: Odion would lead a patrol to monitor Diogo's ship, supported by seventy warriors, their canoes armed with blunderbusses and nets, while Oton consulted the oracle, its shells a guide in the tempest. The patrol set out, their canoes silent as shadows, the water a mirror to the waning moon, the night air thick with the scent of mangrove and resolve. They returned at dawn, the sky painted with gold, with news of the Portuguese retreating, their crew shaken by Odion's musket fire, the air filled with the scent of gunpowder and triumph, the water rippling with victory.

Yet a captured sailor, his face pale with fear, his hands bound with rope, whispered a chilling vow, his words a shiver: "Diogo plans a fleet, its cannons a war on your river, its tide a flood to sweep you away, its muskets a storm." Domingos, holding Tuaso's hand, her fingers warm against his, vowed to fortify the coast, the Warri River, gleaming under the morning sun, sang of resilience, its currents carrying tales of succession secured and a kingdom unbroken, ready for the storms to come, its king and heir bound by love, faith, and the river's eternal flow.

A young warrior, fresh from the patrol, approached with a carved fetish, its wood stained with blood, found on the captured ship. "Ogiame," he said, his voice low, "these bears Ijaw markings, but the sailor spoke of a Dutch trader, his gold buying Diogo's guns. A greater threat brews beyond the sea." Domingos's gaze hardened, his mind racing to Lisbon's courts, where alliances shifted like tides. He turned to Ebi. "Send word to Benin—Oba Ohuan must know. We'll need their warriors, their brass a shield." Ebi nodded, drafting a letter, the quill scratching urgency. Tuaso, her net paused, whispered, "The river warned us, my love. Anthonio's trial proved his worth, but this storm tests us all." Anthonio, overhearing, gripped his spear, his blue eyes fierce. "Father, I'll stand with you, my blood Warri's, my spear its defence." The council agreed, planning a coastal fort, its walls of mud and coral to rise, while Odion trained a river fleet, his canoes a line of defence. Under the Iroko, Domingos and Tuaso stood, Anthonio at their side, the river's whisper their vow, its flow a promise of unity against the coming tide.

CHAPTER NINETEEN
The Tide of Legacy

The Warri River flowed with a quiet reverence under a twilight sky, its waters reflecting the golden hues of a setting sun, as if bearing witness to the twilight of a king's reign, the air thick with the scent of mangrove and the soft hum of evening insects. It was 1640, and Ogiame Dom Domingos, now in his early fifties, stood at the palace's edge, his scarlet Kemeje faded but proud, its fabric a tapestry of battles fought with the Awori, betrayals faced with Emagin, and loves lost with Maria and found with Tuaso, coral beads worn smooth by decades of leadership, their clink a soft prayer against his chest. His hair, streaked with silver like the river's ripples, framed a face etched with the scars of wars, betrayals, and the quiet joys of a kingdom secured, his breath shorter with age. Olori Tuaso, her coral-red wrapper vibrant despite her own advancing years, stood beside him, her hand a steady anchor, her fingers tracing the net she wove for the church's hospital tent, its threads a symbol of healing and hope. Anthonio Domingos, their twelve-year-old son, a towering figure with Maria's sea-blue eyes—deep as the river's heart—and Warri's bronze strength, was the kingdom's heir, his Kemeje adorned with a cross that gleamed in the fading light and coral beads that rattled with each step, a symbol of unity between tradition and faith. The kingdom, strengthened by the Benin alliance forged under Oba Ohuan's brass plaques, its trade routes pulsing with life, and the church's growth under Father João and Sister Clara, thrived, its spirit a river unbowed, its markets alive with the scent of smoked fish and pepper. Yet a new tension gripped Warri—a mysterious illness sweeping the river clans, threatening to unravel Domingos's legacy just as he prepared to pass the crown, its shadow a chill in the warm dusk.

The illness, a fever that left fishermen trembling with weakness, their hands too frail to cast nets, and weavers too sick to work, their looms silent, had struck without warning, its grip a silent curse. Nets lay empty along the banks, markets quieted with the absence of trade, and whispers of a curse returned, echoing the fears of years past when Ikenna's plots darkened the land, the air heavy with the scent of fear and doubt. The chiefs, loyal since Anthonio's trial as heir, their coral armlets a quiet testament, grew restless, fearing the gods' wrath—Oritse Udeji fire or Umale Okun's displeasure—or Portuguese treachery, their voices a murmur of unease. Anthonio, trained by Anomu's stern hand and Temieno's sharp wisdom, led patrols to secure the river, his canoe slicing the water with skill, but his youth—barely twenty—and mixed blood still drew sceptical glances from traditionalists, their eyes lingering on his blue gaze. Tuaso, her healing skills honed with Sister Clara, tended the sick in the hospital tent, her herbs—mint and root—faltering against the fever's relentless grip, the canvas walls a haven strained by despair. Domingos, his health weakened by years of battle—his frame less steady, his joints aching—felt time pressing like a tide, its current swift. He needed to secure Warri's future, to pass the crown to Anthonio, before the river claimed him, its flow a silent judge.

The Fever's Shadow

The palace war room, its walls adorned with Iroko carvings that whispered of Ginuwa's legacy and Benin's brass plaques that gleamed with alliance, buzzed with urgency, the air thick with the scent of palm oil and the rustle of parchment. Domingos sat at a carved table, its surface worn smooth by councils past, a map of the riverlands before him, marked with villages struck by the fever—Ode-Itsekiri, Ale Eko Iwere—its lines a map of despair. Temieno, now in her forties, her dagger a constant companion at her thigh, its hilt worn by use, studied the map, her eyes sharp despite greying braids that framed her face, her voice a current of resolve. Anomu, his scars a map of Warri's wars, leaned on his spear, its blade catching the lamplight, his voice gruff as the river's edge. "Ogiame, the fever spreads from the creeks, its shadow deep. The people say it's Oritse Udeji's anger, his forge cold, or Portuguese poison, their ships a curse. We must act, or fear will break us, its tide a flood." Ebi, his hair white but his mind keen as a hawk's, added, his fingers tracing the map, "Diogo's ship is gone, its sails vanished, but a Dutch vessel anchors at Ale Eko Iwere, its hull bold. They trade cloth— fine linen, dyed blue—but their men ask about our warriors, their eyes greedy. I fear they stir the Ijaw, hoping to weaken us, their gold a blade." Tuaso, her coral necklace glinting like a river's heart, spoke softly, her voice a gentle tide. "The fever resists my herbs, their scent faint, but Sister Clara found a pattern—it strikes where the river meets the sea, its waters tainted. Something poisons the flow, its source hidden." Anthonio, his voice steady as the Iroko's roots, proposed action, his blue eyes fierce. "Father, let me lead a team to the creeks, its currents my guide. I'll find the source—water, poison, or curse, its shadow lifted. The people need their heir to act, my spear their shield." Domingos's eyes, clouded with age, met his son's, a mirror of Maria's gaze, his heart a battlefield of pride and fear. Anthonio's courage was Warri's future, its pulse strong, but the chiefs' doubts lingered, and the fever's toll threatened his succession, its shadow a weight. "Go, Anthonio," he said, his voice a steady drum, "but take Temieno and Adesuwa, their hands sure. The river hides secrets, its depths dark. Be wary, my son, its tide a test." As Anthonio prepared, his Kemeje rustling with purpose, a messenger burst in, his wrapper torn from haste, his breath heavy with urgency. "Ogiame, a stranger seeks audience—a healer from Owo, claiming knowledge of the fever, its cure a hope. He waits at the church, his voice eager."

The Stranger's Claim

The church, its mud walls adorned with coral patterns and a cross that stood tall against the dusk, was a sanctuary of hope, its interior filled with the scent of incense and the murmur of evening prayers. Father João, now stooped but fervent, his hands trembling with age, led the stranger forward—a wiry man named Ovbio, his wrapper dyed with Owo's ochre patterns, its earth tones a contrast to Warri's coral, his eyes bright with urgency, a spark in the dim light. "Ogiame," Ovbio said, bowing low, his voice a river's flow, "I am a healer trained in Owo's forests, its roots deep. This fever is no curse, its shadow a lie, but a poison from tainted fish, carried by river crabs from the sea, their shells a vessel of death. I've seen it in Owo—boil the water, its heat a shield, burn the crabs, their flesh a pyre, and the fever breaks, its grip released." The crowd, gathered for evening prayers, their wrappers muted in reverence, murmured, their coral beads a quiet echo. Sister Clara, her healing tent overwhelmed, its canvas strained by the sick, nodded, her voice a thread of hope. "His words match my findings, Ogiame, their truth a light. The crabs near Ale Eko Iwere are sickly, their shells black with poison, their crawl a sign." Domingos, his heart stirred by hope, questioned Ovbio, his Portuguese years sharpening his doubt. "Why come to Warri, healer, your journey long? Owo is far, its forests distant." Ovbio's gaze held steady, his eyes a mirror of resolve. "The Oba of Owo heard of Warri's strength, its church a beacon, your heir a promise. He sent me to aid, seeking friendship, its bond a bridge. But beware—foreign hands may taint the river, hoping to weaken you, their greed a current." Ebi's eyes narrowed, his mind tracing the Dutch ship. "The Dutch, their sails bold. Their ship trades near the fever's source, its hull a threat." Suspense thickened as Temieno whispered to Anomu, her voice a shadow, "Ovbio's tale is convenient, its words too neat. A spy could hide in healer's robes, his ochre a mask." Domingos, his instincts honed by Lisbon's courts, ordered, "Ovbio, stay with Sister Clara, your hands our hope. Prove your cure, its light our guide, but Adesuwa's scouts will watch you, their eyes sharp."

A Plot in the Creeks

Anthonio, Temieno, and Adesuwa led a flotilla to Ale Eko Iwere, their canoes gliding through mangrove shadows, the water dark and still, the air thick with the scent of mud and the rustle of leaves. The village, once bustling with the sound of nets and laughter, was quiet, its huts shadowed, its nets empty, its people fevered, their breaths shallow. Anthonio, his spear ready, its blade catching the moonlight, inspected the riverbank, finding blackened crabs crawling in the shallows, their shells a sickly hue, their movement a sign of taint. Temieno, her dagger drawn, its edge a promise, spotted a Dutch trader, Pieter, meeting Ijaw raiders in a hidden cove, the water lapping at their feet, the air filled with the scent of foreign cloth. Adesuwa, silent as a shadow, her wrapper blending with the dusk, overheard Pieter's plan, his voice a serpent's hiss: "Taint the crabs with powder from our ship, its bitterness a weapon. Warri falls, its river weak, and we claim the trade routes, our gold a crown." The revelation struck like lightning, a thunderclap in the night. Anthonio signalled Anomu, who rallied warriors hidden in the mangroves, their spears gleaming, the sound of their approach a drumbeat of justice. As night fell, the air thick with tension, they struck, the clash of steel and shouts echoing, capturing Pieter and three Ijaw conspirators, their pouches filled with a bitter-smelling powder, its grains a poison's promise. The battle was swift but costly—two Itsekiri warriors fell to Ijaw daggers, their bodies draped in palm fronds, the scent of blood mingling with the mangrove's dampness. Anthonio, bloodied but unbowed, his Kemeje torn, held Pieter's pouch, his eyes blazing with fury. "This ends now, its tide turned." Back in Warri, Ovbio's cure worked—boiled water steaming with purity and burned crabs sending smoke to the sky halted the fever's spread, villagers recovering as nets filled again with silver fish, the air filled with the scent of life. Ovbio, cleared of suspicion by Adesuwa's watch, bowed to Domingos, his ochre wrapper a banner of alliance. "Ogiame, your son's courage saved us, his spear a shield. Owo seeks alliance, its forests our friend."

The Confrontation

The palace courtyard, lit by a full moon that cast silver over the Iroko tree, hosted a tense council, its roots a silent judge, the air filled with the scent of kola nuts and the murmur of the crowd, their wrappers a sea of indigo and coral. Pieter, bound with rope, his Dutch bravado crumbling like dry sand, faced Domingos, his voice a weak tide. "We meant only trade, its cloth our gain," he lied, his eyes darting, but Anthonio tossed the powder pouch before the chiefs, Iyatsere and Olekun among them, its bitterness a proof. "This taints our river," Anthonio said, his voice a king's, its depth unwavering, "its poison a Dutch blade. They sought our ruin, their ship a storm." Iyatsere, his coral armlets glinting in the moonlight, spoke, his voice a bridge of reconciliation. "Ogiame, we doubted Anthonio's blood, its blue a question, but his heart is Warri's, its river in his veins. He is the heir, proven by fire, his spear our shield." Olekun nodded, his bronze pendants clinking, his voice a rumble of faith. "The river chooses him, as Umale Okun does, its forge his strength. The ancestors smile on his claim." Domingos, his health frail but his spirit fierce, rose, his Kemeje a flame in the night, his voice a river's roar. "Anthonio is my son, Warri's rightful heir, its future bright. His blood blends river and sea, making us stronger, its mix our pride. Let no doubt remain, its shadow lifted." The crowd roared, their faith restored, their coral beads a chorus of unity, the air filled with the sound of ululations. Pieter was banished to his ship, a letter sent to the Dutch governor warning of Warri's strength, its words sealed with coral wax. The Ijaw conspirators, repentant, their daggers cast aside, swore loyalty, their lives spared for labour in the creeks, their voices a pledge of peace.

The Happy Ending

As the fever faded, its shadow retreating, Warri bloomed anew, its fields green with sprouting crops, its nets heavy with fish, the air filled with the scent of harvest and hope. The church rang with hymns, Father João and Ovbio praying together, their faiths united in a chorus of cross and coral, the mud walls a testament to harmony. Tuaso, her nets now symbol of healing, their threads a weave of life, crafted a new one for Anthonio, her pride radiant, her coral necklace a river's gleam. Temieno, her dagger sheathed, its blade a memory of battles, toasted her nephew, her voice a song of joy, while Anomu trained him for the throne, his spear a mentor's gift, its weight a promise. At a feast beneath the Iroko tree, its branches a canopy of celebration, Domingos, his Kemeje bright with renewed spirit, lifted Anthonio's hand, his voice a steady current. "Warri, behold your heir, its river his guide. The river, its flow eternal, the gods, their will our strength, and the cross, its light our faith, crown him, his blood our pride." The drums beat, blending Itsekiri chants with Christian songs, their rhythm a heartbeat of unity, as

Anthonio knelt, his cross and coral gleaming, his blue eyes a beacon. Tuaso, tears in her eyes like river pearls, whispered to Domingos, "Maria sees you, my love, her spirit in our son," her voice a mother's love, her hand in his.

A young scout approached, his wrapper torn from a patrol, his face flushed with urgency, the scent of salt on his skin. "Ogiame, a Dutch fleet was sighted beyond Escravos!" he gasped. "Their cannons gleam, their banners bold, and Ijaw canoes guard their flanks!" Domingos's heart sank, but he masked it with resolve, turning to the council, the war room a fortress of strategy. "Summon the Iyatsere," he said, his voice a steady drum, the air thick with purpose. In the war room, its walls lined with maps stained by time, Ebi, Chief Oton, and Odion gathered, the map a battlefield of ink, its lines blurred by the scout's haste. "The Dutch bring war," Ebi warned, his finger tracing the coast, "their cannons a storm, the Ijaw their allies, their gold a chain." Chief Oton shook his staff, its cowries a river's song, its rattle a prayer. "Oritse demands we guard our waters, its spirit our shield." Odion, his coral amulet glinting, said, "Let me lead the fleet, Ogiame. The river taught me its secrets, its currents my blade." Domingos nodded, recalling a parable from his father, of the Heron and the Sky: "Heron soars above the storm, its patience turning danger to flight, teaching us to rise with wisdom." He devised a plan: Odion would lead a river fleet, supported by ninety warriors and Benin's promised aid, their canoes armed with blunderbusses, while Oton consulted the oracle, its shells a compass. Messengers were sent to Oba Ohuan, the letter sealed with coral, seeking warriors and cannon.

The fleet set out, the river a mirror to the dawn, the air filled with the scent of gunpowder and resolve. They clashed with the Dutch off Escravos, the cannons' roar a thunderclap, the Ijaw canoes a swarm. Odion's strategy—using mangrove cover and Benin's cannon fire—turned the tide, the Dutch retreating, their flagship damaged, the water red with battle. A captured officer, his uniform torn, confessed, "The Dutch seek Warri's pepper, their cannons a bluff to force trade. We'll return with more." Domingos, frail but resolute, met Anthonio on the shore, Tuaso at his side. "You'll lead Warri, my son," he said, his voice weak. "The river is yours." Anthonio, his Kemeje bloodied, knelt, his cross a vow.

CHAPTER TWENTY
The Last Anniversary

T he Warri River shimmered under a golden dawn, its waters a mirror for the kingdom's pride as it prepared to celebrate the final coronation anniversary of Ogiame Dom Domingos, the air alive with the scent of blooming mangrove and the distant call of herons welcoming the day. It was 1641, and Domingos, now in his mid-fifties, stood at the palace's edge, his scarlet Kemeje faded but regal, its fabric a tapestry woven with decades of triumphs over the Awori, trials against betrayal like Emagin's, and loves lost with Maria and found with Tuaso, coral beads worn smooth by the weight of leadership, their clink a soft hymn against his chest. His health, frail since the fever crisis of the previous year, held steady, sustained by Olori Tuaso's unwavering love—her presence a balm—and the kingdom's faith, its pulse a river's flow. Tuaso, her coral-red wrapper vibrant despite her own advancing years, its hue a defiance of time, stood beside him, her eyes warm with devotion, her hands tracing the net she wove for the church's hospital tent, its threads a quiet promise. Anthonio Domingos, twenty, a towering figure with Maria's sea-blue eyes—deep as the river's heart—and Warri's bronze strength, was the undisputed heir, his Kemeje adorned with a cross that gleamed in the sunlight and coral beads that rattled with each step, a symbol of unity between Itsekiri tradition and Christian faith, his leadership proven in the creeks against the Dutch threat. The church, under Father João's aging guidance, his voice a gentle echo, and Sister Clara's healing hands, thrived, its school echoing with lessons and its hospital tent a beacon of unity, the scent of herbs wafting through the air. The Benin alliance, cemented by brass plaques in the palace courtyard, held firm, its trade routes a lifeline, and even the Dutch, chastened by Anthonio's victory at Escravos, kept their distance, their ships a fading shadow. Yet, as Warri prepared for a grand celebration, a shadow lingered—a subtle tension that would weave plots and a twist into Domingos's final day, its whisper a current beneath the joy.

The anniversary, marking twenty years since Domingos's coronation in 1621, was to be a spectacle of Itsekiri splendour, blending riverine traditions with Christian pomp, its preparations a dance of heritage and hope. The palace courtyard, adorned with palm mats that rustled in the breeze and coral-patterned banners fluttering like river wings, buzzed with activity, the air filled with the scent of roasted yam and the sound of laughter. Drummers tuned their Ogume drum, their rhythms to echo Unale Okun's strength and the church's hymns, a harmony of faiths. Weavers, led by Tuaso, crafted nets to drape the Iroko tree, its gnarled branches a symbol of Warri's resilience, the threads a weave of unity. Anthonio, overseeing warriors, ensured the river was secure, his spear a constant companion, its blade catching the dawn, while Temieno, now a greying advisor in her late forties, her dagger still sharp at her thigh, coordinated the feast, her scouts patrolling for Ijaw or Dutch threats, their canoes slicing the water. Ebi, his white hair a crown of wisdom, sorted gifts from allies—yams from Ode-Itsekiri, their earthy scent a promise, ivory from Benin, its smoothness a tribute, and a surprise from afar: a Portuguese caravel, *Santa Maria da Graça*, anchored at the river's mouth, its sails bold against the horizon, bearing gifts from King John IV, Portugal's new ruler after the Spanish yoke was thrown off in 1640, its arrival a ripple of intrigue.

The Portuguese Gifts

The caravel's arrival, announced by a cannon's boom that echoed across the water, stirred Warri's market, its stalls alive with the clatter of trade and the scent of pepper. Captain Almeida, a young officer with a diplomat's smile, his velvet doublet stark against Itsekiri wrappers of coral and indigo, disembarked with a retinue, their footsteps a foreign rhythm. His letter, sealed with the Portuguese crown, its wax a golden seal, praised Domingos's knighthood in the Order of Christ, a title earned in Lisbon, and Warri's faith, its cross a bridge, offering gifts: two bronze cannons, their barrels gleaming under the sun, etched with crosses, a chest of gold cruzados that clinked with promise, a silver chalice for the church, its surface polished to a mirror, and a velvet cloak embroidered with coral motifs, a nod to Itsekiri heritage. The cannons, their weight a silent threat, were a gesture of alliance, but their presence hinted at a price—Portugal sought a renewed trade monopoly, eyeing Warri's pepper, oil, and ivory, its river a prize. Domingos, in the palace war room, its walls adorned with Iroko carvings and Benin's brass, read the letter with Ebi, the map of the Delta spread before them, its lines a battlefield. "John IV honours me," he said, his voice weary, its timbre softened by age, "but Almeida's eyes are like Vasco's—hungry, their gaze a chain. They want our river, its flow their gain." Temieno, her dagger glinting in the lamplight, scoffed, her voice a current of defiance. "Cannons are no gift if they chain us, their bronze a yoke. Let Anthonio meet Almeida, his strength a shield. He'll show Warri's heart, its river unbowed." Anthonio nodded, his cross gleaming, his blue eyes sharp. "I'll welcome them, Father, my voice their guide, but our ports stay ours, their tides our own." The celebration began at noon, the courtyard a sea of colour—indigo wrappers, coral beads, and the Portuguese velvet a stark contrast. Chiefs, led by Iyatsere and Olekun, wore coral armlets, their loyalty firm since Anthonio's trial, their faces a map of pride. Drummers played, blending Itsekiri war chants with hymns, their rhythm a heartbeat, while dancers swirled, their wrappers flashing indigo and red, the air filled with the scent of palm oil and joy. Tuaso, radiant, led women in offering nets to the church, Sister Clara blessing them with holy water, its droplets a shimmer of faith. Anthonio, beside Domingos, carried a carved Iroko staff, a gift from Obawole, the Ife oracle, its wood warm with wisdom. The cannons, placed at the courtyard's edge, drew gasps, their bronze barrels a silent sentinel. Almeida, bowing low, presented the gifts, his voice smooth as the river. "Ogiame, Portugal honours your reign, its years a light. These cannons guard your river, the chalice your faith, the cloak your legacy, its threads a bridge." Domingos, his Kemeje regal, accepted with a nod, his voice a steady tide. "Warri thanks John IV, its heart grateful, but our river guards itself, its current free. Let us feast as allies, not vassals, our bond unbroken." The feast was a cultural tapestry— smoked fish fragrant with pepper, pounded yam rich with palm oil, and palm wine sweet with harvest joined Portuguese wine and bread, a nod to Domingos's Lisbon years, the air a blend of rivers and spires. Anthonio, seated with Almeida, parried trade demands with diplomacy, his blue eyes a mirror of resolve, while Tuaso, her laughter a melody, danced with Anthonio, their bond a mother's pride, her steps a dance of love. Temieno, watching Almeida's men, sensed a plot—their glances lingered on the cannons, their whispers hinting at more than trade, a shadow in the light.

A Plot in the Shadows

As night fell, the courtyard aglow with oil lamps, Ebi's spy, a young fisherman named Oritse, his hands rough from nets, overheard Almeida's men in the market, their Portuguese laced with intent, the scent of foreign cloth a clue. "The cannons are bait," one said, his voice a whisper of treachery, "their bronze a lure. If Warri refuses the monopoly, we arm the Ijaw to raid Ale Eko Iwere, its nets burned." Oritse, heart pounding like the drums of war, slipped away, the mangrove shadows his cloak, reporting to Ebi, who alerted Temieno, her dagger a promise. Adesuwa, her scouts ever vigilant, their canoes silent, trailed an Almeida aide to a creek, where an Ijaw raider accepted a pouch of cruzados, its gold a bribe, promising chaos, the water lapping at their feet. Temieno, her grey braids swaying, rallied Anomu's warriors, their spears gleaming in the moonlight. Under the night's cover, the air thick with the scent of damp earth, they ambushed the creek meeting, the clash of steel a brief storm, capturing the aide and Ijaw conspirator, their pouches revealing Portuguese coins and a letter from Almeida demanding a fort at Ale Eko Iwere, its words a chain. The evidence, stark as the river's truth, was brought to Domingos, who felt a familiar pang—Portugal's games, learned in Lisbon's courts, never changed, their tides a memory.

The Confrontation

At dawn, the courtyard hosted a tense council, the Iroko tree a silent judge, its leaves rustling with the morning breeze, the air filled with the scent of kola nuts and the murmur of the crowd, their wrappers a sea of colour. Almeida, summoned, faced Domingos, Tuaso, and Anthonio, the captured aide trembling beside him, his velvet torn. Chiefs, including Iyatsere and Olekun, stood firm, their coral beads glinting in the light. "Captain," Domingos said, his voice a river's calm before a storm, its depth unwavering, "your gifts mask treachery, their shine a lie. These coins, this letter—Portugal seeks to chain Warri with Ijaw blades, its river a prize." Almeida paled, his smile crumbling like dry sand, his voice a weak tide. "Ogiame, a rogue aide acted alone, his hand a shadow. Portugal seeks only friendship, its bond a bridge." Anthonio, holding the letter, its wax seal broken, stepped forward, his voice a king's, its strength a current. "Friendship doesn't arm raiders, its gold a blade. Leave Warri, Almeida, your schemes ended. Your cannons stay, their bronze ours, but your ship departs, its sails a memory." The crowd roared, their faith in Anthonio unshakable, their coral beads a chorus of unity, the air filled with the sound of ululations. Almeida, outmanoeuvred, his diplomat's mask fallen, boarded his caravel, banished with a warning to John IV, the letter sealed with coral wax and steel. The Ijaw conspirator, repentant, his dagger cast aside, swore loyalty, his life spared for labour in the creeks, his voice a pledge of peace, the water his witness.

The Twist: A Hidden Gift

As the anniversary peaked, the courtyard aglow with celebration, a twist emerged, a current beneath the joy. Among the Portuguese gifts, buried in the chest of cruzados, was a sealed letter, its parchment overlooked in the haste, addressed to Domingos in a familiar hand from a Lisbon friend, António Martins d'Abreu, his companion from Santo Agostinho, their youth a memory. The letter, written in secret, its ink faded but true, warned of Almeida's plot, its treachery a shadow, urging Domingos to trust Anthonio's strength, his leadership a light. "Your son is Warri's bridge," António wrote, his words a bridge across oceans, "as you were mine, your faith our bond." Enclosed was a small coral cross, its surface smooth, a gift for Anthonio, blending their shared past—Lisbon's spires and Warri's river—its weight a promise. Domingos, moved, his eyes glistening with memory, gave the cross to Anthonio in a quiet moment, his voice thick with pride. "Your mother's spirit, her blue eyes a guide, my friend's faith, his hand a memory—this is yours, my heir, its coral your crown." Anthonio, kneeling before his father, accepted, his eyes glistening with tears, the crowd cheering their future Ogiame, their voices a tide of hope, the air filled with the scent of palm wine and unity.

The Last Night

That evening, Warri feasted, its drums blending hymns with Itsekiri chants, their rhythm a heartbeat of joy, palm wine flowing under the Iroko's shade, its roots a witness, the air filled with the scent of roasted yam and the sound of laughter. Tuaso danced with Domingos, her love a steady flame, her coral-red wrapper a banner of devotion, her steps a memory of youth, while Anthonio led warriors in a salute, their spears raised, their Kemejes a forest of pride. Temieno, her grey braids swaying, toasted her brother, her dagger sheathed, its blade a relic of battles, her voice a song of farewell. Father João and Sister Clara blessed the gathering, the church's cross joined by coral nets draped from the Iroko, its mud walls a testament to harmony, the scent of incense mingling with the feast. As night deepened, the courtyard quieting, Domingos retired to his chamber, its coral walls a cocoon of memory, Tuaso at his side, her hand warm in his, Anthonio nearby, his cross a silent vow. His health, long fragile since the fever, faded gently, his breath slowing as he lay in bed, his coral beads warm against his chest, their clink a final prayer. Tuaso held his hand, her tears soft as river pearls, her voice a whisper of love, while Anthonio, kneeling, whispered, "Father, the river carries you, its flow your guide." Domingos smiled, his last words a murmur, his voice a fading tide: "Warri endures... Anthonio, my river's heir, its spirit your strength... Tuaso, my love, its heart..." He passed peacefully, the river's song his lullaby, its waters a mirror to his soul, his legacy etched in Warri's heart, the air filled with the scent of dawn.

Per Itsekiri custom, his death was not announced immediately, its silence a respect for the fallen king. The chiefs, led by Iyatsere and Olekun, convened in secret within the palace's inner chamber, its walls adorned with faded paintings of Ginuwa, confirming Anthonio as Ogiame, his coronation planned to follow tradition, the cowrie staff passed in quiet ritual. Tuaso, her strength unbroken, prepared the palace, her hands weaving a final net for Domingos's burial, its threads a tribute, while Temieno and Anomu guarded the river, ensuring peace, their canoes a line of defence. On the day of the announcement, the courtyard filled, the Iroko tree a witness to Warri's continuity, its roots deep, the air thick with the scent of kola nuts and the murmur of the crowd. Anthonio, crowned Ogiame in a scarlet Kemeje, his cross and coral gleaming in the sunlight, stood tall, his blue eyes a beacon. "Ogiame Dom Domingos walks with the ancestors," he declared, his voice a river's strength, "his spirit in our river, its flow eternal. I, Anthonio, am your Ogiame, by river, its current my guide, gods, their will my strength, and cross, its light my faith." The crowd roared, their grief tempered by pride, their coral beads a chorus of unity, the air filled with ululations, as Warri's river flowed on, its waters clear, carrying the legacy of a king and the promise of a new reign, its roots deep, its future bright under a king born of river and sea.

A young scout, his wrapper torn from a patrol, approached as the ceremony ended, his face flushed with urgency, the scent of salt on his skin. "Ogiame, a Dutch scout ship was sighted beyond Escravos!" he gasped, his voice a wave of warning. "Its flag is small, but its crew barters with Ijaw, their whispers of cannon and gold!" Anthonio's heart sank, but he masked it with resolve, turning to the council, the war room a fortress of strategy. "Summon the Iyatsere," he said, his voice a steady drum, the air thick with purpose. In the war room, its walls lined with maps stained by time, Ebi, Chief Oton, and Odion gathered, the map a battlefield of ink, its lines blurred by the scout's haste. "The Dutch return," Ebi warned, his finger tracing the coast, "their scout a prelude, the Ijaw their pawns, their gold a chain." Chief Oton shook his staff, its cowries a river's song, its rattle a prayer. "Umale Okun demands we guard our waters, its spirit our shield." Odion, his coral amulet glinting, said, "Let me lead a patrol, Ogiame. The river taught me its secrets, its currents my blade." Anthonio nodded, recalling a parable from his father, of the Iguana and the Drought: "Iguana waits as the drought burns, its patience turning scarcity to abundance, teaching us to endure with hope." He devised a plan: Odion would lead a patrol to monitor the Dutch ship, supported by eighty warriors and Benin's promised scouts, their canoes armed with blunderbusses, while Oton consulted the oracle, its shells a guide. Messengers were sent to Oba Ohuan, the letter sealed with coral, seeking vigilance.

The patrol set out, the river a mirror to the dusk, the air filled with the scent of mangrove and resolve. They shadowed the Dutch scout, its crew unaware, and returned with news of its retreat, the Ijaw bribed but hesitant, the air filled with the scent of relief. Yet a captured sailor, his hands bound, whispered a chilling vow, his words a shiver: "The Dutch plan a blockade, their cannons a siege to force trade, their fleet a storm." Anthonio, standing with Tuaso under the Iroko, vowed to fortify Warri, the river singing their future, its currents carrying the legacy of Domingos and the promise of a reign united, ready for the tides ahead.

CHAPTER TWENTY-ONE

Farewell Ogiame

Prologue: The Silent Tide

The Warri River whispered secrets in the dead of night, its waters lapping against the palace docks like a thief in the shadows, the air heavy with the scent of rain-soaked earth and palm oil lamps flickering low, their golden glow a fragile shield against the darkness. It was 1643, and the kingdom held its breath, the river's flow a silent witness to the fading light of its king. Ogiame Dom Domingos, the ruler who had bridged river and sea, his reign a tapestry of unity, lay in his chamber, the room steeped in shadow, his scarlet Kemeje draped over a carved stool, its fabric faded but regal, coral beads resting on his chest like ancient guardians, their clink a fading echo. His breaths came shallow, laboured, each one a battle against the invisible foe that had crept into his body weeks ago—a persistent cough turned to fever, defying Tuaso's herbs with their earthy scent and Sister Clara's prayers, their whispers a plea to the cross. The church's chalice, a gift from Portugal's anniversary tribute, stood on a table, empty, its silver surface cold, as if mocking the bronze cannons outside that guarded Warri but could not save its king, their barrels a silent sentinel. Tuaso, her coral-red wrapper dishevelled from sleepless nights, its vibrant hue muted by grief, knelt beside the bed, her hand clasping Domingos's, her fingers trembling, her eyes red-rimmed but fierce with love. Anthonio, twenty and strong as the Iroko tree, its roots a symbol of endurance, paced the room, his Kemeje unbuttoned, revealing a cross-pendant glinting in the lamplight, a blend of Maria's legacy and Warri's strength. Temieno, her grey braids tied back with resolve, stood guard at the door, dagger in hand, its hilt worn by years of vigilance, while Anomu, his scars a map of loyalty etched across his face, watched the river through the window, his spear ready for unseen threats, the scent of damp wood lingering. Ebi, white-haired and wise, his hands tracing a tattered map of the Delta, consulted Oton, the high priest, whose cowrie staff rattled with chants to Umale Okun, the god of the river, and the ancestors, their voices a murmur in the shadows.

Tension thickened the air like fog, a cloak over the chamber. Whispers from the creeks spoke of omens—a two-headed fish caught near Ale Eko Iwere, its scales a portent, a red moon over Ode-Itsekiri casting an eerie glow—signs the gods stirred, their displeasure a shadow. Domingos's health had declined since the anniversary feast, where Almeida's treachery was unmasked, his body weakened by the strain of banishing the Portuguese captain and securing the cannons for Warri's defence, their bronze a double-edged gift. Tuaso had begged him to rest, her voice a gentle tide, but Domingos, ever the king, had addressed the chiefs in the courtyard, his voice steady despite the cough that racked him, blood flecking his lips. "Warri endures," he had said, lifting Anthonio's hand, "as my heir will lead, his spirit our strength." Now, in the chamber's dim light, suspense coiled like a serpent, its hiss a warning. Anthonio stopped pacing, his blue eyes—Olori Maria's legacy—fixed on his father, their depth a mirror of grief. "Father," he said, his voice a steady current, "the oracle Obawole sent word—he sees shadows, their forms unclear, but your light holds, its flame our guide." Domingos smiled weakly, his hand trembling as he touched Anthonio's cross, its metal warm from his son's chest. "The river calls, my son, its tide swift," he murmured, his voice a fading wave. "But Warri's tide turns with you, its flow your legacy." Tuaso's tears fell silently, her grip tightening as Domingos's breaths grew fainter, a rhythm slowing like the river at dusk. Temieno glanced outside, where warriors patrolled, their spears glinting, unaware of the king's peril—Itsekiri custom forbade announcing an Ogiame's passing until a successor was chosen, lest chaos consume the kingdom, its roots torn. Suddenly, a cough wracked Domingos, blood staining his lips, a crimson tide, his body shuddering. Anthonio knelt, his voice breaking, a son's plea. "Hold on, Father, your strength our shield. The cannons guard us; your legacy guards Warri, its heart unbroken." But the room grew still, the river's whisper the only sound, its current a lullaby. Domingos's eyes fluttered, a final murmur escaping, his voice a fading breath: "Tuaso... Anthonio... the river flows eternal, its spirit my gift..." His hand went limp, the coral beads slipping to the floor with a soft clink, their fall a punctuation to his reign. Tuaso buried her face in his chest, silent sobs shaking her, her coral-red wrapper a shroud of grief, while Anthonio's fists clenched, grief and duty warring within, his cross a silent vow. Temieno, tears in her eyes, her dagger a weight at her side, whispered, "The Ogiame sleeps, his tide turned. We guard the secret until the river speaks, its voice our guide." Ebi nodded, sealing the chamber with a heavy curtain, the air thick with suspense—the kingdom unaware, its future teetering on the edge of revelation, the river's flow a countdown to truth.

Rumors and Shadows

In the days following Domingos's silent departure, Warri stirred with unease, the river's flow seeming slower, its waters darker under overcast skies, the air heavy with the scent of rain and the murmur of doubt. Rumours spread like mangrove roots, their tendrils reaching every corner—fishermen whispered of a king's cough that silenced the drums, their nets idle, weavers spoke of empty thrones in dreams, their looms stilled, the market hushed with fear. The palace gates remained open, a facade of normalcy, but guards stood vigilant, their spears glinting in the dawn, deflecting questions with stoic denials, their voices steady but eyes shadowed with secrets. "Ogiame rests," they said, a refrain repeated, but the silence grew louder, a drumbeat of suspicion. Tuaso, her coral-red wrapper muted by a black shawl, its vibrant hue dimmed by sorrow, moved through the palace like a ghost, her steps soft, tending Anthonio, now twenty-two and burdened with unspoken grief, his blue eyes a storm of resolve. The first rumour erupted in the market, where a trader from Ugborodo, his wrapper stained with salt, claimed to have seen the palace lamps burn low at midnight, their flicker a sign of mourning, his voice a whisper of doom. "The Ogiame has crossed the river," he muttered, drawing gasps from listeners, their coral beads clinking in shock. Word raced through the creeks—Ode-Itsekiri's drummers fell silent, their Ogume drum still, Okere's chiefs gathered in hushed councils, their voices a murmur, the air thick with tension.

Ikenna's old allies, scattered but watchful since his banishment, fueled the fire, their whispers a shadow in the mangroves, stirring doubt among traditionalists. "If the Ogiame is gone, who rules?" they hissed, their voices a serpent's coil. "Anthonio's blood is mixed—will the gods accept him, his blue eyes a foreign tide?" Temieno, her grey braids tied for action, her dagger concealed beneath her wrapper, moved swiftly, her spirit a river's current. With Adesuwa's scouts, their canoes slicing the water, she quelled the rumours in the villages, her voice a thunderclap of authority. "The Ogiame lives," she declared in Ugbolokposo, her eyes piercing the crowd, "his strength our shield. These lies are Ijaw whispers or Dutch deceit, their shadows a lie. Return to your nets; Warri stands, its roots deep." Anomu, his scars a reminder of loyalty, patrolled the river, his spear a beacon, arresting a fisherman spreading tales of blood on the palace floor, his net a symbol of betrayal, his punishment a public flogging to deter others, the crack of the whip a warning etched in the crowd's memory, the air filled with the scent of justice. Tuaso, in the church, prayed with Sister Clara, her tears hidden beneath a veil, the scent of incense a comfort. Father João, his voice frail but firm, debunked the rumours in sermons, his cross raised, "The king endures, as Warri's faith does, its light unbroken." But suspense built— visitors from Benin arrived, bearing ivory tributes, their eyes questioning the palace's quiet, their voices a probe. "We heard of illness," a Benin envoy said, his wrapper adorned with bronze, met with Ebi's calm denial, his white hair a crown of wisdom: "Ogiame rests from the anniversary's labors, his spirit strong. He sends greetings to Oba Akenzua, his ally." Anthonio, his blue eyes stormy with grief and duty, trained in secret with Anomu, his spear throws precise, preparing for the revelation he knew must come, the river's whisper a guide.

A young warrior, fresh from a creek patrol, approached Temieno with a carved fetish, its wood stained with blood, found near a Dutch trader's camp. "The Ijaw barter with foreigners," he said, his voice low, "their gold a threat." Temieno's eyes narrowed, her mind racing to the Dutch defeat at Escravos, their retreat a mask. She reported to Anthonio, who clenched his fist. "The Dutch stir again, their cannons a shadow. We must be ready when the tide turns." The tension was palpable—the kingdom held its breath, the river's flow a countdown to truth, its currents a mirror of fate.

The Secret Selection

In the palace's inner shrine, shielded from prying eyes, its walls adorned with faded paintings of Ginuwa, the air thick with the scent of kola nuts and the murmur of ritual, the Iyatsere and Olekun convened the elders, their coral armlets clinking in the dim light, a sound of tradition. Custom demanded the Ogiame's passing remain secret until a successor was chosen, lest rivals or enemies—Dutch traders, Ijaw raiders, or Ikenna's remnants—exploit the void, their hands a threat. Oton, the high priest, his cowrie staff a beacon, consulted the oracle—a diviner from Ile-Ife, Obawole's successor, a young priest named Adeyemi, his frame lean but his eyes sharp, his staff topped with a brass orisha that gleamed faintly. Adeyemi cast sixteen palm nuts on a woven mat, its threads worn by time, his chants invoking

Orunmila, the orisha of wisdom, and the ancestors, their voices a tide in the shadows. The nuts fell, patterns emerging like river currents, their clatter a language of fate. "The river chooses," he intoned, his voice echoing off the shrine's walls, "its flow unerring. Antonio Domingos, son of sea and soil, his blood blends but his heart is pure, its pulse Warri's own. Umale Okun accepts him, his forge bright, the ancestors crown him, their will our guide." The elders nodded, their faces solemn, their coral beads a quiet assent. Iyatsere, his voice grave as the river's depths, declared, "The oracle speaks, its truth clear. Antonio is the chosen, his tide our future." Olekun, clutching a cowrie shell, its surface smooth as memory, added, "Warri's tide turns with him, its current strong." The selection was sealed in secret, the palace guards sworn to silence, their spears a vow, as suspense hung over the kingdom—the rumours growing, the river's whisper a prelude to revelation, its waters a mirror of destiny.

The Breaking of the Calabash

One moon after Domingos's passing, the national council was called in the palace courtyard, the Iroko tree looming like a sentinel, its roots sprawling, the air thick with the scent of kola nuts and the murmur of the crowd, their wrappers somber black and red, coral beads muted in mourning. Chiefs from Ode-Itsekiri, Okere, Obodo, Ekuobodo, Ugbolokposo, Omadino, Ikpesan, Ijaghala, Kantu, Ugborodo, Bobi, Ureju, and Orere gathered, their faces a map of grief, the people assembled, rumours at fever pitch, markets closed in unspoken mourning, the silence a drumbeat of loss. Iya-tsere stepped forward, a calabash in hand, its clay surface etched with river patterns, his voice booming like a thunder-clap. "Ale Je Efun!" he cried, smashing the calabash on the ground, shards scattering like broken secrets, the sound a crack of truth. "The Ogiame has crossed the river, his tide turned! Ogiame Dom Domingos walks with the ancestors, his spirit eternal!" Gasps rippled through the crowd, tears flowing like the river's flow, the air filled with the scent of sorrow, as the truth dawned, a wave of grief. Olekun raised his staff, its cowries rattling, a prayer to the gods. "The oracle has spoken, its voice clear, the elders have chosen, their wisdom deep. Prince Antonio Domingos is our Oma-Oba, rightful heir by blood, its blend our strength, oracle, its guidance our light, and river, its current our soul!" Anthonio, in a fresh Kemeje, its scarlet a banner of renewal, stepped forth, his blue eyes steady as the Iroko's roots, cross and coral united in his chest, a symbol of unity. The crowd cheered, their grief mingling with hope, as drums beat a new rhythm, their Ogume drum a heartbeat, the air alive with ululations, the river's whisper a promise.

The 90 Days Mourning

Following the announcement of 'Ale Je Efun'—the passing of Ogiame—the Itsekiri people entered a solemn three lunar month period of mourning, cloaking Warri Kingdom in sorrow. A strict ban was imposed on all forms of merriment: no drumming echoed through the air, no parties stirred the night, and all subjects were required to wear their wrappers upside down, a visible mark of grief. The kingdom's spirit dimmed, its vibrancy a shadow, as the air grew heavy with the scent of ash and memory. This period of mourning, lasting until the burial rites were completed and the installation of the new Olu (Ogiame) began, was announced by Iyatsere, who declared 90 days of national mourning. During this time, Warri stilled—its fishing nets lay idle, its market stalls stood silent, and its people donned black wrappers, their coral beads hidden beneath somber cloth.

In the heart of the kingdom, Tuaso led the women in mournful chants, her voice a haunting lament for her love, its melody flowing like a river's elegy. Her coral-red wrapper, once vibrant, now seemed a faded echo of joy. Meanwhile, Anthonio entered Idaniken, a secluded grove where the river's edge met sacred soil, its towering trees forming a canopy of ancient wisdom. There, elders schooled him in the ways of the' Ogiame'—ruling justly, balancing the Christian cross with the sceptre of 'Umale Okun', the deity of the sea, and mastering the river's tides. Their voices, steady and resolute, served as his guide in preparing for the weight of leadership.

Order was strictly enforced during this sacred time. Punishments for defiance were swift and unyielding: a fisherman caught netting in violation of the ban was publicly flogged, his boat set ablaze, its flames a stark warning etched in the crowd's memory. The crack of the whip resounded like a drumbeat of discipline, the air thick with the scent of smoke, reinforcing the kingdom's reverence for tradition.

As Warri grieved, visitors arrived to pay their respects, their presence weaving the kingdom into a broader tapestry of alliances and rituals. Envoys from Benin brought ivory, their wrappers adorned with gleaming bronze. Priests from Ife offered kola nuts, their staffs raised in ritual reverence. Even a Dutch trader, chastened by a past defeat, arrived with bolts of cloth, his eyes wary but respectful. Strangers and allies alike presented condolences, their gifts piling in the palace— ivory tusks, intricately woven mats, and a silver cross from a Portuguese priest. These tributes, symbols of unity and respect, reflected the shared sorrow of a kingdom in mourning. The river, ever-present, mirrored Warri's grief, its tides carrying the weight of a people united in loss, their collective spirit bound by tradition and memory.

The late Ogiame's body, preserved in ritual herbs—palm oil, bitter kola, and mangrove root—its scent a farewell, was taken to Big Warri (Ode-Itsekiri) in the red royal boat, its hull painted with coral motifs, paddled by warriors, their drums muffled, the water lapping a requiem. At Ijala, a sacred grove where the river met the ancestors, he was buried, a young Iroko sapling planted with the inscription carved deep: "Dom Domingos, King of Warri, 1621-1644, Bridger of River and Sea." Tuaso, tears falling like river pearls, whispered, "Rest, my river, your tide eternal," her hand tracing the sapling's bark, the air filled with the scent of earth and memory.

The Final Burial Rites

In the last three weeks ending the 90 days mourning period, Ode-Itsekiri hosted the burial, its rites elaborate as the river's twists, the air thick with the scent of incense and the sound of drums. Communities danced their tributes, a tapestry of farewell—Ode-Itsekiri's drummers pounded ancestral rhythms, their Ogume drum a heartbeat, Okere's warriors performing spear dances, their blades a salute, Obodo's women weaving nets of farewell, their threads a lament. Ekuobodo's chants invoked Umale Okun, his forge a memory, Ugbolokposo's flutes sang of the sea, their notes a tide, Omadino's fishermen offered fish, their silver a tribute, Ikpesan's elders sprinkled kola, its bitterness a prayer. Ijaghala's youth leaped in acrobatics, their leaps a defiance of grief, Kantu's priests burned incense, its smoke a bridge, Ugborodo's coastal dancers swirled with coral, their steps a wave, Bobi's villagers beat ulu okun, its rhythm a pulse, Ureju's group chanted Ulu Umale Okun praises, their voices a hymn, Orere's finale a crescendo of unity, their drums a thunderclap. The rites peaked at midnight, Oton leading a procession to the river, torches flickering like stars, offerings cast into the waters—hot gin for the ancestors, its sweetness a gift, a chalice for the church, its silver a gleam—its surface swallowing the flames, the air filled with the scent of ritual and release. Anthonio, emerging from Idaniken, his Kemeje adorned with a new coral pendant, watched, his heart full, his blue eyes a mirror of resolve, the river's whisper a guide.

A young scout, his wrapper torn from a patrol through the mangroves, approached as the rites ended, his face flushed with urgency, the scent of salt on his skin. "Oma Oba, a Dutch frigate was sighted beyond Escravos!" he gasped, his voice a wave of warning. "Its cannons gleam, its crew barters with Ijaw, their gold a chain!" Anthonio's heart sank, but he masked it with resolve, turning to the council, the war room a fortress of strategy. "Summon the Iyatsere," he said, his voice a steady drum, the air thick with purpose. In the war room, its walls lined with maps stained by time, Ebi, Chief Oton, and Odion gathered, the map a battlefield of ink, its lines blurred by the scout's haste. "The Dutch return with force," Ebi warned, his finger tracing the coast, "their frigate a storm, the Ijaw their pawns, their gold a noose." Chief Oton shook his staff, its cowries a river's song, its rattle a prayer. "Umale Okun demands we guard our waters, its spirit our shield, its iron our strength." Odion, his coral amulet glinting, said, "Let me lead the fleet, Oma Oba. The river taught me its secrets, its currents my blade."

Anthonio nodded, recalling a parable from his father, of the Egret and the Flood: "Egret stands tall as the flood rises, its patience turning danger to safety, teaching us to endure with grace." He devised a plan: Odion would lead a river fleet, supported by one hundred warriors and Benin's promised reinforcements, their canoes armed with blunderbusses and Benin's cannon, while Oton consulted the oracle, its shells a compass. Messengers were sent to Oba Akenzua, the letter sealed with coral, seeking warriors and strategy. The fleet set out, the river a mirror to the dawn, the air filled with the scent of gunpowder and resolve. They clashed with the Dutch frigate off Escravos, its cannons roaring, the Ijaw canoes a swarm, the water churning with battle. Odion's strategy—using mangrove cover and Benin's cannon fire—turned the tide, the frigate retreating, its hull scarred, the air filled with the scent of smoke and victory. A captured officer, his uniform torn, confessed, his voice a shiver: "The Dutch seek Warri's oil, their cannons a bluff to force surrender. They'll return with a fleet, their siege a storm." Anthonio, standing with Tuaso on the shore, vowed to fortify the coast, the river singing their future, its currents carrying Domingos's legacy and Anthonio's promise.

The mourning ended, Warri awakened markets reopened, their stalls alive with trade, nets cast, their silver a sign of life, the air filled with the scent of pepper and hope. Anthonio, now Ogiame, stood with Tuaso under the Iroko, the river's whisper their vow, its tide turning under a new reign, its roots deep, its future bright, ready for the storms ahead, the legacy of Dom Domingos eternal as the river's flow.

Epilogue

The Warri River flowed with a quiet strength under a dawn sky, its golden waters catching the first light of a new day, the air filled with the scent of mangrove and the distant hum of returning fishermen. It was the spring of 1645, six months since Ogiame Dom Domingos' spirit had joined the ancestors, his burial rites at Ijala a memory etched in the hearts of his people. The kingdom stirred awake, markets bustling with the clatter of trade, nets heavy with silver fish, and the Iroko tree standing tall in the palace courtyard, its roots a silent witness to a reign passed and a new one begun.

Anthonio, now Olu Anthonio Domingos, stood at the river's edge, his scarlet Kemeje vibrant with renewed pride, coral beads clinking softly, and the coral cross from António Martins d'Abreu resting against his chest—a bridge between his father's past and his own future. His sea-blue eyes, inherited from Isabella, scanned the horizon, where the Dutch frigate's retreat had left a wary peace, its cannons a fading echo. Tuaso, her coral-red wrapper a banner of resilience, joined him, her hand warm in his, her smile a quiet strength.

"Your father would see this dawn," she said, her voice a gentle tide. "Warri lives in you, my son."

The past months had been a crucible. The 90 days of mourning had united the kingdom, its people emerging with a renewed sense of purpose, their black wrappers replaced by the colours of life. Anthonio had led with the wisdom of Idaniken's lessons, balancing the cross with Umale Okun, his decrees fair but firm—a trader caught hoarding fish was banished, his boat sunk as a warning, the crowd's murmurs a mix of respect and fear. Benin's envoys, their ivory tributes a sign of alliance, had pledged warriors to guard the coast, their brass plaques gleaming in the palace. Even the Dutch trader, his cloth a reluctant gift, had bowed to Warri's strength, his eyes cautious.

Yet shadows lingered. A scout's report had come at midnight, the scent of salt on his skin: "Ogiame, Ijaw canoes were seen with a Dutch flag, their voices hushed." Anthonio's jaw tightened, his mind turning to the captured officer's warning of a siege. He had ordered Odion to strengthen the river fleet, its blunderbusses primed and sent a message to Oba Akenzua. The river, ever a mirror, whispered of trials ahead, its currents a reminder of Domingo's words: "Warri endures."

That evening, under the Iroko's shade, Anthonio gathered the chiefs—Iyatsere, Olekun, Temieno, and Anomu—their coral armlets a circle of unity. "My father's legacy is our shield," he said, his voice steady as the river's flow. "But the tide turns with vigilance." Tuaso nodded, her net weaving a new pattern, a symbol of hope. The drums beat softly, blending hymns with Itsekiri chants, a rhythm of continuity. As the sun dipped, casting a golden path across the water, Ogiame Anthonio Domingos felt the weight of the crown— and the love that sustained it. The river sang on, its voice a promise: Warri's story, like its king, would flow eternal, ready for the storms to come.

Glossary of Terms

Ale Je Efun

The ceremonial breaking of a calabash to announce the passing of an Olu of Warri, signaling the transition of kingship in Itsekiri tradition.

Benin Alliance

A strategic partnership between Warri and the Benin Kingdom, solidified through trade and mutual defense, symbolized by brass plaques.

Coral Beads

Sacred ornaments worn by Itsekiri royalty and elders, representing wealth, status, and connection to the river's spiritual essence.

Idaniken

A secluded grove where the new Olu undergoes rites of passage, learning the wisdom and duties of kingship.

Ijala

A sacred grove near Ode-Itsekiri where Ogiame Dom Domingo was buried, a place of ancestral reverence. It is the traditional burial place of Itsekiri kings with over 500 years of history.

Itsekiri

The riverine people of the Niger Delta, known for their fishing, weaving, and resilient spirit, the heart of the novel's setting. In historic text the word Itsekiri have the following variations: Jakrie, Jakri, Jekri, Sekiri, Chekiri, and Isekiri.

Kemeje

A traditional scarlet robe worn by Itsekiri royalty, adorned with coral beads, signifying power and identity.

Oma Oba

Oma Oba when literally translated in Itsekiri language means son of king. In the English contest its Prince but when an Itsekiri Prince is selected after the passing of an Olu, and he is called Oma Oba, the word signifies Crown Prince.

Ode-Itsekiri

Also known as Big Warri, the spiritual and political heart of the Itsekiri kingdom, home to the royal burial grounds.

Ogiame

The title of the Olu of Warri, meaning "King of the River," a divine ruler chosen by the ancestors and river spirits.

Olekun

The keeper of ancestral rites among the chiefs, his bronze pendants a symbol of his role in preserving tradition.

Olori

The wife of an Olu, a consort who supports the throne with wisdom and love.

Oritse-Udeji

The Itsekiri supreme god, also referred to as God the Creator, a central deity in the kingdom's spiritual life.

Ogume

Traditional Itsekiri drums used in ceremonies, their rhythms echoing the strength of the people and the heartbeat of the community.

Umale Okun

The god of the river in Itsekiri culture, holding significant importance to the Itsekiri and other riverine communities.

Warri Kingdom

The traditional and historic kingdom of the Itsekiri people, founded circa 1480 and lasting until the 1890s as an independent kingdom before the British incorporated it into what is today Nigeria.

Warri River

The lifeblood of the Itsekiri, a spiritual and physical artery whose flow shapes the kingdom's destiny and stories.

Bibliography

Alagoa, E. J. *A History of the Niger Delta*. Ibadan: University Press, 2005.
An exploration of the Niger Delta's cultural and political evolution, including the Itsekiri.

Ayandele, E. A. *The Missionary Impact on Modern Nigeria, 1842-1914*. London: Longman, 1966.
A study of Christian missionary influence in Nigeria, relevant to Warri's historical context.

Bradbury, R. E. *Benin Studies*. Oxford: Oxford University Press, 1973.
Insights into the Benin Kingdom's alliances and trade, including its relationship with Warri.

Edema, Adrian O. "Itsekiri Oral Histories: Tales of the River Kings." *Unpublished Manuscript*, 2020.
Personal collection of oral narratives from Itsekiri elders, informing the novel's cultural backdrop.

Edema, Adrian O. "The Legacy of Ogiame: 100 Articles on Itsekiri Heritage." *Itsekiri Cultural Archives*, 2015-2023.

A series of articles by the author, exploring Itsekiri traditions and history.

Ikime, O. *The Fall of Nigeria: The British Conquest*. London: Heinemann, 1977.
A historical account of British colonization, including the end of the Warri Kingdom's independence.

Itsekiri Historical Society. *Chronicles of the Warri Kingdom*. Lagos: National Archives, 1998.
A compilation of historical records and oral traditions of the Itsekiri people.

Jones, G. I. *The Trading States of the Oil Rivers*. London: Oxford University Press, 1963.
A detailed look at trade dynamics in the Niger Delta, including Warri's role.

Ogbobine, T. *The Itsekiri and the Sea: A Cultural Odyssey*. Benin City: Ethiope Publishing, 2010.
A cultural study of the Itsekiri's riverine life and spiritual beliefs.

Ryder, A. F. C. *Benin and the Europeans, 1485-1897*. London: Longman, 1969.
A historical analysis of European contact with West African kingdoms, including Portuguese influence.

About the Author

Adrian Oritsegbubemi Edema is a proud son of the Itsekiri communities of Big Warri, Ebrohimi, Koko, and Ugborodo in Delta State, Nigeria, where the Warri River weaves its timeless tales. With a deep-rooted passion for his heritage, Adrian brings the rich history and spirit of the Itsekiri people to life through his writing, blending cultural pride with historical imagination.

Adrian holds an HND in Business and Finance from City of London College, a BSc in International Finance from Birmingham City University, and a postgraduate degree in Business from the University of Wales—all earned in the United Kingdom. His academic journey reflects a commitment to understanding global finance, which he now channels into preserving and sharing the stories of his ancestors.

As an accomplished author, Adrian has penned *Ofo Ofa Ni Owun Itsekiri* and *Goldiloks biri Be Meeta*, works that showcase his dedication to Itsekiri culture and language. His passion for historical research has led him to write over 100 articles on Itsekiri heritage, exploring the traditions, legends, and resilience of his people. *DOM DOMINGOS KING OF WARRI* is his latest triumph, a novel that honours the legacy of Ogiame Atuwatse I (Olu Dom Domingos) while celebrating the enduring spirit of Warri.

When he is not writing, Adrian can be found delving into archival records, collaborating with Itsekiri elders, or walking the riverbanks that inspired his tales. He resides in the United Kingdom but remains deeply connected to his roots, inviting readers to join him on a journey through the heart of Warri's past and its vibrant future.

www.ingramcontent.com/pod-product-compliance
Lightning Source LLC
Chambersburg PA
CBHW022029240626
47154CB00007B/2326